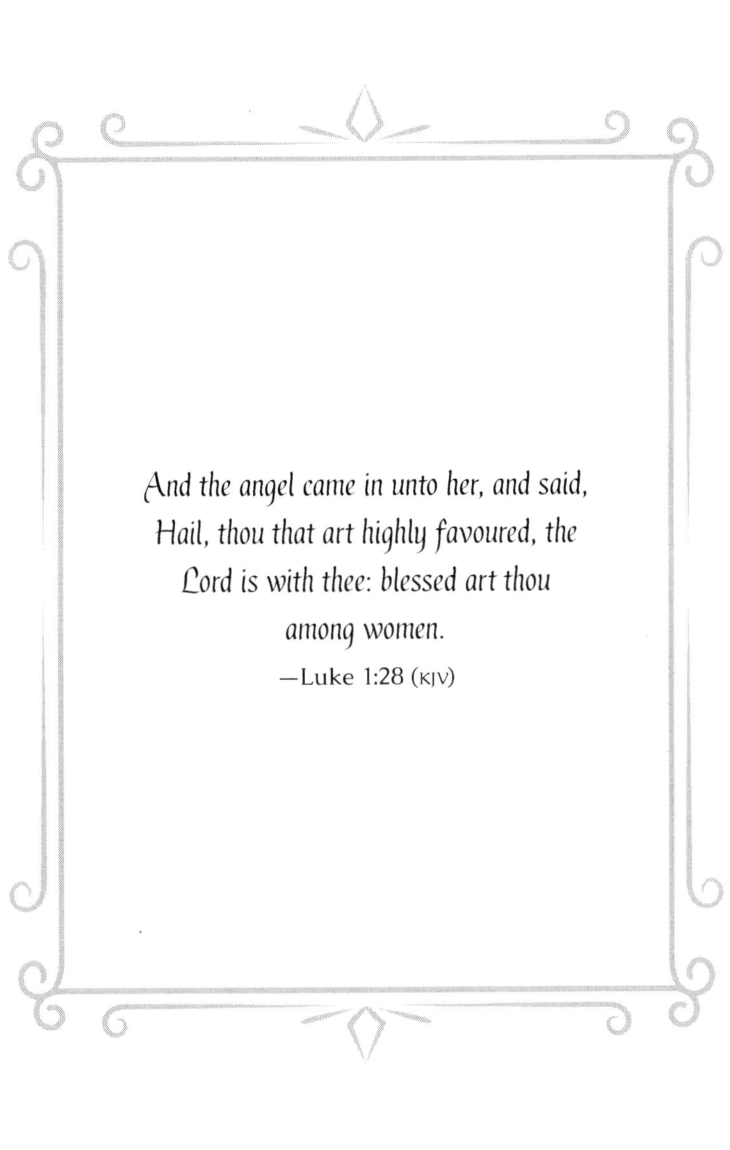

And the angel came in unto her, and said,
Hail, thou that art highly favoured, the
Lord is with thee: blessed art thou
among women.

—Luke 1:28 (KJV)

# Extraordinary Women of the BIBLE

HIGHLY FAVORED: MARY'S STORY

Extraordinary Women of the Bible

# HIGHLY FAVORED

## MARY'S STORY

### Ginger Garrett

# HIGHLY FAVORED

## MARY'S STORY

# DEDICATION

For my mother, Carole

# ACKNOWLEDGMENTS

Thank you so very much to the entire team at Guideposts! The editorial team is simply the best I've ever worked with, and I'm eternally grateful to be surrounded by a group of professionals who are both astute and kind. Special thanks to Jane Haertel, Sabrina Diaz, Ellen Tarver, and Caroline Cilento. Plus, the cover art by Brian Call is stunning. All the writers look forward to each cover reveal!

I also thank my agent, Melissa Jeglinski. I am in awe of her talent and vision, and her patience! And many thanks to my family: Mitch, James, Elise, Lauren, Mom and Dad, plus encouraging friends like Johnna, Sandra and Sharon, Gidget, Beth, and Tracie.

My final acknowledgment is for my grandmother Eloise, who gave me my first issue of *Guideposts* magazine when I was still in elementary school. Stories of faith became the love language we shared. There's an echo of her heart in every story I write.

# CHAPTER ONE

Mary loved every season of the year in Nazareth except one—the wedding season. During the warm months when the flowers bloomed and the grapevines sagged, heavy with purple fruit, it seemed every eligible maiden stood with her beloved under a wedding canopy, and Mary was just a lonely bystander. Never was she a bride. Never was she invited into the story of love.

She frowned to herself as she adjusted her hair yet again, exasperated at the dark curls that continually popped loose, like mischievous toddlers springing up from their beds. How she missed her older sister, who had married last year. Miriam would know what to do with this hair. And today's wedding required that she look her best. Mary's best friend, Rebekah, was getting married. Rebekah was quite wealthy and would look resplendent. All Mary could hope for was to avoid embarrassing herself or her family.

Her mother's poor eyesight limited her ability to offer Mary any help. Using the polished bronze mirror that sat next to the bed she once shared with Miriam, Mary forced each curl back down into place. She'd already run out of combs to secure her hair. Only prayer would help now. She didn't mind praying about her hair. She prayed over everything else, big and small, never even waiting for synagogue or a trip to the Temple in Jerusalem to voice her heart to the Lord.

"Pour out your hearts to Him, for He is our refuge," she sang. She loved the psalms of David, and thankfully, the Lord had blessed her with an excellent memory. Her mind was certainly better than her singing voice. She sighed. Maybe that was why she was still an unpledged maiden. Eligible men didn't swoon over a girl's memory. Besides, there was only one man she was interested in, and he already knew everything about her.

Sitting on the bed, she reached for the sandals lying near the mat. The room was too quiet without Miriam. It had always been the two of them, working by day together at the household chores, then whispering secrets to each other at night when the moon peeked in on them from gaps in the stone walls. The sisters were so close, people joked it was impossible to tell them apart. It didn't help that their father had named them both Mary. To avoid confusion, her older sister chose a variation of the name, Miriam, to go by in the village.

The other girls in the village had giggled behind their backs about having to share a name, as if their family was too poor to have more than one name for the girls. But the younger Mary was named after a beloved aunt, and Miriam after a beloved grandmother, each on separate sides of the family.

And her father took great delight in both daughters. If he regretted his oldest children not being sons, no one ever heard a word about it. He paraded his daughters through town as if he was a man to be envied. In part, he was. Mary knew that everyone thought her older sister was beautiful. Her eyes were the color of richest umber, and her hair had such a sheen that it looked like water flowing down her back.

But Miriam was living in her husband's house now, and with autumn closing in, Mary would be lonely in this tiny upstairs room—and cold. Her sister had taken the best bed coverings with her to her new home with her groom, Cleos bar Jacob. All Mary had left was the hand-me-down covering of her beloved older cousin, Elizabeth. Sadly, this covering was for a child's bed, but the child had never come. Elizabeth, in her old age, was barren. The Lord had never answered her prayers for a child. So many had prayed on her behalf too, Mary remembered. Hope was gone. All that remained was the shadow of grief for what could have been.

But Elizabeth was so much, much more than a barren woman, Mary wanted to tell anyone who would listen. She was kind, generous, and faithful to friends, family, and God.

And if it wasn't for Elizabeth's generosity, Mary wouldn't have this lovely robe for today's wedding. Finished at last with her preparations, she stood and twirled in the early afternoon light. Dust motes danced through the air that looked like a mist of gold.

Suddenly, a nagging fear struck her heart like an arrow.

Would she ever get married? Did anyone want her? Anyone at all? At fifteen, she was past the age of betrothal. Her father said he had saved for her sister's wedding and needed time to save for one more. Secretly, Mary wondered if the truth was more embarrassing…the truth being that no one had shown any interest. Not even the boy she had spent all her summers with, chasing butterflies through the olive groves. Joseph bar Jacob had not sent his father to ask for her hand. He had not even talked to her much recently.

What was Rebekah's charm? she wondered. Every boy in town had made moon eyes over her when they were younger. They still did! Of course, Rebekah's betrothal to Phillip bar Micah had been official for more than a year. And Rebekah was, by law, as bound to her future husband as any legal wife would be. If she had even flirted with another man, Phillip could have had her stoned. Or at least flogged. But Rebekah was so wealthy that Phillip would probably have overlooked that offense. Rebekah was forgiven much on account of her father's wealth. She always had been.

Mary carefully navigated the ladder down to the kitchen below. Her mother was at the table, counting out coins for the week ahead. At least with Miriam gone, it was easier to stretch their market money. Mary pecked her mother on the cheek and walked out, just past the kitchen door.

As she sat in the courtyard's sunshine, she examined her nails. She loved helping her mother in the herb gardens, but it meant her nails usually looked terrible. After finding a fragment of dried flax stalk, she checked to be sure her nail beds were clean then tidied the cuticles. Even if she had the hands of a servant, fresh herbs in the bread were worth the trouble.

Nazareth was abundant with herbs and good produce, and if you knew what to plant and how to care for it, you could feast like a king. Or at least how she imagined a king might feast if a king ate only from a garden.

Today's wedding would be a feast too, for all the senses. The food would be wonderful and so would the music, wine, and the singers. Rebekah, adorned in her bridal finery, would be a vision of happiness. Just the thought of seeing Rebekah under the wedding canopy at last made Mary smile.

Mary decided she would not waste a moment of her friend's day. She might never be a bride, but she would make a joyful companion. Her joy would be her gift. That was the richest gift she could bring, she thought wryly, because it cost her dearly.

Standing, she squared her shoulders, vowing to soak up every bit of happiness that the day offered.

Even if none of it would ever be hers.

* * *

Three hours later, the sun stood like a sentinel of fire above the green hills. Mary pinched the edge of her robe and fanned it, hoping for an autumn breeze to flow down from the hills. Rebekah and her groom stood sheltered under a canopy as they recited their vows. The guests sweltered. At least the herbs would have longer to stay green, since the afternoon sun remained so strong despite the month.

"Let's hope the vows are not long."

The familiar voice in her ear caused her to giggle, lifting the edge of her veil over her mouth to conceal it.

She cut a glance behind her. Joseph bar Jacob sat behind her in the grass. His forehead was dotted with beads of perspiration.

"We still have to watch them exchange gifts," she whispered.

Joseph feigned falling backward, earning a stern look of rebuke from Mary's mother. Even without good eyesight, her mother recognized the voice. Joseph had been a childhood friend of the sisters. Cleos, his older brother, had married Miriam, and for weeks, Mary had felt painfully awkward around Joseph. The match between them would seem inevitable, but they were not at all attracted to one another.

That was what Mary told herself. The truth was, Joseph had shown no romantic interest in her. It was easier to pretend it was mutual. Less painful too. If she were ever to marry, she would have wished it to be Joseph.

With the vows exchanged, the gifts began. Rebekah was already wealthy, and the gifts from her new husband's family were more for the crowd's benefit than Rebekah's. But each family's reputation had to be maintained. Mary sighed, prepared to watch Rebekah gorge herself with gold and finery.

"How are Cleos and my sister?" Mary asked. They had moved into the family home and would not attend social events for some time yet.

"Definitely more comfortable than we are," Joseph complained softly.

Mary shook her head in mock aggravation, knowing Joseph would laugh.

The wedding of Cleos to her older sister had been short and pleasant. Cleos was a good man. A bit hot-blooded at times, as all his tribe could be. What else could anyone expect from descendants of King David? *Yes, Saul had slain his thousands, and David his tens of thousands.* The refrain rang in Mary's head.

Over the next hour, Rebekah received from her father a rich field worth much money and several female servants. The groom gave even more elaborate gifts that everyone exclaimed over.

Mary closed her eyes, partly to escape the temptation of jealousy. She was grateful that next month she would leave to visit Cousin Elizabeth, who was more like an aunt than a cousin. Elizabeth had promised to teach her how to weave. Mary had wanted to try her hand at creating prayer shawls to sell in the market. She had so many ideas for designs! Elizabeth relished these visits from Mary.

There would be no talk of betrothals and babies. Elizabeth would make sure of that, for such talk could be as painful to her as to Mary. Elizabeth was married, true, but she knew how bitter a disappointment with life could be. Just because a woman was faithful to God did not mean life unfolded as she pleased. In Elizabeth's wise and compassionate company, though, Mary would be free to be a girl again, without a care for her future.

At long last, the wine flowed. Joseph accepted a cup of wine from Rubin, who clapped him on the back before Joseph could take the first sip. The wine spilled from the cup, staining Joseph's tunic. Mary winced. Joseph had worn his best tunic today, just as she had. Neither of them had much money. Joseph caught her staring in dismay at the stain. He turned abruptly as if she had offended him. Her heart sank. He had known exactly what she was thinking, but she hadn't meant to injure his pride.

Rubin caught Joseph by the arm. Elbowing him rudely, Rubin chuckled and whispered something in Joseph's ears. Excusing himself at once, poor Joseph was red in the face, all the way to his ears.

Mary had an idea about what Rubin had said. Everyone knew Joseph and Mary were childhood friends, and if marriage didn't bring them together soon, they would be parted forever. They would find spouses in other villages. The fathers seemed reluctant to make the match when neither could offer anything beyond their child. Worse, the awkwardness between the fathers had often made talking with Joseph an exercise in frustration. She couldn't say anything that could be mistaken for flirting. He couldn't say anything that could be construed as a promise.

The two friends who once ran through the hill country together flushing birds into the air, cradling abandoned young rabbits, bringing flowers home to their mothers... Well, at least she had the memories. She might not have Joseph, but she had those years. He was seventeen now, and while some Jewish families waited to marry their sons off, the village knew it was time for Joseph to start his own family. His father had to make a match, and soon.

Mary wrapped an arm around her mother's shoulders, escorting her to a bench where she could sit and enjoy the festivities. Mother didn't have the stamina for parties that she once had. Old age was moving quickly, attacking her mother's every defense, even her joy.

She felt the unknown future wrap around her like a heavy, damp shawl, and she shivered. It wasn't in her nature to be afraid, but lately strange fears had repeatedly, relentlessly tempted her to worry. Often when she was tired or hungry or even simply kneading bread, her mind would wander into fearful and dreadful outcomes. What if her mother died before Mary was married? What if she never married at all? What if she never had children?

What dishonor she would bring to her family! If no one wanted her, what would she do?

She shook herself as if to free herself from such silly imaginings.

Rebekah appeared at her side and led her away from her mother and the bench. "Rubin says you and Joseph have been making lovers' eyes at each other. Shall I create a distraction?"

Mary turned, frowning at her impulsive, spoiled friend. Rebekah had many childish qualities, that was true, but she was one of those rare girls who seemed to have bottled the sun. Everyone basked in her presence. Mary had long ago decided to forgive Rebekah before Rebekah asked, which was good, because some days the poor girl didn't even realize what she'd done.

"Why would I need a distraction?" Mary asked, her voice low. Rebekah was up to something, and it was better not to let anyone else know.

"So you can steal a kiss from Joseph, of course!" She giggled.

Mary shook her head sharply, rejecting the idea at once.

"Or perhaps you already have?" Rebekah pretended to be scandalized. She grabbed Mary's arm and dragged her toward the enormous jars of wine. The wine was of excellent quality, and there was so much that it had stained the ground all around. No one was careful as they poured. Mary sighed. She would have been so careful with such precious vintage. But Rebekah did not understand the value of some things.

"Have some more wine," Rebekah said. "I am drinking until I don't remember a thing."

"It's your wedding day!" Mary scolded.

Rebekah nodded in the direction of the groom's home. A canopy stood on the roof, decorated with fresh greenery and flowers. Jars, presumably holding water for bathing and wine for drinking, flanked a straw mattress. Platters of food sat next to the jars.

Mary gasped. "It's gorgeous."

"We are in Nazareth!" Rebekah snapped. Clearly, she did not agree. Taking a noisy gulp of wine, she gestured with her free hand. "Have you ever seen a wedding in Rome? I have. Those girls are so fortunate. They have everything."

Mary held her tongue. Rebekah would only argue herself further into a sulk.

Instead, Mary wrapped her arm around Rebekah's waist and leaned her head to touch hers. "All the Roman nobility combined could not be as lovely as you are today. I am so happy for you, my friend. I pray God blesses you with many children and that you know happiness in every way."

"We will always be friends?" Rebekah asked, her eyes growing misty.

Mary noticed how Rebekah's words began now to slur. She took the wine cup out of Rebekah's hands and gave it to a passing servant.

Mary smiled. "Of course, silly girl. What could ever part us?"

# CHAPTER TWO

It was just a few nights later that Mary lay in her bed, feeling cold and alone. The thin coverlet was even shorter than she remembered. Now she had to choose whether to leave her toes cold or her shoulders.

The gap between the stones in the wall let a thin beam of moonlight into the room. She turned onto her shoulder and propped herself up to watch the shadows play on the far wall. Unlike her younger brothers, she was never scared at night. She knew how to talk to herself in those moments. It was simple, really. She just borrowed the words from God and repeated them.

*"In the beginning God created the heavens and the earth. Now the earth was formless and empty, darkness was over the surface of the deep, and the Spirit of God was hovering over the waters."* Silently, she recited the scripture in her mind. God had been hovering quite close in that first darkness. What a beautiful thought!

In the darkness now, she wondered if God might hover close by. What would God create here, she wondered? If such a thing were even possible—a brand-new creation—what would it be? Maybe an animal so silly that children would giggle just to see it? Or a new kind of flower? Her mind turned over possibilities until she grew sleepy.

Suddenly aware of her cold toes, she sat up and shifted the coverlet one more time. Hopefully, she would be asleep before she realized her shoulders were cold. Now she was wide awake again.

It was impossible to get comfortable. On the roof sat the bed pallets they had used during the warm summer months. Maybe a full-size linen was there, one that had been overlooked. She might as well go up and see. Without a good cover, she wasn't going to sleep.

She bolted upright.

"Yes?" she called softly. She had thought—but no, it was the late hour and her exhaustion—she thought she heard her name. It was as if the wind itself had called to her.

Her siblings breathed heavily in their sleep. None were awake.

And to think—Mary had called Rebekah a silly girl! She was the silly one, imagining she heard her name on the wind.

Moments later she sat on the roof, looking up at the stars, that endless field of bright lights. She imagined picking the stars like they were wildflowers, collecting them in a straw basket to bring home. The fields had always been lands of wonder when she was a child. Even if it was only Nazareth, she loved it here. Unlike Rebekah, she had no desire to ever leave, or see a foreign city.

She stretched out on a mat, staring at the sky. She had found a good coverlet and was warm but did not want to return to her bedchamber below. The stars were too beautiful.

A shooting star flew from one edge of the horizon to the other. Reaching up with one fingertip, she traced its path, wondering where it was going and what it would see. For a Nazareth girl, such journeys were hard to imagine. She did not know what was in foreign lands or how the people there lived. Did they see this same sky? Did they wonder about other lands? Were they happy?

As she closed her eyes, she heard her name again. That was impossible. She knew her scriptures and knew of a boy who'd heard his name. God had a plan for his life, but she was a nobody from a nowhere-town. She was simply bored, tired, and lonely. *Never a good combination*, she thought.

Sitting up, she scanned the roof for proof that she was alone and then crawled to the edge. She peered at the dark street below. An old dog shuffled along. She recognized the scruffy tail arching over the back. It was the neighbor's dog heading home after begging for scraps at the market. But since the dog was not alert or alarmed, she knew no one was in the street. That old dog would bark at a rock.

She chided herself for her overactive imagination. She'd be useless at chores tomorrow if she didn't sleep. Joseph was probably to blame for her restlessness.

Those childhood years with Joseph, exploring the green hills around the village—how she had lived for those daily walks! They'd chased dragonflies and caught frogs and climbed trees to spy on bird nests. And never once had they confessed to their mothers that they had seen a viper slithering on its belly in the dust. How Mary's stomach had dropped! She had never forgotten the viper's eyes, the slits, the cold, menacing glare. Thankfully she had never seen one again. She had not cared for that day's walk, not at all.

But it was those long walks around the hills of Nazareth that had worn a path in her mind as a child. She had wandered on distant hills, true, but at the end of every day, she was back for dinner. Her days had a rhythm that never varied, and the path was always pleasant. There was no reason to want any-thing different. She assumed she would marry and start a fam-ily here in Nazareth. It would be foolish to think there was anything in God's plan for her. And anyway, what was left to be done? she asked herself.

God was finished with creation. He had worked miracles on the earth and then through the prophets. God was not going to speak again, certainly not to her. He spoke to the prophets and kings of long ago. The age of miracles was long past.

The time of revelations was over too. God had revealed His plan hundreds of years ago, and it had been set in writing. The priests and rabbis knew the words by heart. Now there was only a silent waiting for the Messiah. Elijah would return and a Messiah would come, but she was a woman and had no part in that story.

After all, there was no Elijah to be seen in Nazareth, that was plain. And a Messiah? The priests and rabbis had spoken of the Messiah all her life. The people had been waiting for hundreds of years, maybe four hundred at her count. Whatever God had planned to do, perhaps they had missed it. Perhaps God had grown tired of waiting on them to obey His commands, and He changed His mind. She understood how waiting could sour a mood. Or perhaps the Messiah was not coming, not for another four hundred years. Maybe the prophecy would simply pass her by, like so many other things.

Many things in life might not be meant for her. Marriage might be one of them, she worried. And with that, the blessing of children.

Still…she had felt the sun on her face as a child. She had heard birdsong in the barley fields and seen deer drinking from steady streams, their young folded in among their long legs. She had seen a spider's intricate web, adorned with the morning's dew, sparkling like a diadem as the sun rose behind it.

She'd seen wonders, hadn't she? God was good. The familiar words of Habakkuk came to mind. *"Though the fig tree does not bud and there are no grapes on the vines, though the olive crop fails and the fields produce no food, though there are no sheep in the pen and no cattle in the stalls, yet I will rejoice in the Lord, I will be joyful in God my Savior."*

The wind swept the dried straw across the roof. Well, perhaps the wind was doing a bit of housekeeping, she told herself, smiling, but it certainly was not calling her name. The world was filled with wonders, but there were no more miracles to be had.

But God was good, and she would praise Him yet.

* * *

The next week, Mary had to walk to the well just after midday. Mother was not feeling well and wished for cool water to moisten cloths to lay against her forehead. Mary had already been to the well twice today, however. Mother kept forgetting that. Jars of cool water surrounded her.

It surprised Mary to see Rebekah walking on the dirt path that led away from the village and into the lush green fields. Rebekah saw her too, and her face lit up in delight.

"Come and join me!" she called.

Mary hesitated, looking back in the well's direction. With a sigh, she set her water jug down behind a tall clump of grass and joined her friend.

"I only have a moment," Mary said. "What are you doing out here? Shouldn't a groom hide his bride away with his family for the first few months?"

Rebekah rolled her eyes and kicked at a pebble. Mary flinched. If she had such nice sandals, she wouldn't kick rocks in them.

"I had to find an excuse to escape for a moment. My mother-in-law nags at me day and night. She expects me to clean up after myself, like a common servant."

"She must keep an immaculate house."

"Well, she won't keep her son if she continues," Rebekah groused. "I'll convince him to take a post in Rome. We could have a dozen servants there." Sighing, she crooked her arm around Mary's.

"Tell me everything I have missed," Rebekah continued. "Since my wedding, have there been any matches?"

Mary's face felt hot. "No. And no one has asked my father about marriage for me."

Rebekah groaned. "Men are impossible!"

"I feel I have lost all my friends," Mary confessed. "My sister is married and out of the house. You are married and secluded with your new family. And Joseph? He never makes time to go for walks now. It's as if he wants to be sure that no one assumes we will be betrothed, including me."

Her chin trembled as she spoke. Joseph had been dear to her when they were young. It wasn't fair how time had changed things between them. It wasn't fair that he had no feelings for her, especially since she had stirrings of…what? Affection? Love? She knew her cheeks were red at the mere thought of the word.

"It's your own fault," Rebekah said casually.

Stung, Mary stopped. "How?"

"Men are impossible to live with, but they are easy to catch. You just have to make your desires known." Rebekah stopped too. Hands on hips, she grew serious. "You need to let Joseph know that you are open to a match."

"I cannot! That would be wrong."

"Why?" Rebekah demanded.

"Because…" Mary struggled for words. "Because I want a man who is so desperate to possess me that he lets nothing stand in his way."

Rebekah cocked one eyebrow.

Mary burst into giggles. "My imagination has always been vivid."

Rebekah's face softened, and she reached to touch Mary's arm. "You can't wait for things to happen or just daydream about the future. Especially where men are concerned," Rebekah insisted. "You must make your will very plain. Your will, your way, and your wishes."

"I'm not like you." Mary sighed, shaking her head. "I need to get back to the well. Mother is not having a good day."

Rebekah kissed her on the cheek, and the friends parted.

A nagging thought followed Mary, discouraging her. If she was more like Rebekah, she would be married by now.

Was God waiting for her to change, or did He wait for another reason?

It was the first truly cold night of the season. The sun had hidden behind clouds throughout the day, casting a gauzy light over the hills. When dusk came, the winds came down from the hills, hunting for anyone not tucked in their beds.

That's what Mary told her little brothers, appealing to their imaginations to get them into bed and under the covers. She had an excellent reason, besides her peace of mind at this late hour. She wanted to eavesdrop with no witnesses.

Downstairs, at the kitchen table, Joseph's father, Jacob, was finishing his second cup of wine. Her own father laughed at a shared joke as he refilled both cups.

"Do you think the time is right?" her father, Heli, asked.

"Was it ever a matter of timing?" Jacob shrugged.

Both men stared at their wine.

Were they discussing money? A business venture, perhaps?

"I had hoped there would be more interest." Her father sighed.

"They are shy, perhaps."

Her father nodded. "It is just as well. The extra time has allowed me to make several nice trades at the market. Her bridal gifts to your family will be good."

"And we are ready as well. The gifts for your family will be welcome, I am sure. You have several children more still to feed."

Mary clenched her jaw. They were discussing her and Joseph. Such cold, lifeless terms, as if this were a business transaction instead of a marriage. And worse—the fathers had been watching them for signs of interest? Did Joseph know? Did he think she wasn't interested—because she had assumed he was not interested? She wanted to stomp her feet in aggravation, but that would have given her away and awoken the children.

Why did courtship have to be complicated? Why couldn't men just state how they felt, plainly? But downstairs, that's exactly what the fathers were doing, and she hated it.

What did she really want? The question struck her with fresh force. Did she want Joseph? Did she want marriage? They were not necessarily the same thing.

"How is my other Mary doing?" Her father stood and retrieved a plate of dried figs from a cupboard. After setting them on the table, he sat again.

"She is a delight," Jacob said, helping himself to a fig. "She helps my wife with all the chores, speaks kindly to the children of the other families that we share the courtyard with, and is respectful to Cleos. Now that we know the quality of your older daughter, how could we want any other family to join with ours?"

The fathers bent their heads low and haggled a bit.

Joseph's parents would pay for the wedding, and Mary's parents would receive a payment called a *mohar*. It could be gold, jewels, or even furs and fabrics. Her father could give it to Mary to take into marriage or he could keep it. Mary knew her father needed it.

But her betrothed, Joseph, would offer her a *mattan*, gifts offered to the bride herself. One gift would be a gold or silver ring Mary looked forward to that. It would be her first possession of her very own.

Mary listened as terms of money, land, and several good fleeces were discussed, until the men came to an amount that was agreeable to both. That was the price for her life. Her heart could not be sold. She had to give it freely.

Suddenly, the men lifted cups. "In one year!"

And that was it. Mary was betrothed. She crawled quietly back to her pallet and lay down to think. Sleep would not come tonight, she was sure. She was engaged—what should she feel? She always thought she'd feel elated. But she worried about Joseph's reaction when he learned the news. Did he have any idea what the fathers were discussing tonight? Would he be angry or disappointed? Would he blame her for stealing his freedom? Or be happy to claim her as his wife?

Either way, Mary was betrothed, which was as legally binding as the marriage itself. The rules for her behavior must be strictly observed. She and Joseph could not be physically intimate, but he could call her his wife if he chose. Joseph could divorce her at any time during the betrothal or marriage. She, of course, did not have this option. If Joseph turned out to be abusive and bad-tempered, there was nothing she could do to change her lot. And if she ever made a terrible moral mistake such as adultery, she might be stoned to death.

Love was a dangerous business. When Mary truly understood she was bound to these laws, as well as to Joseph, she felt a shiver of fear pass through her body. She had been a fool to think all she risked with Joseph was her heart.

# CHAPTER THREE

The following evening, Mary was alone downstairs. The younger siblings were in the courtyard playing with their cousins, with her mother supervising. Father had gone to Sepphoris to see about a business deal. Sepphoris made Mary so nervous. Although it wasn't a terribly large city, Rome had sent many soldiers there to scare the Jewish citizens away from tax revolts. Roman soldiers had discipline, not mercy. One might mistake her father for someone else and end his life in the street without warning.

Staying busy, she tidied the front room where guests were received. She'd already tidied it thoroughly a few hours ago, anticipating company. But the day had dragged on with no sign of any guests. Especially the one she expected.

Joseph had not asked to see her yet. Her stomach tumbled as cold nerves shot through her body at the thought of him. What was he thinking and feeling? She had a sudden panicked thought. What if she didn't see him again until the day of the vows? What if he avoided her?

And to think her very life was at risk. She was terrified of making a misstep. She'd always been modest and demure, but the threat of punishment made her every step feel so precarious. It was as if she were trying to walk across a fallen tree hanging over a fast-moving river. Of course, she could walk a straight line on firm ground…but the danger of terrible injury in these new circumstances made the same steps fraught with peril.

Ridiculous! She was being a foolish girl. Mary reminded herself that she would never betray Joseph or her morals. She loved the Lord, and she loved Joseph. She was just nervous. When she saw Joseph's face, and if she saw that big smile as always, everything would be good in her world again.

As she folded a soft beige linen, her mind flashed back to their childhood days, those playful afternoons in the barley fields after the harvest, when rabbits foraged for dropped grains. How she and Joseph loved hiding to watch their twitching noses! She held the linen in midair, a smile warming her all over. If Joseph remembered them the same way, then surely he was pleased about the match.

Heavy footfalls shook the ground. Little bits of pale dried flax straw jumped from the dark dirt floor, falling and scattering into the shadowed corners of the room. Mary could feel the heavy steps all the way from her feet to her thighs. The man must have worn boots to tread with such force.

Who would approach at this hour? The flax all around her continued to jump with each pounding step. This was not a citizen of Nazareth, to be sure. This man wore boots.

Mary looked up. Who wore such heavy armor? Soldiers in Nazareth? Why would they be dressed for war? Her heart thundered as she clutched her tunic with one hand, drawing it under her chin as the steps grew closer. She pressed her lips together to stop herself from crying out. After the stranger passed by, she would run to the door and peek out into the courtyard.

Her family! Her siblings and mother were out there! Fear froze her where she was. Why were they not running inside for refuge? Her eyes darted wildly about, and she wondered what she should do.

A bright light appeared under the door, as if the sun had reversed course and it was now brightest noon. Squinting, she could see the tips of polished boots. The gleaming metal shone as if made of fire. Her fist went to her mouth, covering it to keep herself from crying out. What type of soldier was this?

Before she could blink again, and without sound or movement, a mighty warrior suddenly stood before her. The door had not opened. It was as if he had simply walked through it. The light from his armor blinded her. Dust motes danced in the aura around him like tiny swirling pinholes. Falling to her knees, she lowered her face to the floor until her forehead scraped against dirt. The light was still so bright her eyes watered. Who was this man? How many legions of fighters did he command to be worthy of such dazzling armor? Not even the midday sun shone like this.

Who saw this man enter the home? She was alone with a warrior. A pledged woman! What did this stranger want? She would be stoned for this. What was happening?

"Greetings," the warrior spoke. His voice thundered in the quiet house, and dust trickled down from the roof. Debris fell from the corners of the mudstone walls. Out of the corners of her eyes, she could see the house trembling in this man's presence, just as much as she did. His presence shook everything.

Her sharp intake of breath gave her fear away. He was going to bring the house to collapse.

Immediately, the light softened, almost imperceptibly, allowing her to lift her eyes as far as his boots. Studying them, she noted the strange design. She did not recognize the metal. What were they made of? This was not a Roman soldier.

"You are highly favored," the stranger continued, his voice softer. He had the voice of the rain on a summer night, deep and hypnotic. "The Lord is with you."

Her brain struggled to match his words to his presence. Her body still shook with fear. Glancing at the door, she expected her mother to barge in, yelling. But there was only the voice of this stranger and his strange blessing echoing off the stone walls of their home. Each echo shook a little more debris loose. Nothing was secure in his presence. What did this greeting mean? She was no one important, a maiden betrothed to a man of no political power or wealth. She had nothing to do with wars or revolts.

Gathering her courage, she looked farther up. The insignia on his chest piece would tell her who he fought for.

The chest piece had writing but not of a language she had ever seen. Covered in scratches and gashes from sword fights past, the armor glowed like fire. The air in the room smelled like a raging thunderstorm had just passed through, leaving everything clean and crisp.

He extended a hand. "Do not be afraid, Mary, for you have found favor with God."

He knew her name! She studied his outstretched hand, letting his greeting at last reach her mind. He called her highly favored. He said the Lord was with her.

This was no Roman. Could this be...

He seemed to know the question on her heart, even though it was not on her lips.

Nodding in reply, he told her his name. "I am Gabriel."

Her mind spun, the dawning knowledge unimaginable.

A sudden flash of truth was as blinding and quick as if the angel had drawn his sword. She was not capable of imagining reality. The Lord and His dominion were far beyond anything she could have imagined.

If she had only known how great His power was...her mind darted in a dozen directions at once, overwhelmed. God's reality was extraordinary and beyond all comprehension. A wild impulse seized her, to run and tell the children in the fields that wonders were real. People could not even imagine the grandeur of His kingdom!

"Now, behold," the angel Gabriel spoke.

Mary's attention returned to him, and she smiled, embarrassed. She'd been so overwhelmed with awe and delight that she'd nearly forgotten she was standing in the presence of an angel, a messenger from the royal courts of the Lord Himself. She raised herself to a sitting position, expectant.

He began, his tone soft and deep, like the steady roar of thunder from a great distance. "Do not be afraid, Mary; you have found favor with God. You will conceive and give birth to a son, and you are to call Him Jesus. He will be great and will be called the Son of the Most High. The Lord God will give Him the throne of His father David, and He will reign over Jacob's descendants forever; His kingdom will never end."

Mary cocked her head, trying to absorb and understand the message. His words were as inexplicable as his appearance. A Son of the Most High? From the line of David?

Her mind managed to put together a few words, like a child stringing wooden beads. He spoke of a pregnancy. That was her heart's desire, but she did not understand his meaning. He spoke this prophecy to her, and about her, alone? She was betrothed. There was no mention of Joseph in Gabriel's prophecy. What did that mean? How could she conceive a child without Joseph? Did Joseph play a part in this prophecy? In her future?

Though his eyes were alight with kindness, she swallowed back all her questions. Something about his formidable appearance told her he did not have patience for those who challenged him. Carefully, after searching among her fragmented thoughts, she chose the most important question.

"How will this be, since I am a virgin?"

Gabriel smiled, and his radiance made her stomach drop. She knew she could never stand in the presence of the Lord. Even his messengers carried too much light from heaven. How dark earth must seem to them!

He answered her, "The Holy Spirit will come upon you, and the power of the Most High will overshadow you; therefore the child to be born will be called holy—the Son of God. And behold, your relative Elizabeth in her old age has also conceived a son, and this is the sixth month with her who was called barren. For nothing will be impossible with God."

Watching her expression, Gabriel burst into laughter that shook the walls. Mary gasped, her hands flying to her face. It was all too much! The joy made her heart hurt. Elizabeth—pregnant?! Impossible and yet—reality! Her head felt fuzzy, and her breathing became shallow.

Mary steadied her breath, afraid she would collapse from astonishment or joy or an equal measure of both.

Sweeping her hands across the dirt between them, she felt the cool earth underneath her fingertips. She was not dreaming. She reached out and touched the cool metal of the armor that covered his feet. This was real. Gabriel was real. She could not understand. Until a few moments ago, she had not even understood the true nature of reality. What could she do now but say yes?

"Behold," she replied, and he broke into a smile again, hearing his words echoed back. She pressed her hands to the floor to hold the house down, afraid the house would disintegrate if he laughed again.

"I am the servant of the Lord," she said. "Let it be to me according to your word."

She bowed in submission. When she lifted her face, the room was dark. Gabriel was gone. Stunned, she stood on shaking legs and hobbled to the door. When she flung it open, the evening air hit her like a fetid blast. Turning, she quickly inhaled, trying desperately to catch one last taste of the air of heaven before facing the ruined world.

Her mother sat in the courtyard mending a robe, while her siblings chased each other through the twilight hour. Nothing was out of order. Her mother glanced up, and seeing Mary, smiled in acknowledgment before focusing again on her stitches.

They had witnessed nothing unusual. But Mary had, and she would never be the same. Her life was altered and running swiftly on a new course. She looked at the family she loved, oblivious to the workings of God, and knew she was altogether different than the girl they had seen at dinner.

She was highly favored.

Mary could not sleep. The words replayed in her mind.

*The Holy Spirit will come upon you*

*The power of the Most High will overshadow you*

*The child to be born will be called holy—the Son of God*

The prophecy was multilayered, a weaving that she slowly picked apart, thread by thread in the quiet. What did it mean that the Holy Spirit would come upon her? She remembered the story of David. When Samuel anointed the young David as the king of Israel, the Holy Spirit came upon David. Should she ask a rabbi to anoint her with oil? Gabriel hadn't mentioned a requirement like that.

And what did it mean that the power of the Most High would overshadow her? Gabriel said God's power would overwhelm her, not His love or His mercy. Would it be a frightening, painful event? Simply standing in the presence of His messenger had been terrifying. She couldn't imagine being caught up in His power.

Would she know when the overshadowing was about to begin? Would it happen in front of other people, a public sign from God? Mary dreaded the thought of being a spectacle.

She thought of a hundred more questions she should have asked. One moment, her mind was alive with the thrill of what she had seen and heard, and in the next moment, she was flooded with anxiety. She had no idea how to move forward or what the next step was.

But Gabriel here in Nazareth—that seemed hard to believe. Nothing had ever happened in Nazareth. Scripture did not mention the town. No prophets had ever visited or performed great works here. All that Nazareth had to commend it, perhaps, was the bluest sky. She had spent hours in the grassy meadows, lying on her back, staring as fluffy white clouds, fat as ewes, meandered past. But what was that to a messenger of God, who stood in royal courts above?

And yet it was to this place Gabriel had come! She was certain it was real. To this place, the Son of the Most High would be born! The Messiah, here in Nazareth! Mary's mind was alight with the images that streamed in, of an infant king being born in this sweet and humble place. All the world would know Nazareth as the birthplace of the Messiah.

Then, in the second watch of the night, a new worry demanded her attention. Who should she tell first? Her mother? Or Joseph? Her mother was a devout woman, true, but her health had not been reliable these last few years. She tired from simple tasks, and some evenings she seemed restless, even forgetting the names of her family. Mary's father warned the children to be gentle with her. What if the news was too great of a shock for her mother and she suffered?

But Mary just had to tell her first! Her mother would know what to do, and how best to handle the matter of telling Joseph. The story was unbelievable, Mary knew. Her reputation for good behavior and devout faith were all that would commend her as she revealed the truth. Oh, but if she told her mother, there was no way to shield her mother from the shock! News of a visit from an angel would frighten her, and fright could only drive her deeper into the shadowlands that claimed her in the evenings. No, Mary couldn't risk her mother's health. She needed her, more than ever, but she couldn't risk hurting her.

Her heart ached at the thought. Why hadn't Gabriel told her who she should tell first?

Joseph. It had to be Joseph, then. How would he respond? Silently, Mary counted on her fingers all the potential outcomes. One, Joseph might turn cold as stone and demand to break the betrothal. He would write a certificate of divorce, forcing Mary to live in seclusion, with great shame. Would that void the prophecy?

Or Joseph might demand she be stoned to death. That was his right. She had no defense. She could not tell the rabbis that Gabriel himself had appeared. They would probably throw the first stone, thinking she was mocking them. Surely God did not intend for her to be stoned to death while she was pregnant. Her mind flitted to the story of Abraham nearly sacrificing his son. God tested Abraham. Would He test her too? Or Joseph?

Her stomach twisted. Why hadn't Gabriel told her what to say? Was she supposed to say anything at all?

She twisted in bed and drew the coverlet around her ears, sinking down as if to escape.

"What's wrong?" her youngest brother, Amos, whispered in the darkness.

"I didn't mean to mutter," Mary replied softly. "I'm just replaying a conversation in my head, that's all."

Amos giggled quietly. "Joseph still makes you nervous, after all the years of growing up together? You are very silly, Mary."

Mary bit her lip to keep from crying, but still the tears welled up. She pressed her fingers to her eyelids, rubbing as if she could stop the tears. She was finally betrothed to Joseph, and she could not enjoy a moment of it. Yesterday's worries and plans seemed so trivial now that she had glimpsed the workings of God.

She was going to have to tell Joseph everything. There was no other path forward.

Amos sighed heavily. Mary had awoken him, and the boy would struggle to go back to sleep without help. He was restless and prone to bad dreams.

"Go back to sleep, dear one, and I will keep watch over you." Mary's voice sounded so calm and peaceful.

But now she knew that reality could be so very different.

Mary paced the floor. She'd sent word to Joseph that she wanted to see him, but there was no reply. She fed the children, cleaned them, then shooed them out the door to play in the courtyard. Mother was still asleep in her bedchamber upstairs, so Mary couldn't make noise.

"Gabriel?" she whispered. She was alone, just as she had been when he appeared. Maybe the angel would return if she asked. She needed help.

The door flung open, and Mary clutched her robe at her heart. Her father strode in, beaming with a grin. She wasn't used to seeing him during the day, but there was no work in the fields right now, and he had already been to the city this month to trade.

"What news?" she asked.

Her father sat at the kitchen table. "Pour me something to drink and set out a plate of honey cakes. I have wonderful news to celebrate."

Mary hurried to do as he asked. Maybe Gabriel had appeared to him? Maybe he knew what to do next?

She quickly sat and watched while her father took a bite of a cake. He pushed the plate toward her, but she pushed it right back and shook her head.

"What news, Father?"

He wiped his mouth and then wiggled his eyebrows, teasing her.

"Joseph has gone to Sepphoris to buy you a ring. He has a special design in mind and is searching for a craftsman."

Two days ago, the news would have brought joy to Mary, a sign of his true heart and intentions.

"When will he return?" she demanded.

"I did not ask." Her father seemed surprised at her reaction, or lack of one.

She could barely take the news in. Her own news was so great that there was no room for any other revelation, not even of Joseph's love.

She forced a smile. "I am impatient to see him, that is all. Thank you for bringing me this joyful news in the middle of your working hours."

Her father rose from the table and kissed the top of her head. After taking one last sip of his drink, he strode back out the door.

# CHAPTER FOUR

In the courtyard, Mary watched as the local children played with a kitten that the neighbors had found near the river. The children squealed and fawned over every detail of its creation—the little pink nose, the furry tail, the brilliant green eyes... Mary smiled at their endless capacity for wonder. Noting the sun's position in the sky, she knew it would be lunchtime soon and went inside to prepare a simple meal for the youngest children.

Mary walked inside the house, then paused while her eyes adjusted to the cool darkness. As she shut the door, a blinding, brilliant light struck her, knocking her back against the wood frame of the door. Shutting her eyes against the light, she threw her forearm up as a shield. Her mind spun, trying to understand. She felt she'd been plunged into a strange river.

This was not the light of the sun, nor the moon, nor anything of this earth. It was a living light, slowly filling the room, gently touching her skin. Her mind flitted to the story of the Exodus when the people were led by a pillar of fire by night. Could it have been anything like this?

"Open your eyes, Mary."

A man's voice? No, she thought, not removing her forearm from her eyes. A male, perhaps, but not human. She laughed out loud, without meaning to. This was so strange, like she had fallen into a dream. A sudden, feverish dream that made no sense. What would she see if she looked?

The sensation on her skin cooled, raising goose bumps. That was when she noticed that she was afraid but had no sense of being in danger. It was fear mixed with awe, the kind she had that one time standing in the Temple in Jerusalem when the priests had read from the book of Isaiah about the Messiah and a peal of thunder rumbled in the distance.

"Open them, Mary."

Lowering her forearm, she opened her eyes and couldn't see anything except a heavy mist. It shimmered as if it was made of delicately spun threads, each one brilliantly white.

The Exodus cloud…the one the people had followed by day. She'd assumed it was an ordinary cloud. But then, how could they have known which one to follow? There were always clouds in the sky. Could it have been a cloud like this?

She swept her hand through it. It felt cool on her skin, like river water. It was a fine mist that sparkled like quartz, but so thick it hushed the room, insulating it from the outside world. She felt she was at the bottom of a deep valley and on the top of the highest mountain, all at once. All the extremes she had ever known in the countryside seemed focused here, the air cool and clear. And in the cloud came a noise like a soft rush of wind.

No. Stepping into the center of the cloud, she listened closer. It was the sound of wings. She squinted, turning in all directions, looking through the mist. She saw angels, hundreds of them, hovering at the edges of the cloud, their wings beating. Their voices lifted in praise, and her heart caught in her chest. Was this a vision? How could this be?

She heard footsteps. Not like Gabriel's, heavy with armor. But a man's, in plain leather sandals. The mist swirled, parting for Him. And He stood before her. Her awe was so great now that she could not lift her head to look directly into His eyes. She could only reach for the hand that reached for hers.

The light grew so brilliantly pure, and she wondered how that could be, how white could grow even whiter. It emanated from Him. Shielding her eyes, she passed a hand in front of her face, to look at her skin. She'd never seen herself like this, so clean, so illuminated, reflected in glory. The light did not rest on her but went through her, enveloping her. She became one with the light and made of light.

"I am beautiful," she gasped, looking up and speaking without meaning to. Before she could duck her head in embarrassment, He caught her chin with one finger, carefully, tenderly, and looked her in the eyes.

He laughed. "I agree. I have always agreed."

Her knees went weak with longing. She wanted to live here, in the cloud of glory, with Him, forever. Why, she thought with sudden, great pain, had Eve ever doubted His goodness?

The music began…and she knew it without understanding how that could be. Her body praised in ways she had never experienced, her heartbeat and body tuned to the melody of heaven. She was part of a vast eternal song, her body moving in unison with all the angels and creation. She was just a note in the song, but the song was her native tongue. Standing in His presence, she discovered that she was made of praise.

She had never known that before.

How long she stood in His presence, praising Him, she did not know.

Later, she awoke in a dark kitchen, lying on the floor. Amos poked at her with a chubby finger, demanding lunch. Bleary, confused, she stood up and stumbled about, trying to serve him and his brothers as they came inside, one by one, after playing with the kitten.

After they were all settled with their dried fruit, bread, and milk, she retreated downstairs. Had the vision been real? Yes, she believed it was. Her imagination was not that inventive. Awed, she touched the skin of her arm, hoping to see herself as He did once again. But the overshadowing was over. For that revelation, she would have to live by faith now. Her hand flew to her stomach. Was she now pregnant?

Her womb was as flat as it was yesterday. Perhaps she would have to live by faith for that too. Time would tell if she had only dreamed. But if it was a dream, it was the best dream she'd ever had. She wandered out to the courtyard and sat on a bench underneath the fig trees, letting the afternoon sun slowly warm her. The sun's light was so pale, like old linen, she thought, and nothing at all like the light of heaven.

She heard a commotion on the stairs and looked to see Amos running straight toward her, his little chest heaving from exertion.

"Joseph is coming!"

---

"I have a surprise for you," Joseph announced.

Mary swallowed nervously. It was unfair of God to involve her in His divine conspiracy and not work out the details.

"I have a surprise for you too," she replied weakly.

That was not a good beginning! She chided herself for that, but she refused to keep secrets from him. She originally had a better way planned to tell Joseph of Gabriel's visitation, but the overshadowing knocked all rational thought right out of her mind.

"Your mother is resting?" he asked.

She nodded. If Joseph hoped for privacy, they would not have it in the house. Her mother was not a busybody, but she often heard more than she meant to. Worse, sometimes she misinterpreted what she heard and became agitated. Joseph hated seeing her in distress. Still, unmarried couples could not be completely alone.

Joseph bit his lip, glancing between the house and the path beyond the courtyard that led to the river and the well.

"I will keep my voice quiet," Joseph said, stepping toward the door. "I am anxious to see her now that everything is official. She has always been so good to me."

Mary quickly stepped in front of him, blocking his entrance. "Can we walk?"

Joseph frowned but then nodded. "Of course." He grabbed a water jug. "We will say we're going to the well."

She smiled at his thoughtfulness. He hated gossip as much as she did, but he knew that now it could have serious consequences for her. She had to be very careful. *Never mind me,* she thought. Money was at risk, so people were paying more attention. A trip to the water well was public enough to avoid scandal. Half the town would be on the same little path.

Still, this was Joseph, an honorable man who had no intention of causing scandal…and he wanted to be her husband. Her stomach flipped with pleasure at the thought. She repeated the word in her mind—*husband.*

As they walked, Joseph spoke of his journey to Sepphoris and signs of recent Roman activity. He did not seem bothered by Rome or its soldiers. The reason was simple—Joseph was a carpenter and builder who lived in a small town. He didn't see much sense in protesting Roman taxes when he rarely had enough money to tax. Maybe when he had his own shop, he would make more, she thought.

"And," he concluded, "I have designed a wedding band for you."

She gasped with delight, clapping her hands. "What is it? Tell me of the design!"

He laughed, shaking his head. "No. You won't see the details until we exchange vows. But let's just say that it will remind you of our childhood days and our very best memories together."

"Silver or gold?" she asked.

"You'll have to wait." He looked at the horizon, ignoring her, then shifted the weight of the water jug to his other hip.

"Twisted strands or a plain engraved band?"

He set his jaw. "Not even a Roman centurion could get those details from me."

"Ah, but a Roman centurion doesn't know how to properly tickle you," she said, reaching her hands like claws to his ribs.

He leapt away, trying to maintain his grip on the jug.

A neighbor on the path chuckled as she passed them.

"Now, what is your surprise?" he asked.

Reality hit her like a sharp blow to her cheek. Stopping, she stared wordlessly at him.

"What is it?" He cocked his head, waiting. "Did you forget something back at home?"

Her gaze swept the ground at her feet, as if the answer would be there. When she glanced back up at Joseph, his eyes narrowed. He knew something was wrong.

"I had a strange…I suppose you could call him a visitor," she began haltingly.

"A visitor? What did he want?"

She pressed her lips together. They were terribly dry. The roof of her mouth was as dry as leather too. Her mind knew what she had to say, but the words traveling the distance between them, the mere arm's length, seemed impossible. She couldn't do it.

"Go on," he prompted.

She grabbed his elbow and steered him off the path and waited for a moment of complete privacy.

"I think I'm pregnant." Oh, that was not how she planned it. She should have told him of Gabriel first. Or the cloud.

His face fell and drained of color. Folding his arms, he leaned back on his heels.

"Tell me of this visitor." He spat the words out.

"It was an angel." *Help me, God*, she prayed, fumbling about for words, telling of Gabriel, what he said would come to pass, who the child would be…and the words sounded like the ravings of a desperately ill woman. In the traitorous afternoon sun, the words sounded like lies. But if Joseph had seen the light of heaven, if he had known what real light looked like and heard the voices that sounded like thunder harmonizing across the hills…he would believe. He would know she spoke the truth. But in this ruined sun that fell across a fallen world, the holy prophecy sounded too strange, too outlandish, to be believed.

She blurted everything, and then she repeated it all in case she had left something out. Joseph's face never changed. He looked like a statue, his face frozen in shock and despair. His intended bride was pregnant, but not by him. And he had likely just spent his entire savings to design a perfect ring for her.

He dropped the water jug, and it shattered into a hundred pieces at their feet. He turned and walked back to the village alone. She dropped to her knees as her tears fell. She had not found the right words, and she had no prayers left. She'd done as Gabriel had instructed, but it had cost her the love of Joseph. Now she would wait to find out if it would cost her life.

The baby might be born and hidden away, like Moses was, and then she would be stoned to death. Why hadn't Gabriel told her the price of her trust? But if he had, would she have done as God asked? But this was the Son of God, and she was nothing but a nameless girl from a nameless town. Why shouldn't she be sacrificed? Wiping her cheeks with the back of her hand as she picked up the shards, she just had one regret.

She wished she could have seen the ring.

***

The rain was unrelenting. Everyone commented on that, heads poking out from doorways, eyes squinting up at the sky. Winter always brought rain, but this was remarkable. The dark skies never lightened, and lightning lashed the clouds over and over.

Mary did her best to stay warm, but she made sure her mother had the thickest coverlets. Mother had grown thinner. Mary focused on keeping her warm and urging her to eat.

Mary did not like the dark skies or constant rain. It was as if the world she once loved now conspired against her. Why? Because of the overshadowing? Because she carried the Son of God in her womb? Why did she feel afflicted instead of favored?

When her monthly courses were absent, first she felt relief that she had not imagined the angelic visitation, and then she felt anxiety. Joseph had not stopped by for nearly three weeks, not even once. Little Amos noticed his absence right away. He adored Joseph. Mary made a fast excuse. Men who were about to be married often worked long hours, she claimed, to provide for their new wives. Her excuse was partly true. Joseph traveled every week to Sepphoris for work.

Amos did not know better, but Mary did. And soon, all the gossips in Nazareth would buzz about Joseph's sudden turn of heart. He didn't want the work. He wanted to avoid her. Suspicion would fall on Mary. Joseph was a sensible, clear-thinking boy from an excellent family. If he rejected her, the wolves would be at her door in a heartbeat, Mary feared.

When her second monthly courses did not arrive, she knew she was further down a path that had never been walked. No one could help her or give her advice. Even if she wanted to confide in someone, she couldn't. The situation was too strange—or too holy, perhaps—to explain in ordinary words. A lonely month passed without a visit from Joseph.

She muddled through each day as best she could, mourning the future she once shared with Joseph. Another thing had changed since the overshadowing—she found it harder to live in this world. She had always loved the deep color of the green field grasses, and the delicacy of a single petal on a flower she discovered on a walk, the sweep of an eagle's wing when it took flight. But these were shadows of things to come, or perhaps shadows of the past, of what once was in Eden. Standing in the Overshadowing Presence, she had glimpsed such beauty. She sensed that it was this perfection that God was leading His people to.

To have seen such light! To have felt the warm rushing glow of His presence! And to have inhaled the air around Him, sweet and crisp and clean. That was a world no one could understand. And day by day, the memory faded and she could not bring it back. She had to continue living on this side of the veil, but this world was so dark and cold.

She did not know what Joseph would do.

Now she waited every day, not for the sound of his footsteps but for news of his decision. Would he quietly divorce her, sending her away to die in shame? Or would her death be a public event? Where was this favor of God that Gabriel had spoken of?

It was two more long weeks before she had her answer.

# CHAPTER FIVE

The floors were a mess. Mary threw handfuls of dried flax on the threshold floor to keep the mud from being tracked in. Standing, she pressed her hand to the small of her back. She'd spent hours bent over today trying to deal with the relentless rain and its effects. The rain came as a steady drizzle, a dull gray curtain pulled across the courtyard. Leaning her head against the doorpost, she thought of happier times and younger days, when the world was green and Joseph slipped his hand in hers whenever the climb was too steep for her.

"Oh, Joseph," she whispered, "I need your hand in mine."

Like an apparition from a folk tale, she saw him walking through the courtyard. His beard and hair were longer, and he looked thinner. She noticed that immediately. Still, she couldn't stop her heart from leaping at the sight of him drawing near. Before she could stop herself, she called out.

"Joseph!"

He flinched at the sound of her voice. As he approached, she noticed something else. He was pale. He must not have slept well. Had he been wrestling with a terrible decision? Maybe, but now it was clear he had made up his mind. His jaw flexed as he looked at her.

Her stomach dropped. She backed away from the door, not wanting to hear his decision. It had cost him too much—it could not be good.

Joseph walked past her, into the house. His eyes had a glazed look. Not waiting for an invitation, he moved through the interior rooms. Sitting at the kitchen table, he wiped the mist from his face and stared up at her as she stood before him.

"You have decided to divorce me?" she asked, then glanced at the corner. Mother was resting comfortably, tucked up with several coverlets. Amos sat at her feet, playing with a wooden lion. He jumped up and embraced Joseph, and Joseph whispered in his ear.

Amos nodded reluctantly and returned to the corner with his mother.

Mary raised an eyebrow.

"When we are done talking, I promised to take Amos to the river to look for frogs." Joseph looked at Amos, who nodded in approval. "Until then, he will give us privacy."

He motioned for her to sit. Reluctantly, she did.

"I have had a dream." His voice was quiet but flat. Then a smile cracked his pale, worn features, but there was no mirth in his face. "Like my namesake, yes?"

Mary's thoughts flitted back to the stories of Joseph during his time in Egypt.

"Joseph dreamed a dream, and he told it to his brothers, and they hated him even more," Joseph said quietly. Mary recognized the words. Joseph repeated words from the rabbi who had first taught him the story.

"What was your dream?" Mary reached across the table and took both his hands in hers. She couldn't help herself from offering comfort. That was her nature.

His hands were so cold.

"The angel of the Lord appeared to me in a dream," he said quietly. When he lifted his face, he looked into her eyes.

Goose bumps raised on her arms. Joseph had been visited by the same Presence of God that had overshadowed her. She did not know why God appeared in a dream to Joseph instead of sending Gabriel. Maybe she'd had so many questions after Gabriel left, he was afraid to return!

Mary glanced to the corner. Amos was absorbed with his toy, and Mother was watching him. They had heard nothing.

She pressed her lips together to keep from smiling. This was not a funny moment, but the relief of knowing she was not alone in this overwhelming turn of events…the relief broke through all her fears and worries. She was not alone. Just like when they were children, the climb was too steep, and somehow, Joseph was here to help her.

She exhaled, her body slumping forward over the table. She wasn't alone anymore.

"I did not see His face," Joseph said. "Just a brilliant light. Light is not the right word, though. The brilliance was alive, and brighter than anything I ever thought possible."

Mary nodded. She knew. Her cheeks were wet. Reaching up to wipe them, she realized she was crying.

"But His voice!" Joseph whispered, withdrawing his hands and then covering hers. Joseph was back. Her Joseph, the man she loved and who loved her.

"Have you ever heard a voice like that?" He leaned across the table, the intensity in his eyes burning.

She nodded, not trusting herself to speak. The tears streamed down her cheeks.

"The voice of the Lord said to me, 'Joseph, descendant of David, do not be afraid to take Mary as your wife, for the Child who has been conceived in her is of the Holy Spirit. She will give birth to a Son, and you shall name Him Jesus, which means The LORD is Salvation, for He will save His people from their sins.'"

Mary put her head down on the table and wept. She would not lose Joseph. He would marry her! She had been prepared to be obedient to the Lord, even unto death, but losing Joseph's affections had been stunningly bitter.

But now she knew. God illuminated the unexpected path and gave her a beloved companion for the journey. God was so, so good!

Joseph's warm hands rested on hers, comforting her in the chilled room.

Outside, the rain rattled and hissed.

She felt his strength, the weight of his arms, as he waited for her to finish crying. When she had, he stood and beckoned her into his embrace. Mary bit her lip, glancing at Mother, wondering if this was allowed. But Mother had nodded off and Amos was distracted in his playtime, so Mary collapsed against

Joseph's chest, his arms encircling her waist, lifting her up, her head pressed against his chest. For the first time since Gabriel's announcement, she let herself be weak. She let someone else take the burden that was her body and her life. Joseph was strong, his muscles made resilient through years of carpentry. She felt the power that lifted her, coming from him body and soul.

"I am here," he whispered. "Now, dry your tears. We must plan. When is the baby due?"

"Summer." She kept her face pressed against his robe. He hadn't seen her for nearly two months, and her face was red with tears. She wished she hadn't cried. Did he still find her attractive? Or was he too simply obeying? That thought chilled her to the bone. She needed to know.

She pushed away to look at him. His face was an honest one. He had never been able to get away with a lie, not even as a boy. He would always turn bright red.

"Do you want to marry me?" she demanded.

Joseph pursed his lips before a smile spread across his face. "I don't want to, no. I have to."

Before Mary could exclaim, he held up one hand.

"I have to, Mary. I cannot live without you. You are the one I always dreamed of spending my life with. You are the one who makes the world come alive for me. There is nothing even Gabriel could ever say to you that would change that."

"Nothing?" Mary cocked an eyebrow.

Joseph laughed. "Well...I hope he's done making announcements to you."

She embraced him, and this time she let her arms wrap tightly around his waist. Having her best friend and her betrothed restored to her in one day was a miracle.

"Summer?" Joseph's voice was barely a whisper as he continued in thought. "We cannot move the date of the wedding, at least not by much, or else the village might guess you are pregnant."

Joseph always saw how the pieces fit together. With a fall wedding date, she would give birth before the vows. That would be disastrous. But if she asked her father to change the wedding date, to accommodate a summer wedding, people might suspect she was pregnant. Neither outcome promised a long life for Mary.

Mary was lost in her thoughts. Joseph's gentle touch on her arm, so hesitant, as if she was a delicate new flower he had only today discovered, brought her focus back.

"You are carrying the Son of God. You have found favor with the Most High," he said. Hearing the words from his mouth made her stomach contract. She did not know if it was excitement or anxiety, but he was validating what she had experienced.

She was not alone anymore in the revelation. She marveled again at that. What a blessing it was to have a companion when called by God to a lonely road.

"I am the one to protect you both," he finished. "Why that task was given to me, I do not know. I am not a soldier or watchman. I make things with my hands. I labor for others. None of this makes sense to me either."

She smiled. He understood so well!

"Are you still going to see Elizabeth?" he asked suddenly.

She nodded. "I delayed because the rains came so early. The roads will be nothing but mud."

"The rains are almost over. Make plans to go at once. Do not write to me or send any messages. That will give me time."

"Time to what?" she asked.

"Time to convince our families to move the wedding date up. If you are out of town, and we have no communication, everyone will assume I am an impatient man. I will play the part."

The idea sounded clever enough. He had not visited in nearly two months, so no one would imagine she was pregnant. Even if they did, they wouldn't dare accuse her, because of the potential consequences. Besides, everyone in Nazareth knew he had no opportunity to be alone with her. Some were already wondering if he had lost interest. She always seemed to hear the unkind whispers.

"Aren't you done yet?" Amos jumped up. "Those frogs are waiting for us to catch them!"

Mary and Joseph looked at little Amos, his hands on his hips.

Joseph burst into laughter and walked to the door.

"I love you," he said to Mary. "When you told me…I am sorry…I forgot what we shared." He clearly struggled to guard his words in front of Amos.

He had never said the words of love to her before today. She felt her face warming. "I hate leaving. I will miss you."

"You will not tell me you love me?" he asked, a playful tone in his voice as he frowned.

Amos pretended to gag. Joseph gave him a nudge in the ribs.

"You have to have something to look forward to," she replied.

He and Amos charged into the rain, on their way to the river. If anyone saw them together, they would know that Joseph was a family man, still committed to Mary.

The rain poured down in thick sheets, obscuring everything visible, and this time, Mary was glad for it. No one would see the tears of relief and gratitude running down her cheeks.

---

Her father, Heli, traveled with her. Walking alone, he could make the journey in five days. But they would join a caravan for safety. It would be a journey of up to ten days if the caravan had many small children. Mary was excited to see Elizabeth. Gabriel had said Elizabeth was pregnant too.

At her age! Mary didn't breathe a word to her father about this. Would it be obvious when he saw her? All of Nazareth would talk about that when he returned with the news. What a welcome relief that type of chatter would be.

There were a great deal of woodlands to cross over on the way to Capernaum. Nazareth didn't have the best roads, not like the bigger cities, the ones the Romans cared about. But the roads were not as muddy as she feared, and the almond trees had buds. As she and her father picked their way through tall evergreens, she paused in the last afternoon and glanced back toward Nazareth.

"Don't turn to salt," her father teased.

"I so rarely see Nazareth from a distance," Mary replied, grinning at his jest. "The hills are graceful, are they not? They look like flowing water."

"You have always had a big imagination." He kept walking, not looking back.

Mary swallowed, struck with the tension of that truth. She had always been the one to wonder and look for the hand of God everywhere she went. If her father found out the truth of her child—no, *when* he found out, for how could she hide the Messiah?—would he think she had made up the story of His conception?

How would she prove to him that she was telling the truth? How could she ever prove to anyone what had happened, or who he was? Once again, she wished Gabriel had lingered and revealed more of God's plan.

She rested a hand on her stomach, then quickly moved it, faster than if she had touched a flame. Only pregnant women did that. She had seen the gesture enough to know what it meant. She must stop her impulses before they gave her away.

"What can your enemies take from you?" Father asked.

He loved to pose these questions to his children. Mary got so little time with him alone that she did not mind that she'd heard this one before. Many times, in fact.

"My money," she replied, stepping over a thick rock that had the decency to reveal itself before any travelers tripped. Too many rocks on this path were half-buried. When the

Romans loved Nazareth like a city of their own, the roads would be better.

"And?" Father nudged. Mary looked up from her careful navigation of her way.

"My possessions too."

"Ah, but my darling little Mary, what wealth can you always safeguard, even from your most devious enemy?"

"The Word of God. I hide it in my heart." She sighed as a cardinal flitted past, scavenging for food. "I just wish I could go to synagogue to be taught by the rabbis. If I was a boy, I would know the scriptures by heart."

"There is a scripture you haven't committed to memory?" He acted shocked, although it was a silly exaggeration. He knew how good her memory was.

She memorized whatever she learned, but she knew there was still more scripture.

"If you want to practice, let us sing the psalms together as we walk," he continued. "The first one to forget the words has to refill the water jugs at the next well."

They spent the rest of the afternoon working their way through King David's words. How close that long-dead king felt when she sang his verses! She knew the Messiah would come from David's line, and she was of David's line, but the lineage worried her. How would the future scribes record it? Would they know who fathered the child, or would they assume it was Joseph?

Someday, would it be easier for people to think that Joseph had fathered the child? She had no proof, except the child in her womb, and He could not testify yet. She was alone with this secret, and secrets always had a price, even noble ones.

When they arrived in Jericho, her father booked a room at an inn, and she settled in comfortably. Father had lost the contest and drawn water at the well, but she was still worn out. The noise of the city grated on her nerves. King Herod was building a winter palace. Her exhaustion seemed strangely magnified, but perhaps that was from being with child.

She did not know and could ask no one.

Tired from the pregnancy, the day's travel, and the secrets that weighed on her, she was grateful for the warm soup and the straw pallet in a quiet room that the innkeeper provided. Downstairs, the inn had a large common area where families ate and drank. As the sun set, Shabbat was upon them. It should have been a time of quiet rejoicing and good food, but perhaps not everyone observed Shabbat like in her village. The inn was noisy.

Still, the inn was a welcome refuge, and she thanked the Lord for providing for her needs. She would be able to eat and sleep indoors for the Sabbath, which was wonderful. After this she'd travel for a week without seeing another inn. For now, on this Shabbat, her needs were met. Perhaps, being the mother of the Messiah, every detail was being taken care of, like this inn, and she just needed to have more faith.

Perhaps she did not need to worry, not at all.

Or was that a foolish mistake? Did she need to be more vigilant or more trusting?

She was the first, and the last, mother of the Messiah.

The only certainty was that she was completely uncertain how to do this.

The morning after the Sabbath, Mary and her father set out again on the Jordan Valley Road. The first stop was a synagogue, where they would find other Jewish families who were making the trek south. There was always safety in numbers. The road led to Jerusalem, although this time, she would bypass that city and go on to the hill country.

She was thankful for that, for the road into Jerusalem was used by Rome for public torture and executions. The empire crucified men along the road as a warning to citizens entering the holy city.

The synagogue was a beautiful sight, cleansing the gruesome thoughts from her mind with its brilliant white limestone, the morning light washing across the stones like a creamy white paint. Compared to the one near Nazareth, this synagogue was huge. The columns were taller than any building in Nazareth, and the walls stretched quite a way. She wondered how many families came here to listen to the rabbis.

The instruction for boys had not yet begun for the day, so she entered through the south door, and what she saw took her breath away.

Mosaics made of tiny colored tiles covered the walls in every direction and the floor as well, pictures of biblical tales.

Dozens of scenes from scriptures, painted in vivid color! She saw Samson holding up the gates of Gaza, and on another wall, she saw the Red Sea parted, with Pharaoh and his men frozen forever in their moment of terror. She moved quickly from mosaic to mosaic, wanting to see it all before school began. Standing before a huge mosaic that would run the length of the entire city of Nazareth—that's how it seemed to her, at least—she gasped and reached for her father's hand.

It was Noah and his ark! The animals, in pairs, approached the ark from every direction. Her breath stopped in her chest as she reached out to touch the images. Animals she had only heard of but never seen were depicted.

"Is this...," she whispered to her father, who stood next to her, equally intrigued.

"An elephant?" He grunted. "I think so. I have never seen one, though. I doubt the artist got the proportions right. No animal could be that big."

She laughed at the thought of a pair of elephants—if they really were so big—getting onto a boat and the boat still floating.

"What's this one?" she asked, stepping farther down the wall to a different animal in the mosaic, pointing.

Her father came and leaned to peer closely at the mosaic. "A cat—see the tail? I have never seen one with stripes. The artist must have had quite the imagination."

The first boy arrived for his lessons. Her father took her by the hand, and they returned outside to find a caravan to travel with.

She wanted to go back and ask the rabbi about the animals. How much more to this world was there yet to discover? She pitied herself for a moment that she was just a Nazareth girl, and to Nazareth she would soon return.

Why did it seem men got all the best adventures?

# CHAPTER SIX

**M**ary squinted at the sun overhead as she crossed a dry field, the grasses brown from winter scratching at her calves. She was eager to make it to Elizabeth's home before sunset. After six days of walking, she was once again on the cusp of Shabbat. In a few hours, she would need to rest and observe the Sabbath. And she desperately needed to rest. She could not tell her father, but her feet and ankles were swelling and painful. Was this because of the pregnancy, the long walk, or both?

With great relief she caught sight of the house of Zechariah at last. Her father must have sensed the urgency, for he walked ahead of her. But neighbors intercepted him at once, slowing his progress. Mary did not understand why the neighbors would prevent them from going at once to Elizabeth. Worried, she hurried toward the house. What had happened?

She caught snippets of conversation as she walked.

Apparently, Elizabeth's husband, Zechariah, had suffered a devastating illness and could no longer speak. Zechariah had gone to serve at the Temple and had come out a broken man. The neighbors came rushing over to prepare Mary's father for the shock and to help translate Zechariah's gestures.

The prickles of anxiety that stung her stomach did not abate. Gabriel had promised that Elizabeth was pregnant. But Mary knew the power of God and what even the mere presence of His messengers could do to the human heart and mind.

If Zechariah couldn't speak, would Elizabeth be stricken too?

Mary entered the home. An oil lamp burned on the first table near the door. Letting her eyes adjust to the light, Mary moved toward the kitchen. Elizabeth was not there. Hearing soft voices in the loft, Mary went to the ladder and climbed the short distance. Her nerves were like twine pulled tight. She watched from the shadows, looking for any signs of distress.

Elizabeth sat on a bench in front of a dressing table, her maid behind her working on her hair. Her glorious, long white hair was loose, cascading down her shoulders. Elizabeth rested her hands on her abdomen, covered by a lovely robe, touching her rounded belly with such reverence that Mary felt searing grief. She wanted to touch her belly the same way but could not! No one could know she was pregnant.

Elizabeth looked up just as her maid reached for a section of hair to comb. Mary stepped out of the darkness. Elizabeth's eyes met Mary's and both women gasped in delight, startling the maid.

Mary rushed across the room and hugged Elizabeth, then rested her hands on Elizabeth's round abdomen.

"Elizabeth, my beloved friend!"

A great kick resonated against her palms. She must have looked surprised, for Elizabeth threw back her head and laughed. The joy on her face was so radiant, so brilliantly pure, that Mary knew at once Gabriel's words were true. This woman had been touched by God too, for only God could make a woman that beautiful.

Quickly dismissing the maid, Elizabeth held Mary's hands in hers and lifted her head as if praying.

"Blessed are you among women, and blessed is the fruit of your womb! And why is this granted to me, that the mother of my Lord should come to me? For behold, when the sound of your greeting came to my ears, the baby in my womb leaped for joy. And blessed is she who believed that there would be a fulfillment of what was spoken to her from the Lord."

Tears sprang to Mary's eyes. Elizabeth made a soft tutting noise and drew her in for an embrace. Mary sat on the bench next to her friend, rested her head against Elizabeth's shoulders, and let the tears fall. She was tired from the journey, but the tears were not from exhaustion. No, she was overfull with the shock of seeing Gabriel's words fulfilled, with the joy of Elizabeth's face, with the impossible made real. God had swept decades of barrenness away from Elizabeth as easily as Mary might have swept a stone away from the door.

And to be in the presence of a friend who knew God's power, in such a similar way to Mary, was like a homecoming. Embracing Elizabeth was a reunion with someone who had been to the same distant land. No one could understand Mary right now the way Elizabeth could.

A flood of praise rose in Mary's spirit. She had planned on telling Elizabeth so many things. But praise crowded out every other thought, until there was just joy, and God, and the thanksgiving between friends.

"My soul magnifies the Lord," Mary said.

Elizabeth nodded. She must have felt the same way. They were sisters in this divine conspiracy of grace.

"And my spirit rejoices in God, my Savior, for He has looked on the humble estate of His servant. For behold, from now on all generations will call me blessed; for He who is mighty has done great things for me, and holy is His name."

As Mary poured out her praise, she saw in Elizabeth's eyes a recognition of something Mary had not anticipated. Mary feared how other women might react to the news that she was carrying the Messiah. But Elizabeth was her one friend who shared in this miracle, the miracle of God pouring His presence and power out on women! Mary was highly favored, and Elizabeth was pregnant in her old age. God had done such astonishing things for both that they stood in awe of Him. As they stood together and contemplated God's goodness, they could not stare at each other in comparison or envy.

How had she never known that? Facing the wrong direction provoked envy, not one's circumstances.

As Mary poured out her praises alongside Elizabeth, she knew women would sing these same praises someday, because God was here, and God was coming, and He was a God who favored women.

"His mercy is for those who fear Him from generation to generation," Mary went on. "He has shown strength with His arm; He has scattered the proud in the thoughts of their hearts; He has brought down the mighty from their thrones and exalted those of humble estate; He has filled the hungry with good things, and the rich He has sent away empty. He has helped his servant Israel, in remembrance of His mercy, as He spoke to our fathers, to Abraham and to His offspring forever."

After a long moment, Mary felt the peaceable energy that seeing a good friend can bring. She grasped Elizabeth's hands. What had Gabriel said to Elizabeth? Why had Zechariah gone mute?

"Tell me everything," Mary exclaimed. "How did it happen?"

Elizabeth blushed furiously, her eyes widening.

"Oh!" Mary giggled. "I don't mean that!"

"You didn't seem shocked that I am pregnant," Elizabeth said. "Why? It's all anyone can talk about in the village. I can't leave my house without everyone crowding around me, hoping for answers that I don't have. I didn't cure my barrenness. I don't have special cures for other women. Some of them get angry."

Mary nodded, listening. "If they knew that Gabriel, an angel of the Lord, appeared to both of us, they would be angrier still. They would demand that he visit them too."

"Gabriel? An angel?" Elizabeth repeated slowly. "No one named Gabriel visited me. I have not seen an angel."

Mary held her breath, the surprise stunning her. "But Gabriel told me you were pregnant."

Elizabeth cocked her head to one side. "Curious. Tell me everything about that visitation. But first, tell me of the wedding."

Mary looked down at her hands, twisting them in her lap. "I am not married."

"But you are with child."

Mary nodded, and to her dismay, tears sprang to her eyes. "Yes. That is what I must explain. You are perhaps the only person who can understand. I fear for my life if anyone discovers this."

"Look at me!"

Elizabeth's tone was sharper than Mary expected. Mary wiped her cheeks as she looked at her friend.

"Pregnant and with a crown of white hair! Impossible, isn't it? We can understand very little of the ways of our Lord. But Mary, I know this—you are carrying a holy child. You do not need to live with such fear."

"I'm so worried that something could go wrong," Mary said, her breath choking her like the searing hot air from an oven in summer. "Gabriel told me what the future was, but he did not tell me how to live in the meantime. I have so many questions, and questions make me afraid."

Elizabeth chuckled softly and rose from the bench. She walked to a table underneath the window, poured a drink for Mary, and brought it over to her.

"Do you know what it is like to wait for a blessing that never comes?" Elizabeth asked. "I waited so long that in time, I had to give up. I had to face the reality of my limitations. When you give up like that, there is a hollow place in your heart where the hope once lived."

Mary took a sip of her drink, feeling it wash down to her stomach. She was weak and tired.

"You are afraid because you think you might lose what God has granted," Elizabeth said. "I am here to tell you: God is not concerned with our limitations. He has none. And if His power granted you this gift, then His power will sustain you. This is your calling, that you trust in His power above your own."

Mary beheld her sweet friend and knew that she was wise and strong. The combination of years of barrenness and faithfulness had made her so. The heartache that left Elizabeth feeling so empty had made room for an incredible reservoir of God's love and truth. That wisdom poured out to Mary, anointing her like a fragrant oil.

Mary was so grateful for this trip.

⁕⁕⁕

As the days passed, Elizabeth gave Mary great strength and encouragement. Elizabeth recounted the story of Zechariah serving in the Temple. How on the Day of Atonement, when Zechariah entered into the Holy of Holies, he came face-to-face with Gabriel. Whatever had transpired between them, Zechariah could not communicate.

No messages came from Joseph, as planned. Yet Mary was disappointed. Had she hoped that he would get a message to her, despite the risk? Yes, she admitted. She always heard tales of men driven to dangerous deeds by passion. Maybe he didn't feel passion for her. He might marry her out of a sense of duty, despite what he had said. That thought left her cold. The visit from Gabriel had changed everything.

God had blessed her in a remarkable, unprecedented way, and it had driven an awkward wedge between her and Joseph. She knew it was there. Joseph wasn't just marrying her now, he was entering into this mystery. Their lives were no longer their own, and neither was their love. God had called them both to something bigger.

Not so long ago, she had looked forward to three months with Elizabeth to get away from the village chatter of marriage and babies. Now, it was all Mary and Elizabeth could think of, and they whispered to each other late into the night. Mary confessed her worries about Joseph. Elizabeth had been married long enough to tell her of how married love changes, that it was always going to happen anyway, and Mary should embrace the seasons of love. Mary noticed that the closer Elizabeth's due date crept, her friend had trouble sleeping.

One night, when Elizabeth could not get comfortable, Mary adjusted the linens, balling them up and wedging them under Elizabeth's belly. While she did, Elizabeth spoke of the blessing and burden of grace. Elizabeth's miracle was hard for her body to bear up under, but what joy.

"When you missed your monthly courses, did you imagine you were pregnant?" Mary asked.

Elizabeth laughed, disturbing the maid. Zechariah had returned to the Temple for service, so the women were alone.

"My courses stopped years ago," Elizabeth said. "I did not believe I was pregnant until I felt the baby move. Can you imagine the shock? To feel a baby moving at my age! Zechariah had gone back to the Temple to serve his second week of service. I had to wait for his return. I was worried that if I told anyone else, they would send for a doctor, and give me herbs for a brain malady."

Mary exhaled quietly. Poor Elizabeth. She had kept a secret too, afraid of how others would react. God's grace was wonderful, but it was not always easy.

"My life will forever be divided between the days of prayer and the days of fulfillment," Elizabeth continued. "What I had never known, what I wish someone had told me, was that God's grace would strike faster than a bolt of lightning across the sky and be more powerful than a legion of Roman soldiers."

Shifting on her mat to get comfortable, Elizabeth sighed in the dark. "Thank God for my waiting days. They made me strong. And I needed that strength to endure such a turn of events."

Mary checked the bedding around Elizabeth one last time, making sure she was as comfortable as she could be. Mary had never been afraid of God before, but until now she never understood His power. She had understood more about His beauty as expressed in His creation. Now she understood that God could upend His creation, for His own reasons, at any moment.

"The baby will never get to hear his voice," Elizabeth whispered.

Mary knew she was talking about Zechariah, who remained mute.

"But if nothing is impossible with God," Mary said, remembering the words of Gabriel, "then perhaps there is more to come in Zechariah's story. One word from God is all it would take. Haven't we seen that? One word can shatter strongholds and situations that seemed hopeless."

Mary knew this was true. She had seen the radiance that surrounded Gabriel. His presence seemed to energize the air itself. Even the smallest bits of dust sparked and danced.

Zechariah had stood in the presence of an angel and paid a high price. She did not understand what had happened.

Mary was grateful that Gabriel did not appear to Joseph in person, but rather, the Lord spoke to Joseph in a dream. If Joseph had lashed out in anger when Gabriel appeared with the news that his betrothed was pregnant, Gabriel would not have stood quietly by. He had looked to be more of a warrior than a messenger.

The women slept, although Elizabeth's sleep was fitful. She needed naps the next day and every day after that.

Slowly, over the final few days together, the women came to agree on one more point— God's will did not always feel like a safe place to be in the middle of. When anything is possible, it felt like anything might happen. Those were not quite the same thing, Mary reminded herself. When she could only imagine the worst, God saw the possibilities.

Elizabeth's time for the birth crept ever closer. They counted each sunset with growing anticipation. How many more days until the baby arrived?

Without warning, Elizabeth's waters broke, and the pains began. The maid ran to fetch the midwives, and Mary held Elizabeth's hand through the tearful afternoon. The pains stole her friend away, leaving her breathless with agony.

Elizabeth moved further into that dark valley of childbirth where she was beyond anyone's aid. It was a place where God alone could save her. Many women died here. Everyone in the room, including the midwives, felt the tension. It was written plain on their faces.

When the baby emerged, he cried. A midwife rushed from the room to find Zechariah, for only the father could name the son. A fresh tear rolled down Elizabeth's face at the mention of her husband. Mary comforted her friend, even as she turned away the feelings of jealousy that temped her. Everyone celebrated the boy's birth as a miracle. Mary could not even reveal that she was pregnant!

Moments later, Zechariah's voice filled the room. Outside, in the courtyard, he sang a praise so loud, so clear, that Elizabeth's face grew completely still even as the midwives worked to clean her.

"His name is John," a priest shouted, clearly delighted.

"Praise be to the Lord, the God of Israel, because He has come to His people and redeemed them," Zechariah sang.

Elizabeth bolted upright in bed, gasping in delight at hearing her beloved's voice once more. And Zechariah sang a song of praise that hushed everyone and everything, even the infant.

"God has raised up a horn of salvation for us in the house of His servant David, as He said through His holy prophets of long ago, salvation from our enemies and from the hand of all who hate us—to show mercy to our ancestors and to remember His holy covenant, the oath He swore to our father Abraham: to rescue us from the hand of our enemies, and to enable us to serve Him without fear in holiness and righteousness before Him all our days. And you, my child, will be called a prophet of the Most High; for you will go on before the Lord to prepare the way for Him, to give His people the knowledge of salvation through the forgiveness of their sins, because of the tender mercy of our God, by which the rising sun will come to us from heaven to shine on those living in darkness and in the shadow of death, to guide our feet into the path of peace."

Elizabeth and Mary held each other's gaze. Elizabeth had received a second miracle! Zechariah wasn't just speaking. He was shouting and singing, leading the entire village in praise. And to think that Gabriel had said it was Mary who had found favor with God! Mary wanted to laugh. Gabriel didn't tell her that this favor was going to be so expansive! God's favor was flowing in Israel, drenching women, all those who turned to Him.

Mary's heart lifted in joy. Women had never been allowed to even get close to the room of His presence in the Temple. And here He was, pouring grace upon grace on them!

Oh, God was good.

A midwife returned to the room carrying the infant, the boy Zechariah had named John. Elizabeth was being cared for further by the midwives, so Mary held the infant, looking into his eyes, as he blinked drowsily against the light of this new world.

"We are bound together, you and I," she whispered, gently rocking the baby. "We are all bound together now by God's grace."

Her thoughts turned to the babe now growing in her own womb and the days to come. She would give birth in Nazareth, surrounded by her mother, sisters, and the old village mid-wives. Would there be any rejoicing? Would they suspect that Joseph was not the father?

When she had handed the infant back to the midwife, Mary paused to kiss Elizabeth on the forehead.

"You rest," Mary said. "I have to plan my return journey."

"I will pray for you. For the events to come." Elizabeth nodded sagely, saying no more in the presence of the midwives.

Mary still had to keep her secret. She had to return home, to a wedding meant to hide this secret. To a husband who would not claim his marriage rights. To an unknown future.

It was like waiting for a cat to pounce, not knowing if the cat had sharp claws.

# CHAPTER SEVEN

**M**ary took a deep breath as she and her father approached Nazareth. Spring rains had made the grass and trees lush and green. The sun was warm on her face. Summer was here at last.

A sour lump rested in her stomach, as if she had eaten a heavy meal. What if Joseph had changed his mind? No, she reminded herself. Before she left for Elizabeth's, he said he loved her and intended to marry her. He said an angel visited him in a dream.

But was that enough? A dream was not as powerful as a visitation.

Joseph stood waiting at the main road leading into Nazareth. Her heart jumped. She felt painfully alive with nerves, her smile forced and frozen as she watched his face for a sign of his feelings.

His eyes met hers, at last. And he smiled. Her father's hand reached out and grabbed her arm.

She looked down, surprised. Her father smirked, and Mary realized she had been preparing to run toward Joseph.

"Keep your composure, my daughter," he said. "After a few years and a few children, you'll run in the other direction."

She elbowed him playfully in the ribs. "Never!" Yet she was grateful he couldn't see the creeping blush she felt growing on her cheeks. She wouldn't wait years to have children. She wouldn't even wait for the wedding.

When they met, Joseph gave her father a greeting first, which Mary found disappointing, even though it was traditional and proper. The men exchanged handshakes and kisses on the cheek.

Next, Joseph kissed her on the cheek but no differently than he had her father. That was how she imagined it, at least. She bit her lip, picked the edge of her robe up from the dust, and walked toward her home.

Father, mercifully, let Joseph walk with her, and he stayed several paces behind to give them privacy.

"We have to maintain the illusion," Joseph said softly. "This must look like an ordinary betrothal, made between our fathers. It should look like a business arrangement. I cannot reveal my true feelings."

*And it's not my child,* his face seemed to say. Worries buzzed around her like invisible gnats. She caught him stealing a glance at her abdomen, which was concealed by her tunic and robe. It was still fairly easy to conceal her pregnancy as long as she wore her loosest tunic. Her abdomen had a gentle swell, even now at about seven months. Toward the end it would be harder to hide, but she couldn't worry about that now.

"Do you still have feelings?" she whispered, not looking at him. "I didn't get any message from you while I was away. Nothing."

He kept pace at her side, but he did not touch her. He kept himself entirely apart. Had his heart cooled in her absence? She could not blame him, she reminded herself. Her situation was too strange, too fantastical. What man would dare raise the Son of God? If he thought he was worthy of the task, he'd be a fool. If he understood how unworthy and unprepared they both were, he would refuse altogether.

God had put Joseph in an impossible position. Mary bit the side of her cheek. If Gabriel were here, she would risk his wrath and chide him for doing this to Joseph.

"You know why I couldn't." Joseph's voice sounded wounded.

She cut a quick glance at him. His eyes were clear and bright. He looked sincere.

"I've had time to think through many details," he continued. "When I had my dream, I knew why we must do this. But now I know how too. Before I tell you the plan, please know that I cannot touch you while you are pregnant."

Mary stopped. "Not even a kiss? A kiss on the cheek?"

"Not a real one. I love you and I will marry you. But I cannot be your husband, in any sense, while you are carrying this child."

Her mouth fell open.

"Is there a problem?" her father called from behind.

If he only knew!

"No," Mary called back, forcing a smile yet again. "Joseph is teasing me, that's all."

"I've known her so long that it's easy to get a reaction," Joseph said, tipping his head slightly in sweetest deference. But it was deception, Mary thought. Joseph had to hide the truth, to hide her, to hide what was happening. How did they get to this point, and how would they ever get past the wedding, all the way to the birth, without touching each other?

Her father laughed. "Married life will be quite an adventure for you both."

Mary wanted to scream. Adventures were afternoon walks through sweet spring grasses. This was so different. This was a jail cell with no key to be found for the lock.

Joseph cleared his throat. She glanced at him, her eyes narrowed with frustration. "I have good news, though. The plan? God has favored us with some bad news."

"I am confused," Mary grumbled.

"Caesar has proclaimed a census. Updating the tax rolls," Joseph said, sounding strangely delighted, especially considering how the Jews felt about paying Rome's taxes. "But there is word he is also trying to assess how many people are in his empire, especially men of fighting age. He might have to oppose Persia if they become aggressive. By Roman decree, I must return to my family's city to register."

Mary thought back to Joseph's lineage, the lineage he shared with her—King David.

"Bethlehem? You're going to Bethlehem?" She'd be big as a house before he returned!

"No. *We* are going to Bethlehem," he replied calmly. "It is perfect. We will marry immediately and leave for Bethlehem. You will have the child while we are gone. We will return after a few months, when the baby is still little. No one will be entirely sure of the birth date, because no one from Nazareth will be there to witness the birth."

"My father will never let me go with you. Your mother will never let me go!" His mother would expect Mary to move in and begin to help with the family chores. Mary's father would be outraged that Joseph swept Mary to Bethlehem, cheating her out of her newlywed year.

"When you are my wife," Joseph said, "no one's authority will be higher than mine."

"When will you tell them?" Mary asked. Her head hurt. And she was starving. She needed food and time to think through everything Joseph had just told her. If she left home to have a baby, she would not have the village midwives, or her mother and sisters. She would be alone. Utterly alone and in a new city.

How could that be God's plan? It was terrible!

"It's going to be all right," Joseph said softly, as if he read her mind. "God will provide."

She was back home, on her sleeping mat, drifting to sleep when she realized something. Joseph had never answered her question.

When was he going to reveal his plan to the families?

She pressed a hand to her forehead, as if to make room.

Now she had one more secret to keep.

---

Joseph's mother delayed the wedding. She insisted her husband build a different, more elaborate wedding canopy, saying it would be good for the family business. Joseph was trapped. Three more long weeks passed before the wedding could take place. Mary watched her abdomen grow, knowing every day brought her closer to discovery and dishonor. Finally, the day arrived.

Her sister Miriam fussed over the delicate linen, with the glass beads along the edges. Draping it over Mary's head, she stepped back to inspect her work. The other women in the chamber sat, watching.

Earlier that morning, Rebekah had sent over her own maidservants to attend to Mary. The girls had heated a metal rod and used it to soften her maddening curls. Then they braided her hair and looped it around to form a knot at the back of her neck. Rebekah had loaned her a pearl necklace and gold hoop earrings as well.

Clucking like a mother hen, her sister turned and reached for the comb that sat on the dressing table.

"We don't have time," Mary insisted. The wedding procession was outside, their noise unmistakable. Her sister ignored the tambourines, singing, shouting, and clapping as she carefully teased out individual curls to frame Mary's face.

When her sister had arrived that morning, she had found Mary already dressed in her wedding tunic, with a beautiful robe draped over it. The robe too was a gift from Rebekah. Mary was grateful she'd had an excuse to dress herself in private before anyone arrived. No one could see her abdomen. It was now unmistakably round.

"I brought perfume," her sister said, rummaging through her bag. Once she found it, she poured a thick oil into her palm and used two fingers from her other hand to dab the oil onto Mary's neck and chest.

Pinching the tunic's fabric to pull it away from her body, Mary twirled for the women in the upstairs chamber, who applauded. Mary's mother rose unsteadily from a bench to kiss her, and Mary gently hugged her then helped her sit. The maids tutted and fussed over her mother while Mary inspected herself in the bronze mirror.

From the stairs, Rebekah crooked a finger and beckoned Mary to follow her downstairs, alone. Mary hesitated. Her nerves were too thin for inappropriate jokes. These were not ordinary wedding nerves. She carried the weight of her secrets, worried that her abdomen might give her away. But no one had noticed. No one had expected to see her fully naked, probably, not even as she dressed, because she was a girl of such pious modesty.

If they only knew what she protecting. It was not her modesty.

Downstairs, Rebekah dipped a hand into the bag at her waist and produced a tiny clay jar with a stopper. She pressed it into Mary's hand.

"What is this?" Mary asked. Rebekah shushed her, as her eyes darted toward the stairs warily.

"Blood. From our cook when she was preparing last evening's meal," Rebekah whispered.

Mary's brows knotted together. She was both confused and repulsed. Thankfully, the stopper was secured in the jar.

Rebekah grabbed her by the forearm and pulled her close to whisper near her ear.

"If you do not bleed on your wedding night, people will talk. Some of the stricter rabbis may call for you to be stoned," she urged. "The law demands we be pure, and this is the proof. Joseph must wave the bed linens outside the chamber."

Panic struck Mary's heart. She knew that during the wedding feast, she and Joseph would retire to an upstairs bedroom chamber. It was expected that they would consummate the marriage. But Joseph would not, not while she was pregnant with the God-child. But if Joseph did not pretend to consummate the marriage and prove her virginity to the crowd, she could be stoned to death.

Why, oh why, had God not warned them of this complication? Why had God not given them directions for this too? Mary knew where the child came from and what His name was to be, but what good was that information if neither mother nor child survived?

She thanked Rebekah for this gift even as she pushed it back to her. "You are thoughtful. I appreciate you trying to protect me from gossip." She did not mention that Rebekah was trying to protect her from the law as well.

Rebekah's face was clouded. "Mary, you must take this seriously. Not everyone bleeds. I don't want to see your good name ruined. Of all our friends, you above all have earned it."

Without thinking, Mary embraced her friend, hugging her tightly.

Suddenly Rebekah pushed back, a dark frown changing her expression. She slipped a hand to Mary's abdomen, and just as fast, Mary pushed it away then froze.

Rebekah's eyes opened wide.

"Oh Mary," Rebekah exclaimed under her breath. "What have you done?"

---

The wedding procession had been small but noisy. Mary's mother blinked in surprise at the merrymaking, and more than once Mary had to remind her that today was her wedding day.

As Mary approached the courtyard of Joseph's home, the noise from his family joined hers. More tambourines rattled as local girls danced and sang. The littlest boys ran and acted silly, until their mothers caught them by the napes of their robes. The sun was warm and brilliant gold, making everyone in a good mood after weeks of cold spring rain.

"What a beautiful day for a wedding!" Joseph's mother said as she kissed Mary on either cheek. Mary returned the kisses dutifully.

She could barely look her future mother-in-law in the eye. Mary wanted to tell her of the God-child she was carrying. Wouldn't that thrill her above any news of a wedding? To know that her son's new bride was going to have such a special child, a grandchild to raise and love, one that would be mighty among the people?

"God's favor is upon us," Mary replied.

Joseph took her by the arm and led her to stand under the wedding canopy placed in the middle of the courtyard. Mary smiled at his father in appreciation. The wood canopy was ornately carved, and a credit to the family name.

His grandmother grumbled as she walked past. "Summer is not a pleasant time for a wedding. The bugs always bite old people first."

"You are not old." Joseph scowled dramatically as he pretended to chastise her. "And besides, it is a very pleasant day. Not a bug in sight."

"Phh," was the only reply from her. Then the old woman winked at Mary, and Mary decided she liked her very much.

"I suppose for a bride this lovely, I wouldn't expect you to wait the full year," the grandmother muttered.

Mary felt a surge of warmth in her chest. What gracious, sweet words, spoken just as her nerves were failing. She had wanted her own mother to tell her how beautiful she looked. Mary took good care of her but missed her. How was that possible? To devote so much attention to her mother and yet feel like she hadn't gotten to spend any time with her?

A tear slipped down Mary's cheek. The crowd nudged each other, smiling at the sight. They probably thought it was love and sentiment for her wedding, but it was loneliness and fear. She had never expected to be married without her mother being truly present. And she had never expected to be married while she was secretly carrying a child. To think that it was a God-child…well, she would have been incapable of imagining that not long ago.

Everything about today, about her wedding, was so unexpected. For everyone. The census that Rome had decreed had forced the date to change. And the biggest surprise, Mary knew, was coming.

Or was that the second-biggest surprise? She knew what Joseph was about to do.

Joseph stood under the arbor. She took her place at his side. Wind stirred her tunic, and Joseph angled his body to shield her from the little crowd. As he did, their eyes met. What did she see in them? Was it love? Or the shock of being swept into God's divine conspiracy? She had never experienced either before now. She didn't know which was which, or what the future held. She did not even know how to read Joseph anymore, just as he no longer could see her as an ordinary girl from their ordinary town. God had changed her. She had to see herself the way Gabriel said that God saw her. Otherwise, she would lose her nerve from the pressures of these secrets. And Joseph?

God had instructed him to marry her as his wife. What did that make them to each other? Necessary?

She didn't want to be necessary, or a sign to him of his obedience to the Lord. She wanted to be loved as an ordinary woman, and as an ordinary wife. But she was neither.

She looked into his eyes and saw a glint of the radiance from Gabriel's presence reflected in them. Blinking, she tried to clear her mind before she looked again. But there it was, that same radiance that had marked Gabriel as having stood in God's presence. Joseph's eyes held that same brilliance, one that she had not seen before when he looked at her.

It was love. Abounding, deep, and steadfast.

She looked up in the direction of the sun, which had gone behind the white gauze of clouds. Even shrouded, the sun was a welcome guest today, and its soft light warmed her face. Looking then at all her family and the people from the village gathered to witness the vows, she saw little glimmers of this radiance. The faintest little sparks that until an hour ago had been invisible to her were all around, alive in the people and the air itself.

Love surrounded her.

Drawing a deep breath, she accepted Joseph's outstretched hand. She was ready.

# CHAPTER EIGHT

The wedding feast was wonderful. That's what everyone kept telling Mary. She had no appetite, even if her stomach growled with hunger. The thought of food made her nauseous. This was not morning sickness like other expectant mothers suffered with. She was past that point in her pregnancy.

This was nerves. She was married now, in every legal sense. Now Joseph had to prove himself one more time, breaking with tradition to safeguard her good name.

Yet he let the wedding feast continue for so long. She was hungry, nauseated, tired, and on the verge of, crying at any moment.

Her father raised a cup of wine. "Mary the younger has been a joy to raise and a blessing in our home. May she be both to you as well." He tipped the cup toward Joseph's parents.

Everyone cheered and drank to the toast. It was not her father's first toast of the evening but probably his fifth. He wouldn't stop, Mary knew, until the wine ran out.

Her father slapped his palm against the wood table loaded with food. Mary could tell he was summoning his words for another, more boisterous toast. This time there would be mention of future babies, no doubt.

If he only knew.

Joseph appeared at his side and rested one powerful hand on her father's shoulders. Her father quieted and looked up with a quizzical expression.

"I have an announcement," Joseph said. His voice was loud enough that conversation ceased everywhere in the courtyard. Even the musicians stopped playing and looked at each other, confused.

"I am taking Mary to Bethlehem," Joseph said. "For the census."

"The House of Bread?" Mary's father asked, referencing the oldest name for Bethlehem. "Why? We have enough here!"

Laughter scattered among the guests.

"We do indeed," Joseph replied. "A wedding feast to be remembered! My family line runs through Bethlehem, and so it is to Bethlehem that I must return now."

"But you only today married!" Mary's mother exclaimed.

Mary winced with pain. Her mother struggled to understand daily events. Why did she have to be lucid at such a painful moment?

"Mary will come with me." Joseph's tone was firm, as if cutting off protests before they began.

The words sucked the breath from the crowd. Mary knew this was unheard of. A bride and groom leaving town immediately? No, Mary should be moving into his house this very night, not setting out on a journey.

"But why?" Mary's father asked. "Not everyone is returning to their home city. And you are not required to present yourself in Bethlehem right away."

Joseph bowed his head. "True. But being of the line of David means I take special care to protect the records of my family name. I must go to Bethlehem and register there, as his descendant. It must be on record."

Across the room, Rebekah caught her eye and cocked her head to one side, as if asking a question.

Mary immediately looked away. Her mouth was dry as sand. She accepted a cup of wine from a servant and took a sip. Clearing her throat, she forced a smile.

"It should delight you," she announced, before looking directly at her father. "The Roman empire will have a record that your daughter and her new husband are of the line of David. They will know we come from kings. Your grandchildren's lineage will be indisputable."

Turning to her mother, she continued. "What a wonderful way to begin a marriage, wouldn't you agree? I can only think this is a wedding gift from the hand of the Lord. And I will bring back soil for your garden too. Our food will be grown in the soil that nourished David."

Her mother drew her shawl tightly around her waist, leaning back in her seat, a cloud on her face.

"You will bring soil to me as well," Joseph's mother spoke at once.

Mary turned and nodded, heat rising in her face. She didn't like being spoken to as if she were a servant. Maybe that's what married life would be like in this woman's home. Mary could read the excitement in her eyes, though, even from across the room.

A garden that other women envied? Mary could tell that sounded good. And a daughter called to David's revered homeland? Mary saw the thoughts racing through her mother-in-law's head. This would be a point of pride. If...if her mother-in-law never discovered the truth.

"We are under Rome's control," Joseph's mother said, shrugging.

"When will you leave?" her father asked. His voice was softer now.

Mary would miss him. He was a tenderhearted father. Tears sprang to her eyes when she realized she would return to Nazareth but never again to his home.

Their eyes met, and she saw tears forming in his eyes as well.

Mary excused herself to go up to her bedchamber just beyond the stairs to pack. As she passed Rebekah, her friend reached out, as if for a quick, tearful hug.

Rebekah hissed in her ear. "How could you let the pregnancy continue? You could have gone to Sepphoris and bought medicine!"

Mary nodded and smiled, as if Rebekah had whispered words of good wishes into her ears.

"No, I could not." Mary looked at her friend, willing her to understand. "I have to do this. Someday I hope you will understand."

Rebekah pressed a hand to Mary's cheek. "Bethlehem is a long journey. Be careful." She looked as if she was saying good-bye to Mary forever. "I could have helped you. I wish you had told me."

Mary's chin trembled. The friends had always looked out for each other when they traveled. Even when going to Jerusalem for Passover, they stayed side by side. The boys knew it was safer to pester other girls when Mary and Rebekah were together.

Mary took hold of Rebekah's hand and clasped it between her own against her heart.

"Whatever you think happened, you are wrong, my friend," she whispered. "You know me."

Rebekah slowly shook her head. "I thought I did."

The first step on the road out of Nazareth was the hardest. Mary refused to let herself glance back over her shoulder, knowing the families watched as she and Joseph departed. If Mary saw her mother crying, she'd leave Joseph's side and run back to her, telling her everything. Mary would explain that this was the only way to protect the baby and her good name.

Mary could not look at her mother, not even one more time, for fear of her heart breaking. And she knew, in her heart, that her mother might not survive until the return journey in a few months. *Please, God*, Mary prayed silently. *Let her live to see this child.*

Joseph had arranged for an inn on the first night. They would only walk a few hours away. Joseph wanted to have Mary ride a donkey, to spare her another journey by foot, but it would arouse too much suspicion. Instead, he promised he would provide a donkey for her once they were safely away from Nazareth.

Late that night, Mary realized what the journey gave her—she no longer had to hide her pregnancy. She could allow the wind to blow her tunic close to her body. She was married now, and everyone would assume that this was a normal pregnancy. Mary smiled to herself at that all-too-human mistake. People assumed many things. But she was highly favored. How could anyone guess the way God moved in her life? She thought of Elizabeth, with her white hair, now cradling a newborn.

With the inn in sight, Mary sang psalms to the unborn child, reciting the psalms of David.

"You have energy left?" Joseph sighed. "I am exhausted."

"He will know the sound of my voice, and the scriptures will be familiar," Mary replied. "The sound of my voice, and the Word of God, will be His shelter. Both will sound like home."

"You have had a lot of time to think about this pregnancy," Joseph replied, sounding both impressed and distant.

He was tired, having just pulled off a daring escape plan. She reached for his hand—and this time, he did not pull away. She smiled, relieved, grateful to be married at last. Even if all he would allow was his hand to hold, she was grateful.

"It's not a pregnancy," Mary said, letting her other hand rest on her belly. "This is Jesus, the Messiah."

Her pace quickened now that the inn was so close. Joseph pulled at her hand.

"No need to rush," he said. "The stars above are so beautiful. Besides, no one waits for us at the inn."

Mary smiled bravely, even as her heart sank. Family, friends, and home were behind her.

Only the unknown future lay ahead.

***

Mary had never been to Bethlehem. Jerusalem was the farthest she had ever traveled, and Bethlehem sat below Jerusalem.

The first full day's journey led them into the Jezreel Valley. They traveled along the river's route through the Jordan Valley to avoid Samaritans. True to his word, Joseph had arranged a donkey for her. A wedding gift, he called it.

She called it Balaam in case the donkey felt encouraged to talk. The days were long and boring. Joseph wasn't talking as much as he did when they explored the hills of Nazareth. He seemed so much more serious and always on alert. She missed his playful side. But then, maybe he missed things about her too. Or about his hopes for the newlywed year. Sharing a bedroom—but not a bed—was not what any man expected.

The next day, crossing through Jericho, she thought of the walls that fell. Then they traveled uphill for an entire day heading toward Jerusalem. The pains in her back and low abdomen increased as her body struggled to handle the jostling. As the donkey walked uphill and downhill, she struggled with her balance, her swollen belly catching her off guard.

On the second day, they were still three hours outside of Jerusalem when darkness fell. Joseph grew frustrated—she could tell by the tight line of his mouth. He had not counted on her being so slow. She was usually nimble.

"We will camp here," he said.

She watched as he made camp. Helpless, really, to do anything to assist, she sat and then noticed as the stars came out, forming a canopy of light overhead.

She thought of Rebekah's wedding, how her friend grumbled at a wedding canopy made from inexpensive fabric.

Joseph sat beside her, removing his sandals to shake the dust out.

"Look," Mary said shyly, pointing overhead. "God has spread a wedding canopy over us."

Joseph leaned against her, his face softening as he nudged her with his shoulder. "So He has." He was impatient with the slow pace, not with her. She traveled nearly half the speed she usually did. Even she was frustrated.

"How many times have you been to Bethlehem?" Mary asked. Joseph had the route picked, the inns chosen, and seemed to have no doubts about the journey.

"Never." He shrugged.

Her mouth fell open. What if they got lost? They could walk forever! A robber might get them, or a Samaritan! Mary's emotions surged, and tears formed in her eyes. This was unlike her.

Ducking her head, she spotted a green stem poking from the earth, its bud curled tight. Even in the shadows, she could see that the summer flowers were here. Her heart lightened as she thought of that. Flowers in summer had always been such a joy. She couldn't help but think that flower had been planted there just for her, by God's grace. She had stepped into a strange new life, it seemed to say, but there would still be flowers.

Joseph put an arm around her. If he couldn't touch her like a husband would, at least he would touch her like a friend, Mary thought. That was yet another small comfort.

Had she ever appreciated small comforts before this? The Lord surrounded her with them, and their effect on her heart was noticeable. A small comfort could do the work of a hundred greater graces when your back was bowed with trouble, she thought.

"Praise God," she whispered. Praise the God of small comforts. The words of a psalm sprang to mind, and she sang them to herself.

"If I should say, 'My foot has slipped,' Your faithfulness, LORD, will support me. When my anxious thoughts multiply within me, Your comfort delights my soul."

How different it was to sing a psalm on the open road rather than in her kitchen in Nazareth. She had never been to Bethlehem and was uncertain of the route, but the words of praise made her feel at home, even on the road. Her soul had its home in God's Word.

Would that be enough, she wondered, when all else turned dark and strange?

***

The Jordan Valley was beautiful in early summer. The farther south they traveled, the greener the world seemed. Her sweet donkey could barely constrain himself from stopping to sample the fresh grasses every few minutes.

Joseph had a dim view of this impulsive behavior.

"That donkey is going to delay our trip by a day or more," he grumbled.

She stroked the beast's scruffy fur along its neck. "He's hungry. It was a long winter."

Water in a nearby river gurgled across smooth wide stones, as if laughing at Joseph's impatience. Joseph tried to maintain his scowl, but Mary's donkey brayed at him.

"I think he's arguing with you." Mary laughed. "Maybe a rest would do you good too."

Joseph shook his head. "I want to be at the edge of the Jordan Valley by sunset. There will be plenty of vendors in the village, and with land this fertile, they will have good provisions."

"Will we need them? We will be in Jerusalem after that."

"It's a sharp climb into the city from the east. We will make it by nightfall tomorrow if we don't stop. But something tells me we will be stopping a lot."

Mary tipped her head in acknowledgment. "I can't sit on a donkey all day. I can't walk that fast either. The baby isn't due for a few weeks yet. I think. But my body feels heavy and slow."

Joseph stopped and turned to look at her.

"You think?" he asked, repeating her words. "You don't know exactly when the baby is due?"

Mary stopped her donkey, who was all too glad to find another clump of fresh grass to devour.

"No," she replied, her tone betraying the defensiveness she felt. "It's a holy child. Does that change the length of the pregnancy? I don't know. Elizabeth and I guessed the arrival date as best we could. But even if it were a natural pregnancy, I couldn't tell anyone else about it. No one in Nazareth told me what to expect. I've carried this secret, this child, alone!"

Tears fell, and she raised her hands to hide her face. She didn't mean to become so emotional. Her emotions were unreliable, and she wasn't sure if it was the circumstances of her marriage or this pregnancy, or both.

Joseph walked to her and stroked her arm. "Forgive me. I assumed that women knew these things…I don't know, I suppose by instinct. That was foolish of me. You were isolated from your friends and family and unable to ask all your questions. I wish I could help you."

She couldn't bring herself to look at him. Silence hung heavily between them.

In a sudden movement, he grabbed a shawl from her saddle pack and draped it over his head.

Scrunching up his face so that he appeared to be a shriveled old woman, he spoke in a silly, high-pitched voice. "Got a question for me, dearest girl? I will assist you as best I can."

Mary peered between her fingers, giggling. "Yes, I do. My husband and I are wondering, when is the baby going to come?"

"When it's good and ready!" Joseph shouted, pretending to be irritated by the question.

Mary nearly fell off her donkey laughing. This Joseph was her childhood friend that she remembered. He was such fun and so kind to her, always.

She reached over and yanked the shawl off. Resting it on her lap, she scolded him good-naturedly.

"Don't wrinkle my shawl. It's bad enough that it smells like a donkey."

They walked together in companionable silence. She was grateful that somehow they had navigated her emotional outburst and the frustration of the circumstances. Maybe married life wasn't going to be so complicated. She just had to remember one thing about Joseph. Before he became her husband, he was her dearest friend.

He could still be that no matter what unexpected roads the marriage might take.

# CHAPTER NINE

The next afternoon, they made the sharp turn west, toward the ocean and the eastern gate to Jerusalem.

Joseph kept her in the middle of the road, shielding her from the sights of the crucified. She held her robe to her nose, unwilling to breathe the stench of the dying.

As she entered the beloved city riding on the donkey, the baby kicked. The sun shone like a proud sentinel over the watchtower looming above the gate. Would her child enter this city by the same gate when He revealed Himself as the Messiah? Or would people immediately recognize His divinity at His birth? Sitting tall, she surveyed the faces of the Pharisees and Sadducees who wandered the streets. No one marked her approach with any interest. To them, she was just a common woman, and her child was just another child.

But Elizabeth had known at once that Mary carried the Messiah. Why didn't these holy men? Why had God chosen to work among women and not these men of the law?

When they finally stopped for the evening at an inn, Mary was grateful to be done with the hardest part of the trip, that steep relentless climb into Jerusalem. The innkeeper promised to feed and water her donkey well, because the poor creature looked as tired from the climb as Mary felt.

Outside the inn, a young woman wailed and cried. Joseph winced as he heard the noises of someone in such pain.

"What is happening to her?' Mary asked, feeling the baby shift. Maybe he was restless after a long day of riding.

"Nothing," Joseph replied. "The innkeeper told me of a demoniac who roams this area. She is the youngest daughter of a perfumer from Magdala. Her name is, or was, Mary, but now she only hurls curses and steals for bread."

Mary shuddered. What a world she was bringing her son into!

"That is why we got a good price on this room." Joseph sighed. Flinching as another ear-splitting, unearthly wail shattered the peace, he clapped his hands over his ears.

"Because we have a window facing the street," Mary concluded. Joseph nodded.

They endured the awful sounds until evening prayers. The young woman grew strangely quiet. Mary ventured to peek outside the window. As the sun set over the limestone walls, the city sparkled and looked like it was made of gold.

The innkeeper's wife served a good stew with lamb and barley bread. Mary was hungry but found it hard to finish her bowl. Her abdomen didn't have as much room as it used to. And her thoughts kept returning to the woman who was afflicted with demons. Mary rested her hand on her belly, praying that her Messiah-child would be protected from women such as that. She sounded dangerous.

That night, once again, Joseph slept on the floor. How odd to have a man who was not her relative in the same bedchamber! Marriage, she was discovering, caused a hundred different adjustments to her daily routine. When she finally slept, she dreamed of Nazareth and fields of wildflowers.

She dreamed of the life she left behind. When she awoke in the night, she was sad and homesick, and didn't dare tell Joseph what else she was feeling.

Painful contractions rippled across her abdomen at unpredictable intervals.

Joseph slept, and she did not awake him. This might be the last good sleep he had for many months.

---

Rough-looking shepherds watched Mary and Joseph approaching Bethlehem as their sheep grazed. The men looked hard-used by life, with threadbare robes and faces weathered by the sun. Seeing her tunic drawn tight against her belly as she rode, they nodded respectfully, and her heart softened as she considered their lives. Alone by day, awake by night, these men guarded helpless animals against wolves and mountain lions. One of the men held a wooden staff as thick as her arm. How many times had he used it to bash the head of an animal who bared its teeth?

She glanced at their flock. The sheep looked healthy and fat. A few had distended bellies. She guessed they were due to give birth. Some of the lambs would be sold for sacrifices at the Temple. What a sad thing to send one of these sweet babies to die for the sins of men!

Just ahead, Roman soldiers walked the streets, deep in conversation, making her skin crawl. What were they saying? She rested a hand on her belly, and their eyes glanced over her frame.

Bethlehem was larger than she imagined. Was it because David had been a young shepherd here when Samuel the prophet anointed him as king? This was the land where David shepherded his sheep, forgotten and overlooked. Except by God.

The city had walls, fortified by King David's grandson, Solomon's son Rehoboam. The Judean mountains sat dark and brooding in the distance. Palm trees and scrub brush lined the road into the city.

Bethlehem was a noble city, yes, but so dusty! She longed for a bath at the inn when they finally arrived. She had to have a bath before the birth, certainly. Her robes itched with all the sand and grit that had stolen into the folds of the fabric.

The wind coming from the Mediterranean Sea had blown the dust around, rather than cool the air.

Joseph asked a Roman soldier where he must register. The soldier looked at Mary, his eyes roaming over her belly again. A chill shot down her spine despite the day's heat. Instinctively, she pulled her robe tight across her body to hide her frame. These Roman guards had no right to look upon the God-child she was carrying! They would never share in this blessing! Indeed, the Messiah would deliver the Jews from oppressors like these!

The noise of the street seemed so loud after the silence of the road, and everyone was speaking Hebrew. That was a shock after the years of hearing Aramaic in Nazareth.

The long silences on the road that led to Bethlehem had given her time to ponder the four hundred years of silence since the time of the prophets.

She looked up at the clouds, wondering what the dead prophets could see and know. And, she wondered, what would the birth be like? Would Gabriel return and tell her how to raise the child?

A thought struck her with such force she nearly toppled off her donkey. Saying yes to God had broken every tradition of man, for she did not ask her father for permission to obey. She had not even asked Joseph, her betrothed, for his permission to bear this child. She had said yes to God and allowed God to establish the path for her future. That was a thing unheard of, especially in a little town like Nazareth.

Joseph insisted they find an inn and eat a midday meal. They could shop at the market for supplies later. For now, he wanted Mary resting comfortably. Everything else could wait. He left her at the corner of a market stall and headed out to secure an inn.

Mary did not need the time to think. She had thought too many thoughts already. Tonight, at dinner in the inn, she'd overwhelm Joseph with her chatter! One question she had— should Joseph approach a local rabbi and reveal that the infant was the Messiah—or would a rabbi instinctively know?

She pressed her lips together to keep from crying out as a pain in her belly rippled through, all the way to her back.

She knew that Joseph had seen the winces of pain. She was uncomfortable and scared, as her body stirred, like the air before a storm.

She couldn't go into labor, not yet! Not until she was safely in an inn and the local midwives had been called. How disreputable to give birth to the Son of God on the side of the road! She chided herself to maintain control. Joseph would return any moment, and she would be at an inn, with plenty of help.

Scanning the street, she did not see Joseph. He was probably negotiating for the best room for the God-child's birth. The world had held its breath for this moment for four hundred years! She did not doubt that this story would be told for hundreds of years to come.

She wished she had prepared more, including buying clean and proper linens for the child. She hadn't dared buy anything in the markets before this in case word reached her parents and they figured out the timing. Traders all seemed to know one another.

Joseph returned and took hold of the donkey's reins. He mentioned an inn at the far edge of town.

When Mary saw the inn, she breathed deeply for the first time all day. She was almost there. Joseph would make all the final preparations. All she had to do was hold on. The incredible journey, the astonishing fulfillment of Gabriel's words, was about to reach its climax.

She would soon see the face of God.

Joseph opened the stable door, then turned to Mary. Shocked, Mary felt a tear slip past her defenses. If she cried now, she might never stop. This was not how the birth should go! The Messiah, the King of the Jews, deserved a decent birth. He deserved all the honor that the Jewish people could give!

Had she or Joseph made a mistake? What should they have done differently?

Any other woman would have made sure the birth would be appropriate for the Messiah...Mary's anger turned toward herself. She was a foolish girl not to have prepared more efficiently!

"Can you bring me something to drink?" she asked Joseph, her voice tremulous. A sheep raised its head from its stall, blinking at the light.

He nodded. "Yes, of course. The innkeeper has sent for a midwife. Stay strong, my love."

Mary sat on the straw-ridden floor, defeated. She pulled her shawl down around her face and shoulders, wrapping herself against the sight of the stable. How could she give birth here? It was impossible. Not even the poorest woman in Nazareth would think of that.

She fought tears, but they overwhelmed her last defenses. She wept, from homesickness, from pain, from the longing to have a word from God. This could not be His will! But every contraction came stronger than the last. Even if an inn opened its doors now, she would never make it. The God-child was coming.

She shifted to all fours, rocking back and forth, trying to ease the contractions. This was strange to her. She had seen women give birth, and they had screamed in agony. This pain was not like that. Her body shifted like the stars in the heavens, everything moving into new places. Each contraction was a blinding burst of light, and while it was not comfortable, she could bear the strange sensations.

Joseph returned just as her waters stained the stable floor.

He rushed to her side, frightened.

"It's not blood," she whispered. "Just my waters."

He nodded, mutely, but the color had drained from his face. The dark, dirty stable floor made it impossible to tell the difference between blood and water.

"The midwife cannot come," Joseph said after a moment. "The innkeeper will send salt and wine for the baby when it is born."

"Where is the midwife?" Mary asked weakly. She wanted to ask where God was too, but pressed her lips together. Fear made her feel like a small child. How could such a momentous event happen in such a forsaken place?

A young horse peered over his stall door. His warm brown eyes were fringed with black lashes. He seemed to be held rapt by her. Mary was comforted by his luminous eyes, which seemed steady and calm.

The horse belonged to a Roman soldier. She knew this, not just because it was a majestic animal but because of the smell of peas and boiled barley that wafted from its stable. The Romans bought good food for their animals. Still, she thought, it seemed like a kind creature.

The other animals, including her own donkey, quieted, keeping vigil as Mary labored. Every creature in the stable was alert, ears twitching back and forth, their heavy breaths the only noise they made. The straw stirred around the stall doors as they exhaled.

Did the animals sense what was happening? Was that even possible?

Suddenly she heard a sound that made her blood run cold. Outside the stable, in the hills nearby, a mountain lion screamed. The horse kicked against the stable walls, nervous at how close the predator was. A sizeable gap in the roof above made the sound even louder, and it seemed the lion might break down the door at any moment.

Joseph stood and went to the door. Peering outside into the starlit night, he sighed in relief.

"The shepherds are on the hill," he called back to her. "They keep watch. Nothing will come near us tonight."

Mary nodded. It was time to push. The Lamb of God was coming.

A few minutes after Mary had delivered her son, the innkeeper's wife arrived and offered to assist with the cord and first bath. Joseph declined her offer but accepted the supplies she had brought.

Joseph took the infant from Mary and wrapped Him in linens. "The bath will wait," he whispered to the baby. "For now, we just want to hold You."

Mary could not stop staring at the infant's face. Was this the face of God?

Above her, through the gap in the roof, moving lights danced. She heard a singing that was not of this world, and her heart leapt.

Joseph stood still, as if listening with his whole body. He handed the baby back to Mary, careful not to touch her directly, and went to the stable door. He opened it and peered into the night.

"Angels," Mary whispered. "I think we are hearing angels."

"There is a bright light outside, near the shepherds," he said. "It is like a thick cloud that shines. I cannot see what is at the center."

The infant Jesus opened His eyes. Light from above illuminated His face.

Mary's heart filled with awe at her son's expression and the light reflected in His eyes. This was the light of a thousand angels, filtering down through broken wood beams that crossed overhead. His little face was bathed in the glow of heaven.

Without warning, He cried, a little bleating noise, and she treasured the first sounds of the Messiah, who sounded like a little lamb separated from the herd. She held Him to her chest, her heart breaking with sorrow that this dark, broken world surrounded Him.

Joseph walked back to Mary.

"His name is Jesus, for God is with us to save." Joseph named Him, just as any natural father would do. Mary knew nothing was natural about this. She felt a pang of guilt too that this son was not Joseph's son. That was not God's plan.

And yet His plan was good. "God saw all that He had created and declared that it was very good." She recited the words of Moses from the book of Genesis. Surely God in heaven looked down at Jesus and was speaking words of love. Mary wondered if Gabriel was present by the throne of God, if he watched to see the face of God in this new creation.

She looked up at Joseph, and radiant love had transformed his face too. Mary closed her eyes in thanksgiving. Joseph was not the father, but there was no wall between him and the infant Jesus. Love had filled the space between them.

"I will protect you," he said to them both, speaking into the night air. Mary wondered who else—or what else—might be listening. The encounter with Gabriel had forever altered her awareness. Even if she was now unclean, and would be for seven days after the birth, Joseph could touch her with his words.

Falling back on the straw, Mary wished her tired mind could find the words to express her gratitude to God. He had delivered the child, but hadn't He also delivered Joseph in an important way? Joseph was fully committed to the infant and to her. Pride could have sabotaged the plan, but Joseph submitted to the Lord's will and was gifted with the task of protecting the Messiah and Mary.

What a warrior Joseph was. So much had seemed wrong since the day that Gabriel visited her. So much had been unexpected. Yet God delivered them, together. A family, alone in a stable, the face of God revealed at last.

# CHAPTER TEN

A knock came on the stable door. Startled, Mary awoke. The innkeeper's wife stood at the door, her face visible in the moonlight. She talked in a low voice with Joseph. After closing the door, Joseph came to Mary.

"The innkeeper says the shepherds are at the inn, wondering about a child that was born. The shepherds are telling everyone an unusual story. They say angels appeared in the sky. It's well past midnight, into the second watch, so not a lot of people are awake. But there are Roman guards inside at the inn, drinking, laughing at the shepherds."

Mary hated the thought of a Roman guard laughing at the noble working men who had guarded the area through the night. "Bring the shepherds here."

He bit his lip before replying. "Are you sure? The shepherds are attracting attention. I don't want the Roman soldiers to hear reports of a Messiah born under their watch."

Suddenly, Mary wanted exactly that. The Messiah, the King of the Jews, had been born while those men had been drinking.

Moments later, the shepherds entered the stable. They looked even rougher than Mary remembered. And yet their faces glowed with a radiance that she knew reflected an encounter with heaven's hosts.

They approached Mary tentatively, feet shuffling along the dirty, straw-covered floor. When they spied Jesus wrapped in milk cloths, asleep in the wooden feeding trough, they fell to their knees in worship.

Mary and Joseph looked at each other, startled. Jesus was just a baby. How could He have such an effect on men?

Joseph rested a comforting hand on the shepherd's shoulder. "Tell me what happened."

The man rose unsteadily to his feet, his joints obviously causing his pain and stiffness. Mary studied his face with compassion. He had deep lines around his eyes and forehead, and scars that crisscrossed his forearms. Shepherding was hard work for even a young man. She pitied this elderly man—and then stopped. God had swept him into a miracle. He was not a man to be pitied, even if his joints ached.

"We were awake, of course," the shepherd began, struggling to keep his focus on Joseph. He kept stealing awe-filled glances at Jesus.

"We heard the lion," Joseph said.

The shepherd nodded. "It's unusual for them to come so close to the city. We don't know what they were hunting, or what drew them here. But we stayed awake and kept watch over the flock. And then..." His voice trailed off as his eyes glazed, as if seeing a wonder.

The youngest of the shepherds rose to speak.

"An angel of the Lord appeared to us. We had never seen one before, but when you see one, you know immediately who it is. What it is," the boy said, sounding astonished even now, hours later. "Then the glory of the Lord shone around us, like a brilliant light. We were terrified."

He laughed at the thought, looking at his elders. "We were so frightened! Perhaps he heard our knees knocking together, because the angel said to us, 'Do not be afraid. I bring you good news that will cause great joy for all the people. Today in the town of David a Savior has been born to you; he is the Messiah, the Lord. This will be a sign to you: You will find a baby wrapped in cloths and lying in a manger.'"

Mary exclaimed softly. The milk rags that Jesus was swaddled in were not God's second best. They were part of His plan! What a comforting thought.

The young shepherd continued. "Suddenly a great company of angels, thousands of them, appeared with the first angel, praising God and saying, 'Glory to God in the highest heaven, and on earth peace to those on whom his favor rests.' When the sky went dark, we talked among each other and decided we had to come and find this Savior. The Messiah!"

Joseph and Mary exchanged surprised glances. Why would God announce the birth of His son, the Messiah of the Jews, to shepherds? Why wouldn't He announce it at the Temple in Jerusalem?

But this was the city of David, who had been a shepherd before he was a king. "The Lord is my shepherd," Mary softly said, echoing David's words.

The men openly wept as they looked at Jesus and repeated the famous psalm. They were filled with a sweet emotion Mary wondered at. Perhaps God had done something they never expected either. God rewarded years of lonely work with a glimpse of His glory.

"I think I understand," she softly said to them. God had called her to be a vessel for His creation power—and that overwhelmed her. She had to turn her thoughts away from her faults and her failings, to focus on His calling and His gifts.

She could not explain why God chose her to bear this child. She couldn't explain why God revealed the birth to these shepherds either. God's plans were beyond her understanding. But she felt a deep sense of relief. If God rejoiced over the birth, she hadn't failed.

Somehow, for reasons she did not understand, giving birth in a stable was acceptable to God. The Lamb of God had been born while shepherds watched over the flock nearby. And Jesus sleeping in the feeding trough, in the House of Bread, somehow this made sense to the Lord too. Perhaps Jesus was like the manna of heaven that fell upon the Israelites in the wilderness, she mused. Like that manna, it was unexplainable how He came to be here, but so welcome. The Jewish people would rejoice. Joy would overwhelm the Jewish leaders.

She nodded, her eyes growing heavy. His ways were mysterious and beyond comprending.

"Go in peace, my friends," Joseph said, noting how tired Mary was. "But stay away from the Romans. If they take an interest in the infant, things may be complicated. Best if the Romans never know He is here."

The words nagged at Mary for reasons she did not grasp. She felt herself sliding into a restless sleep, the bloodred capes of the soldiers snapping at the edges of her dreams. The Roman empire would find out that the Messiah had been born. They would know her son was the Messiah, the King of the Jews.

What trouble would that bring?

***

The innkeeper found them a room the following night. Joseph arranged to pay for their room by making much-needed repairs, both to the inn and the stable. With his skills in carpentry and construction, he had a good eye for what could be done on the innkeeper's budget and with access to the materials available in Bethlehem.

Mary settled into the tiny room as Joseph went to the town center to register for the census. She worried about Joseph making his way through the Roman soldiers who patrolled the streets. As much as the Romans loved to talk about law and justice, often a soldier's sword was the first and final verdict a commoner received.

With one hand on the door, Joseph stopped and looked back at her. "Did Gabriel give you any instructions about revealing Jesus as the Messiah?"

"You know he didn't," Mary replied, a bit hurt Joseph had to ask. "I told you every word of that encounter." Would she always feel uneasy around Joseph about the circumstances of the pregnancy? She had concealed nothing.

"I am not questioning your honesty," Joseph replied steadily. "I am just wondering how to proceed. If word continues to circulate that He is the King of the Jews, that could be dangerous. Should we conceal His identity?"

"Even from our own people?" Mary asked, disappointed.

"Yes, I think so. Until we have clear confirmation from God, we are better to wait."

Mary looked at the sleeping infant. The angels declared that the child was born to all people, and great joy was upon the earth. All of heaven celebrated the birth.

But Joseph was right. The birth of the Messiah was good news, but it was God's news to share, not hers. She had to protect Jesus and trust God's timing.

Bethlehem was a stop along the way to the southern cities of the empire, so Roman soldiers passed through here every day. If they took the stories of the shepherds seriously, the news would reach Rome and Caesar quickly. Thankfully, no one paid much attention to shepherds. Or women, she thought ruefully. God was moving mightily, but it seemed He spoke to people who were forgotten and overlooked. When would that change?

The infant Jesus slept fitfully. Mary wondered if He was disoriented. The earth was vastly different than it had been at creation. And the Messiah had never experienced life in a body before. What did hunger feel like to Him? Or cold? Mary wished, above all, for someone who had more knowledge of the scriptures and prophecy, someone who could describe why the Messiah was born in these circumstances, and if the Son of God was more of a title or a literal defini-tion of His being.

She remembered her teaching from her own mother and father, what bits they had taught about the Messiah. She had a few passages committed to memory, but surely the scriptures had much more to say.

Isaiah had recorded a passage that the Jews held onto with fervor and longing.

*For to us a child is born, to us a son is given, and the government will be on his shoulders.*

*And he will be called Wonderful Counselor, Mighty God, Everlasting Father, Prince of Peace.*

*Of the greatness of his government and peace there will be no end. He will reign on David's throne and over his kingdom, establishing and upholding it with justice and righteousness from that time on and forever.*

Isaiah had written those words hundreds of years ago, when the Assyrians fell for the last time. Isaiah was her favorite among the prophets because his words were those of someone careful with the language as well as the message. That had made memorizing his passages a delight.

How had Isaiah, or any of the prophets, seen the future? How had God revealed His truth and His plan to those men of long ago? No mention was made of Gabriel, but then, no woman had ever been swept into God's plan as dramatically as Mary had.

A cloud passed over the sun and the room darkened. Jesus turned His little eyes to the window, now in shadows.

Mary shivered, not from the sudden drop in temperature but from what else she knew about Isaiah. The prophet who saw such glory was murdered, sawed in half by the enemies of the Jews. That was what her people believed, although his body never returned for burial. The sacrilege of killing a prophet in such a cruel way, and treating his body with indignity, horrified her.

She reached out and picked Jesus up, turning her back to the window, cradling Him against her chest.

Why was she tasked with bringing this child into such a cruel and violent world? If she could not protect Him, her love for Him was a terrible, terrifying burden. Tears fell onto the swaddling cloths that Jesus was still wrapped in.

This first week after the birth brought many strong, unruly emotions that surprised her. The reason for her tears on many days? The Jewish law. She was loath to admit it, but she often resented the law. Declaring a woman unclean after childbirth was hard in ways she hadn't expected.

Being unclean meant that anything Mary touched became unclean. Poor Joseph could not even hold her when she needed comfort. She had to be deliberate with her movements when he was in the room, and at meals.

Her time for sacrifice and purification at the Temple was weeks away. After that offering, she could go in public with no worries. The first seven days kept her away from Joseph. The rest of the time kept her away from the public.

She would manage, she thought, trying to maintain her composure. The room had limestone walls, which gave them quiet privacy, so no neighboring customers complained about the baby's noise.

A small window above her head allowed light in, and the returning sun reflected pink and green on the limestone. Joseph said that was how he knew the stones had come from Jerusalem, for the limestone there was unusually beautiful.

The infant watched the play of colors on the walls with wide brown eyes. Mary wondered what He thought, or if a child this young even had thoughts.

Even though He cried at night, He settled easily. As soon as she sang to Him or stroked His petal-soft cheeks, He calmed and quieted. Just a touch of love was enough.

And so, the first seven days passed with Mary and Jesus in a room in the inn, and Joseph working for their keep.

---

Mary counted the days until they traveled to Jerusalem. There, Joseph would buy a sacrifice in her name, to cleanse her of ritual impurities, restoring her to full community. He would present Jesus at the Temple and arrange for a sacrifice in Jesus's name. Joseph had to redeem Jesus.

Being the firstborn child, Jesus was, by Jewish law, dedicated to the Lord and His service. Thankfully, the Levite clan served in the place of all firstborn sons.

Mary knew, however, that Jesus would serve the Lord. His service would be eternal.

Joseph had worked for several people in town, earning money for sacrifices. Mary knew two doves were sufficient, but Joseph was determined to offer a perfect lamb in Jesus's name. The shepherds had one in mind and offered it for free, but Joseph insisted on paying full price.

She smiled to herself, reflecting on how Joseph took pride in this son. God had blessed Joseph with an amiable spirit to adapt to the strange reality of God's will.

The innkeeper was careful to hand things to Joseph only, and Mary reused the same utensils and cups as much as she could.

On the eighth day, she bathed for purification. Now she was subject to the laws of purification. For thirty days she could not visit the Temple or any sacred space to the Jews. But she determined to remain both patient and calm, even as her mind spun.

The law no longer made sense now that Jesus was here. She could hold God in her arms, but she could not approach the Temple? Maybe God would provide answers someday, at least to her. God had not revealed how the Messiah would reveal Himself or rule His people. Since all she had was the law and the prophets, she would follow those until a greater revelation arrived.

On the eighth day, Joseph brought a rabbi to circumcise the baby. Mary pressed her lips together, worried about Jesus. The law brought such pain! The commandment dated back to the time of Abraham, commanding that on the eighth day an infant male be circumcised.

She hated that the Messiah could not break the laws that He had come to fulfill. He would save His people, but He was so tiny, and felt such pain.

Surely the Messiah would take the pain out of the law someday?

At last, after forty days, it was time to go to Jerusalem. The journey was about five miles, and the climb was not as steep as the road from the hill country into Jerusalem. Mary packed for the trip, feeling the lightness in her body, hoping the journey would be good for her. She was eager to leave the tiny room, stretch her legs, and walk among her people.

She wondered if signs and wonders would appear in the heavens, announcing the Messiah arriving at the Temple. Would the ground shake? Would angels fill the sky once more? Her stomach knotted with anticipation.

This was going to be a day to remember.

# CHAPTER ELEVEN

The journey to Jerusalem was a quiet one.

"What are you thinking, Joseph?" Mary winced even as she asked, because there had been a time when she would have known his thoughts even from afar. God's will had driven a wedge between them, that was how it seemed to her. It was not fair that each of them had to wrestle with His will in their own way. Would God bring them together again? She dared not dream it, but her heart sent the prayer to God.

Joseph held the donkey's reins loosely in his palm. The donkey had no intention of racing away. He was content to plod along with Mary and the infant on his back.

"I have never traveled this road," Joseph replied.

"The road to Jerusalem?" Mary asked. "You've been many times. But you are right that you have never traveled from Bethlehem into the city." Like Joseph, she had always approached Jerusalem from the northern area of Nazareth, entering through the eastern gates.

"That is not what I meant." Joseph sighed. "I feel the weight of shepherding you and the child. I am called to lead you on a road I have never traveled. I am called to raise a son that is not mine. And yet I have prayed two things my entire life."

Mary looked at him, concealing her pain. She smiled softly, a sign for him to continue.

"I have prayed for the Messiah to come to our people," Joseph said, the sound of wonder in his voice. "And I prayed that God would grant you as my wife."

Her heart warmed. "So, the road is unfamiliar, but you are happy to walk it? With me?"

He looked at her and nodded. "I need time to understand my role. The angel who appeared to me in the dream didn't explain everything or tell me how to do this."

Mary laughed, then covered her mouth with her free hand. "I don't mean to laugh, but that is what I have been saying to God for over a year now."

Joseph chuckled, and the silence that fell between them now was one of companionship. They shared the same burden.

She closed her eyes and thanked God. Even moments of earthly pain and confusion brought them together if they sought the Lord. It was a small miracle, but it was a miracle.

They approached Jerusalem at twilight. She was thankful that the dusk covered the sight of the dying men on their pitiful crosses. No one should have to look at that horror.

But Jerusalem—what beauty! The city glowed, lit with golden rays from the sun. The radiance seemed to come from the stones themselves, as if they were alive, as if they spoke in a language that was felt in the heart, not heard by the ears. Jerusalem at this time of day was a city of golden light.

Many people spoke Aramaic, and Mary was relieved to hear her native tongue.

She held the infant Jesus in her arms, while Joseph carried the sacrificial lamb, to protect it from the crowds that did not pay attention to their steps.

Joseph hurried her and the babe through the crowds to the Jaffa gate. The massive doors would close when the sun set. No one wanted to be stuck outside the gates, left on their own at night. Too many wild animals, thieves, and troublemakers would be on that side.

Joseph worked his way through the street to an inn near the famous Hezekiah casement wall.

When Hezekiah had built this wall to defend the city against an Assyrian attack, he had cut several homes off from the city, leaving them outside of the wall, outside of his protection. There was no room for them in his plan. She felt that keenly now in sympathy. Hezekiah's wall was not as beautiful as the ones that David built. Instead, his men built two narrow walls and dumped rocks in the gap between them. It was crude but fast and effective.

The inn that sat next to the casement wall was inexpensive. But Joseph promised that the beds were comfortable and the hospitality warm.

When the innkeeper accepted Joseph's money, Mary released a breath she did not realize she had been holding. She had been worried that the innkeeper would deny them a room. Whatever God's purpose in that past misfortune had been, it was over. She and the infant Messiah had a room at this inn.

The family passed the night in deep and restful sleep.

The next morning, Joseph and Mary carried Jesus and the lamb, walking the narrow pathway that led to the Temple. Beggars lined the street, pleading for alms. *I have no money,* Mary wanted to say, *but I bring you a Messiah!* But, she reminded herself, this was God's son, and He must reveal His identity. She and Joseph had agreed on that, as it seemed wise. She chose to trust God for each next step and would try not to get ahead of Him.

Once they passed through the main area, Joseph would be able to enter the men's courtyard and get close to the center of the Temple, the Holy of Holies, the resting place for the shekinah, the glory of God.

She envied him but only for a fleeting moment. The glory of God had come down from heaven and rested on her when she conceived Jesus. She had entered a cloud of glory that men had only seen from afar.

"I wish I could show You the first Temple," she said to Jesus as they walked. "But Nebuchadnezzar of Babylon pillaged it then later destroyed it."

She felt silly recounting the history to a baby, especially one that might have been an eyewitness to the events of history. What did the Son of God know or remember?

"This one was rebuilt under the eye of Zerubbabel, in the reign of Cyrus the Second," Mary said, concluding her history lesson. "It is called Herod's Temple because many years later, Herod the Great added onto the structure. But I will never call it that. It does not belong to Herod. It belongs to You."

She drew His swaddling cloths higher above His face to shield Him from the glare. The amount of white stone and gold overlays made this Temple blinding in the afternoon light. No one could stare directly at it.

Entering through the gate called Beautiful, she felt her heart pound in her chest. Any moment now, God would move. The Messiah had come! Joseph would take Jesus through another gate into the men's courts in a moment, but this moment was hers.

She cradled Jesus in her arms, looking in all directions. She wanted to see His little face illuminated by all the gold that lined the Temple fixtures, to have just one moment alone with Him before the rush of excitement that news of His arrival would bring.

An old man hobbled toward her, and she stepped aside to let him pass. He stopped, craning his head as if hearing a far-away sound. Snapping his head to look her in the face, he cried out. His gaze lowered until he was staring at the infant Jesus. The man gasped.

Mary looked at Joseph in confusion.

The man reached for Jesus and lifted Him into the air. "Praise be to the God of our fathers!" he cried.

Mary was so shocked she couldn't move. Joseph's mouth hung open, but he didn't move either.

The man continued his praise.

"Sovereign Lord, as You have promised, You may now dismiss Your servant in peace. For my eyes have seen Your salvation, which You have prepared in the sight of all nations: a light for revelation to the Gentiles, and the glory of Your people Israel."

Women milled past them, hardly paying any attention.

"I do not know you, friend," Joseph said, resting a hand on the man's arm to draw his focus away from the baby. When the man looked at Joseph, Mary stepped forward and took the infant away from him. She cradled Jesus tightly to her chest.

A broad grin broke out across his wrinkled face. "My name is Simeon. The Lord spoke to me recently and promised me I would see the Messiah before I died. I hardly dared to believe that I had heard Him correctly! But here He is, the Savior."

Mary was startled and chewed her lower lip for a moment. She expected a grand display from the Lord. Instead, He had whispered in an old man's ear.

Simeon stepped closer, motioning for Joseph and Mary to lean in.

"This child is destined to cause the falling and rising of many in Israel," he said, "and to be a sign that will be spoken against, so that the thoughts of many hearts will be revealed. And a sword will pierce your own soul too."

Simeon was looking directly at her when he said that. Not Joseph, she noticed. Why would a sword pierce her soul but not his?

As Simeon prophesied, a tiny, wrinkled woman shuffled toward them. She smacked a few gossiping women on the legs with her walking stick to encourage them to move out of the way.

"Anna!" Simeon called. "He is here!"

Anna seemed to immediately know who Jesus was, and not because Simeon told her. Mary, less reluctantly this time, handed the baby to Anna, who gazed at the infant with such adoration that Mary's heart melted. The love in the old woman's eyes was immeasurable.

"She has no family," Simeon confided to Mary quietly. "Widowed decades ago. She stays here, fasting and praying."

A woman without a husband or children had no voice in this world. Mary felt pity for her but then remembered the shepherds. *These dear, kind souls,* she thought, *are such unlikely sentinels who keep watch for You, Lord. These are not powerful or important people. Why have You revealed Your secrets to them?*

Although the ground did not shake, nor did angels appear in the sky above the Temple, Mary contented herself to see Jesus received by the two people who waited for Him. While everyone else was busy with the business of the Temple, these two had not missed the heart of it all, the heart that beat right now in a tiny, human body.

After rushing home from the market in Bethlehem, Mary waited upstairs in her room at the inn, her heart pounding so loudly she could hear it in her ears. Sensing her unease, perhaps, Jesus was restless, so she set Him on the sleeping mat underneath the window, where He could watch the shadows play on the wall.

What Mary had seen today was strange and terrifying. Where was Joseph? He would know what to do. Certainly, it was time to return home to Nazareth, for today's events, strange events in an unfamiliar city, had shaken her to the core.

As she had been buying bread, she saw the expressions of the women all around her in the market. Eyes widened. Mouths fell open. Hands flew to mouths. A low roar of gossip moved from stall to stall.

For through the market strode camel riders in dark cloaks, olive-skinned men with kohl-blackened eyes and many amulets around their necks. Mary turned, observing them, her knees weak from fear. She'd heard of these men but had never seen one. Judging from the reaction of the other shoppers, neither had they.

Zoroastrians. Priests from the land of the Persians, these men obsessively followed the path of the stars and believed in fantastical fables. They did not believe in the one God, the God of the Jews. They believed, however, in signs.

Mary shrank back into the crowd, pulling her robe over her baby's face. The tallest man, surveying the crowd from his perch, pointed a long, bejeweled finger at a boy. Crooking his finger, he beckoned the boy to approach. Mary felt sorry for the boy, who had gone pale.

The rider spoke in a strange, guttural language. Neither Mary nor the boy understood it. The riders whispered to each other. The man tried again, this time using Aramaic.

"We are looking for the king."

The boy burst out laughing, then caught himself, scowling, perhaps realizing the man was not joking. Swallowing nervously, the boy shook his head. "There is no king here. This is the Roman Empire. We have a Caesar."

The riders conversed in their strange language once more. "We have seen a great sign. A king has been born in this city."

No one replied. The market was silent except for the rustle of birds and cries of animals.

The riders surveyed the crowd with growing frustration.

"We will find him," their leader announced.

Did they think all of Bethlehem was keeping a secret?

*No,* Mary thought, *only me.* As soon as they moved on, she hurried to the inn. Behind her, she could hear low whispers. A few of the women she had frequently bought from pointed at her. Mary heard snippets of what was said—rumors of shepherds who said they saw angels in the sky and immediately ran to find Mary and her child.

What was God doing? She wanted to scream. Why would He bring priests of another faith to her doorstep in such a dramatic way? Jesus's identity wasn't being revealed as much as it was being exposed. That didn't feel good. Plus, what would the other Jews think of Zoroastrians recognizing the Messiah before they did?

Joseph returned from his local job before the evening meal. She did not even wait for him to wash before telling him everything. While she was still speaking, someone rapped on their door.

Joseph cracked it open and peered out. Mary spotted the innkeeper's wife. She cast a wary eye at Mary.

"This cannot keep happening," the woman said.

Joseph reached into the bag at his waist and produced an extra coin. "We will not be any trouble for you."

Mary gritted her teeth. They needed that money for bread. What were they going to eat and drink tomorrow? Nothing, it seemed, until Joseph returned home with his day's wages.

The woman looked at the coin, then at him. "Get downstairs and deal with it. If trouble comes to my inn because of your child, you will be thrown out, and not by me. It's the Romans who will come for you! These men are from Persia, an enemy state to the Romans. The Persians are the very reason the census has taken place!"

"Would you want me to speak with them in private? In here, perhaps?" Joseph asked, his tone even and peaceable.

"No! What are you thinking?" she snapped. "They are unclean by Jewish law. They cannot enter my inn!"

Joseph turned back and looked at Mary. She knew what he was thinking.

"I know the perfect place," Joseph said. "No one will look for us there."

# CHAPTER TWELVE

Mary paced the floor, anxious for Joseph's return. She hated the thought of him being alone in that dark stable with those men. They seemed so untrustworthy, but maybe that was only because they were priests of that strange religion.

But she didn't pace long. Within ten minutes, Joseph returned and insisted she come to the stable—with Jesus. He carried the baby and explained as he escorted her through the inn.

"They have come from Herod's palace after having an audience with Herod himself!" He sounded as if he felt the same dread and awe as she felt. She'd never known anyone who had stood in Herod's presence. "They have gifts for Jesus. Gifts worthy of any great king. Gold, incense, and myrrh."

Outside the stable, she paused. Resting a hand lightly on the wood, she blessed the old wood beams that had sheltered her son on His first night here on earth.

And He was born to be King, she knew. What king turned away foreign tributes? Even a devout king accepted them. She remembered that Solomon was visited by the Queen of Sheba. That woman was not a Jew, so this perhaps was not entirely new.

Once again, she wished she had asked more questions of Gabriel. Her country-girl manners did not equip her for raising a king.

Entering the stable, she studied the men as they turned to face her. She was relieved to see that when not perched on camels, they were not so tall and able to look down on her. She exhaled, the sound echoing in the room, making the leader smile.

He stepped forward and bowed.

"I understand you must be nervous meeting strangers like us," he said kindly. "But please, try to imagine how nervous we have been to meet a great king."

When he lifted his head, she searched his face for any hint of deception or mockery. She found none. The other men too seemed sincere.

Still, she did not relax her hold on Jesus, and Joseph stood just slightly in front of her. No one could hurt Jesus without going through Joseph first.

The leader gestured to several chests that lay in the far corner. "May I present our gifts?"

Joseph nodded.

The younger of the priests stepped to the chests and opened them, one by one. She was delighted to see fine robes and sandals in one, much like the beautiful linen robes these men wore. Of course, they wore pants under their robes too, which looked silly to her. But the next three chests took her breath away.

The first chest contained chunks of raisin-colored resin.

"Myrrh," Joseph whispered to her. "A lifetime's wages' worth."

Mary had never seen myrrh, but she remembered the story of Joseph, how his brothers threw him in a cistern then sold him to a traveling caravan of myrrh traders, Ishmaelites journeying to Egypt.

The gift, although honorable for a king, troubled her. Myrrh was a spice associated with betrayal and suffering.

She gently rocked Jesus in her arms, thinking. Joseph had saved the Israelites, but he lived in Egypt. It had been a sad life for a Jewish boy who wanted to return home. She never wanted to see Egypt, that land of slavery and suffering. She never wanted her son to suffer torment.

The priest brought a chunk of myrrh to Joseph for inspection.

She declined to touch it. Would her son be like a second Joseph? Would he too save the Israelites despite their betrayal?

The next chest contained another resin, this one milky white.

"Frankincense," she whispered to Joseph. He glanced back at her, nodding. That was burned at the Temple as an offering to God. Mary wet her lips nervously. The men were acknowledging Jesus as God. Mary felt a twinge of fear. For anyone else, this would be blasphemy worthy of being thrown out of the Jewish faith forever. Or worse, if such a thing were even possible.

The final gift made Joseph's knees buckle. She saw him lose his steadiness then replant his feet. The final gift was a chest full of gold pieces. She'd only seen one or two pieces of gold in her lifetime. This chest held so many she could probably sweep her hand through it without touching the bottom.

Suddenly, they were wealthy beyond all imagining.

Talking into the evening hours, Mary watched as the priests held the infant Jesus, their faces radiant with joy. These were not Jewish men—why would they receive a Jewish child with such unabashed delight? Although it broke with Jewish law, this act of letting an unclean man touch the child, she thought this was what God would want.

She hoped she had not misjudged. So much wealth, so suddenly, so unexpectedly, might have clouded her judgment. Everything seemed surreal. The priest's robes were woefully out of place. The fine fabric, embroidered with gold threads, was collecting straw and dirt with every movement around the floor.

"How did you know?" she whispered to their leader. Jesus had fallen asleep in his arms.

The man smiled, never taking his gaze from Jesus's serene face.

"We live with our faces upturned to the heavens," he whispered back, "searching for a sign of the world to come. A sign appeared in the heavens, telling of a great king born in the east. We departed at once. I have watched the sky my whole life, hoping for that which I could not name. Now I know what it is I hoped for. His name is Jesus."

"What is your title?" the youngest priest suddenly asked of Joseph.

"I suppose you could call me a *techton*," he replied, using a word that they might know at once. A techton was more than a simple carpenter. Joseph could build nearly anything with his hands.

A laborer was not what these men expected. They whispered among themselves.

"You are not of royal descent?" the leader asked.

"We are of the house of David, the Jewish king, father of Solomon," Mary spoke up.

"Ahhh," the man said, nodding gravely. They expected to see a king, and met a baby in a stable, birthed by a common woman. The father was a day laborer. This did not fit their expectations.

But something beyond this troubled Joseph. She could see it in his eyes.

Later in the evening, when the wise men had returned to their own inn, in the cover of darkness, Joseph brought the chests up the stairs at the inn, one by one. Once the door was closed and locked, then Joseph spoke.

Jesus slept on the straw mattress, content after a feeding and bath.

"What troubled you tonight?" Mary asked quietly. She didn't want to wake Jesus, and a softer voice could sometimes help Joseph sort his thoughts.

"The reality of all this," Joseph said. He stood beneath the small window, looking up at the sliver of sky visible. He glanced back at Jesus.

Mary sat on the bed, and after a moment, Joseph came to join her. The oil lamp flickered and sputtered, the oil running low.

"You were favored of God and chosen to bear Him," Joseph said. "I was chosen to protect you both. But I must admit that I do not know how. I do not know the way He would have me take."

Mary loved him all over again for his worries. He was wealthy now, yet all he could think of was how to protect his family and serve God.

"Not knowing the way is the way." Mary rested her head on his shoulder. "That is faith."

⟡

Early the next morning, Joseph prepared to go to his local bricklaying job.

"We don't need the money," Mary objected.

"We don't need attention," Joseph countered, his voice soft to avoid waking Jesus. "People from Nazareth are not wealthy."

"The wise men will leave now, though, yes?" she asked.

He nodded.

"Why don't we return home?" Mary asked. There was no need to remain in Bethlehem. They had registered for the census and presented Jesus at the Temple.

Joseph cocked his head to one side, thinking. "I could return to my tools and my woodworking."

"In Nazareth, surrounded by family and friends, we'll be safe," Mary said. "No one there will think that Jesus is a king. Not with me as His mother. I'm too boring."

Joseph looked at her and scowled. "Boring? Mary, you have led me on the journey of a lifetime! Of a thousand lifetimes!"

They giggled together like children.

That night, Mary watched Joseph sleeping. He still hadn't shared her bed, even though Jesus was born. He slept on a mat next to hers, and most nights, she was too tired to argue. She didn't know—neither of them did—when the time would be right to share a bed as a married couple. That was one more detail Gabriel had omitted.

In the third watch of the night, as dawn broke pink and yellow in the east, she watched Joseph as his breathing came in fitful stutters. Was he having a nightmare? She rose and knelt next to him, shaking him gently, calling his name.

He jerked awake, leaping to his feet, his eyes darting around the room.

"Is he gone?" he asked, holding one hand to his side, as if he had a stitch.

"Who?" Mary asked softly, trying not to wake the baby.

Joseph's ragged breaths filled the chamber.

"Pack your things," he said. "We have to leave."

Mary patted her bed, urging him to sit.

"Now!" he demanded. "Herod's men are coming to kill the baby."

Jesus woke and cried.

Joseph ran to the window and strained on the tips of his toes to look out.

Mary was on her feet in a flash. Stuffing their belongings into the saddlebags her donkey had carried here, she made quick work of deciding what she needed. As she moved about the chamber, Joseph emptied the sturdy leather satchels he used for his tools and refilled them with the contents of the gift chests.

"The angel of the Lord appeared to me again as I slept," he explained as he worked. "The same one who explained to me your pregnancy. The angel spoke with such authority! He said, 'Get up! Take the child and His mother and escape to Egypt. Stay there until I tell you, for Herod is going to search for the child to kill Him.'"

Joseph held open the door of the chamber as Mary, carrying Jesus, passed through. He grabbed the bags and closed the door behind him. His labor already paid the bill.

"What route will we take?" Mary whispered. She could not even bear to think of the destination. Egypt. The land of slavery. Nor could she bear to think of Herod's men coming to kill her son. She could only focus—*must* only focus, she decided—on the very next step.

"We will travel south to the port of Hykkos," Joseph replied.

"What will the innkeepers think when they discover we fled in the night?" she whispered. "What will they say?"

By now they were outside, passing by the stable. In a few hours, the market would be open, and the women would be at their stalls with their children.

Joseph stopped and looked at her, a somber, searing sadness in his eyes. "Herod is sending Roman soldiers to Bethlehem. The gossip will not be about us for very long."

Mary felt a shiver of terror and hurried with Joseph away from Bethlehem.

Joseph's plan was to find a trade caravan deporting from the port of Hykkos for Egypt. He hoped to join the caravan, paying for protection using the gold from the magi. If anyone grew curious about their business, they would claim to be spice traders. The magi had given them plenty of myrrh and frankincense.

They set out with the eastern rim of the world turning red as dawn approached. The first full day of travel promised bad weather. Still, what could Mary do but move forward? The storm would be at her back, at least. It was as if the dark forces of the skies were following them, biting at their backs as they fled. Maybe Herod didn't know they were fleeing, but something wicked, something far more powerful, did.

Conserving resources, Joseph bought one donkey in the next town. He chose to walk. He refused to spend the gold. Besides, one donkey made them look poorer.

That was an asset when concealing so much wealth. And yet the greatest treasure was not in the leather satchels. A mighty and feared king was overturning a city searching for Jesus at this very moment.

She shuddered and refused to think of it.

"Three days' journey, and we are out of Herod's jurisdiction," Joseph promised.

*Will we feel Herod's shadow lift from our backs?* Mary thought.

As they traveled, trying not to stop, Mary repeated the words like a refrain. "Just three days. Just three days. Hold on for the third day. Hold on for that sunrise," she whispered.

The donkey was skittish as thunder growled in the distance. Mary placed a steadying hand on the beast's warm neck, talking in a low, soothing voice. Jesus was fast asleep in His sling wrapped across her chest. Storms had little effect on Him. She bent her head and kissed Him softly on His forehead, just visible between the folds of linen. "In three days," she promised Him, "you'll be out of his grasp. That's not such a long while, is it?"

*Lord,* she prayed silently, *let this child live to see the sunrise on the third day. The third day seems so far off, when all around are storms and strange faces.*

As the donkey plodded along, she focused all her will and heart on the thought of that waiting sunrise. Jesus would live to see it. She would give her life to make certain.

But she hadn't told her family about her pregnancy and why she went to Bethlehem with Joseph. She'd never said goodbye, and now she never would. Setting out toward a horizon she had never seen, she felt more alone with every step. She was not just leaving Bethlehem. She was leaving everyone and everything she had once known.

# CHAPTER THIRTEEN

"D"id you ever hear a rabbi read from the scroll of Hosea the prophet?" Joseph asked on the second day. "'Out of Egypt, I called my son.'"

"My mother did not like that scroll," Mary answered.

Joseph laughed. The scroll of Hosea said much about an unfaithful woman, besides the prophecy about the Son of God going to Egypt.

"I don't understand why we are being sent to Egypt," Joseph admitted. "But the angel gave me explicit instructions. I am thinking of Hosea's words, trying to understand why we must go to Egypt. It's driving me mad trying to make sense of it."

"Nothing makes sense anymore," she muttered. Sand had blown into her robes and was making her uncomfortable. The baby seemed to be having the same problem. The second day of the journey was worse than the first.

"Egypt is the land of slavery and the land of Moses's Exodus. Now the Messiah flees for protection there?" Joseph continued, thinking out loud.

"I struggle with something else," Mary admitted. "Jesus is the Messiah. We did everything God asked. Why has so much gone wrong? Every time God answers a prayer, it only raises more questions."

Joseph sighed, although she couldn't tell why.

"I think we misunderstood what it meant to be favored," he said finally.

"Go on," she replied.

"We are driven from home, without friends and family, hunted. Still, we know God is with us. We have the Messiah under our watch to raise."

"What are you saying?"

"It's a mystery that is unraveling truths wherever I turn," he replied. "Yet I don't understand it all. Not yet. For example, look at what we've lost, then look at what we have left. We have each other, and we have God. Before this, I never knew God was so real, so present. What else have I never known? Maybe I never really knew you either. You have far more strength than I ever realized."

Mary's heart softened. Suddenly, it wasn't the gold or incense that made her feel rich—it was his words.

On the evening of the third day, they arrived in Hykkos. Mary expected to feel relieved. Instead, she was exhausted, sore from riding all day and sleeping on the ground at night, and uncomfortable from the sand and grit that got into her robes, hair, and mouth when the winds blew.

She longed for an inn. She wanted to sleep, with Jesus tucked safely in her arms. Peaceful dreams would surely come now that they had escaped Herod's reach. But Hykkos offered no peace.

What she saw was a seaport filled with slaves—terrified prisoners of war—and slave traders. She pulled the edge of her robe around her face and slipped off her donkey, wanting to be close to Joseph. She clutched Jesus tightly to her chest, hoping no one took notice of her little family. These men had hard, cold eyes.

"I have to find a caravan to join." Joseph tilted his head down to her as he spoke. His eyes never left the slave traders unloading a crop of prisoners of war off a ship. The shackled men were blond. Mary guessed they were from northern Italy. She'd heard so much about the light-haired men from that region. No doubt they'd rebelled against Caesar, and this was their reward.

She angled her body to look away from the ship and to the water. The turquoise waves lapped against the piers and edges of the beach. She wondered how big Solomon's ships must have been. He'd used this port to bring in the cedars from Lebanon for his construction projects. But his Temple now existed only in her imagination, and in the hearts of every Jew.

Her thoughts turned to her mother. Was she well? Did she miss Mary—or even know she had gone? Mary wanted to send word of where she was, or where she was going, but she couldn't. Herod searched for Jesus to kill Him. Mary had to disappear. Her family must never know what happened to them.

Would they know, someday, that Jesus was her son? Or would she be dead when He revealed Himself as the Messiah?

Joseph had taken but three or four steps away to negotiate with a trader who seemed to have an official air about him. If he did not lead a caravan, he might know one. Mary stayed with the donkey, protecting Jesus, not caring that the gold would start a riot if the men discovered it.

A slave trader bowed before her, catching her off guard. Her heart caught in her throat. Glancing at Joseph for help, she couldn't catch his eye. The trader waited at a polite distance.

Swallowing nervously, Mary tipped her head to acknowledge him.

His face was weather-beaten, whether by sun or sea, she didn't know. His eyes were dark and heavily wrinkled, as if he had spent years squinting in the shadows. He wore thick kohl on his eyelids, which gave him an exotic appearance, one she found disconcerting.

"Forgive me for startling you," he said kindly.

Mary did not speak but nodded sharply.

"You look weary," he continued. "I do not wish to make assumptions, but you look as if you need a good meal and a comfortable inn."

Mary's knees weakened at the thought of a bath and hot dinner. She nodded her head in agreement, this time with more vigor.

"It would please me to show you and your husband to the inn that the best merchants stay in. We are here so often, we always have rooms waiting for us."

He called himself a merchant? He traded humans, not commodities. Her eyes narrowed in contempt.

Joseph returned to her side, his eyebrows raised, looking alarmed.

Mary explained the man's offer, bile at the back of her throat.

"We cannot accept your offer," Joseph said.

"I understand," the man said, turning to leave. He stopped, speaking over his shoulder. "I only wondered…do you come from Bethlehem?"

Mary's blood ran cold. "Why would you ask that?"

The trader turned back. "You haven't heard? But then, news travels faster over water than land. Herod slaughtered all the infant males in that city. No male child under two is alive. I saw your child, and by the look of your robes and your donkey, you made a hard, fast journey."

Joseph folded his arms, drawing himself up to stand over the man. Mary hadn't realized until then how much taller Joseph was. She was glad he had a bit of King David's hot-blooded temper.

Her mind flashed to Bethlehem as the men squared off. The mothers and sons she met in Bethlehem suffered because of her, because of Jesus.

"Is there anything else?" Joseph demanded.

The slave trader withdrew a gold piece from the bag at his waist. "I can offer one piece if it is a girl, two if a boy. A boy would bring a high price in a town of bereaved mothers." His gaze wandered over Jesus like the baby was a fatted calf. "Best keep Him close. Plenty of unscrupulous dealers won't even be willing to pay."

Revulsion turned Mary's stomach. Her grip on Jesus tightened, making Him whimper.

The slave trader grinned, an unpleasant, sickly sight.

"Herod's men were liberal with the directions to kill the infant boys in Bethlehem. Seems they had a bit of practice in the villages along the way. The hills are filled with the graves of young boys. Plus, the mothers who died with them, out of grief or those who tried to resist."

She swallowed back a dry heave.

"What grieving mother wouldn't pay for a handsome baby boy? Your child could take the place of any of them."

"No. I would never sell Him!"

The longer the trader focused on Jesus, the more his face changed. A deep pain surfaced in his eyes that shook her. Suddenly, his entire demeanor changed as he bolted upright. His face cleared, and he spoke with urgency.

"Go to your caravan and sleep with their watchmen tonight. Do not go to any inn," he warned. "Traders want the baby alive—not you."

"Thank you," Joseph replied tersely.

Making their way quickly through the busy port, Mary kept hold of Jesus, and Joseph kept hold of the donkey, the saddle-bags filled to the brim. After finding the caravan, they paid the agreed-upon price and slipped into the line of camels and donkeys. Food and water were brought in, and their donkey was eager for both.

Mary sat on the ground, thankful for a safe place to sleep. Grit in her hair was a small price to pay for living through the night and keeping Jesus safe.

"He was bold to talk to you," Joseph said, lowering himself to rest beside her. "He should have addressed me as your husband."

A prickle of irritation made her roll her eyes when he glanced away. "The man had plans to buy Jesus, or worse, and you're worried about your honor?"

"I've been praying for a sign, and I got one." Joseph sighed, a weary smile breaking on his face. "It's time for me to become your husband."

"What?" Mary blurted, confused. And hungry. It had been a long day, this third day of running, and now that she was sitting down for the evening, she wanted to eat and sleep. Or eat while she slept, if that was possible. She had no energy left.

Then she realized what he meant. A frown of confusion crossed her face.

"When I saw him talking to you, I thought he was interested in trading you, not the baby. The thought of any man trading you enraged me so fast, I wanted to throw him into the sea," Joseph confessed. "If there had not been witnesses, I might have."

Her heart lightened. He loved her, even if she was grumpy, hungry, and covered in grit.

"I realized," Joseph continued, "when we arrive in Egypt, we will start new lives. We can be the married couple we once intended to be. I was always ready to lay down my life for you and Jesus. Now I am ready to be a husband, not just your protector."

Joseph's fierce devotion moved her. Becoming husband and wife in every sense would mark the beginning of a new marriage. Was she ready?

She had to be. Following God's will was a new adventure every day.

* * *

The following week, the blistering heat of Egyptian sun ruled her every waking hour. How long since she had last eaten? Yesterday, Mary realized. The water was almost gone too. She urged the poor donkey on, carrying Jesus in a sling across her chest, His face shielded from the sun. She spied a shimmering turquoise horizon, and her mouth ached, despite her mind telling her it was only a mirage.

Her tongue was thick, dry as sandal leather. She lifted the water flask and drained it, mentally apologizing to Joseph. She wanted to wait, but without water, she could not produce milk. She had to sustain Jesus. Jesus, above all else.

Her mind could think only in short bursts.

A merchant traveling with the caravan caught her eye as she pondered these things. His leering smile unsettled her. She drew her veil farther across her face, angling her body away from the man so that he could not look on the young Messiah as well.

"Beautiful," the man murmured.

Joseph did not hear.

Mary bit her lip and continued to look away. Rudeness to strangers offended the Lord. But this man unsettled her. He was not a Jew. His garments of dirty purple linen told her he might be a Phoenician.

Suddenly Joseph was at her side. Had he seen the man's lingering smile? Mary stepped back, sheltering herself and the baby behind Joseph.

"What do you want?" Joseph asked, his voice hard.

"A little entertainment." The man shrugged. "Long day's journey, you know."

Joseph's hand went to a dagger tucked in his belt, a recent purchase from another caravan member. "If you bother my wife again, I will gladly entertain you."

The man's eyes widened as if shocked at the suggestion of violence. "This woman is your wife? My apologies. She falls under your protection." He bowed his head. "Even so, a child of this age, and a beautiful mother who is both fertile and unscarred by Roman horrors…We don't see many in these parts."

The man reached into the bag at his waist and produced a handful of gold coins. "There are ways for a man to be rid of his burdens and find himself rich. When you return home, no one will question you. Few women and children survive long voyages. And everyone loves a widower. Especially the young women so eager—"

With one powerful punch, Joseph drove him to the ground as he was speaking.

Taking hold of the donkey's reins, Joseph quickly urged the beast through the crowd. Many laughed as the slave trader picked himself up.

"I shouldn't have done that," Joseph murmured, his face red. "We don't need more enemies."

Mary forgot about her thirst and the sun. Enemies surrounded them. Only together with God would they stand a chance of seeing Jesus safely to Egypt.

---

Joseph found a trader who offered better protection in exchange for repairs to their wagons. Late in the night the following week, Joseph slept as Mary nursed Jesus and sang Him back to sleep, wishing she had more psalms memorized. She enjoyed the peace, though, watching both Joseph and Jesus sleep comfortably and without care. How grateful she was that Joseph was a carpenter and builder—what other skill would be so useful for a refugee?

The word hit her hard, breath forced from her lungs. Refugees. Would they ever have a home again? Perhaps that depended on how long Herod lived.

Mary knew she was part of a grand story, His story, the story of the Jewish Messiah. But what would be told of her? She did not rule or lead like the great men of scriptures, or even Deborah or Esther. No, she simply trusted. Because she trusted, she obeyed. In this age of chaos and evil, confusion and pain, why should a woman's trust be remembered? No, it was too small an offering.

The leader of the caravan passed by, checking on them. He did not stop for conversation. Instead, his eyes roved over the little family, and Mary nodded in acknowledgment. His face softened at the sight of the infant sleeping in her arms.

She did not feel the need to draw her veil over Jesus's face. A bittersweet smile crossed the leader's face.

Jesus had unpredictable effects on people, she noted. Perhaps the leader missed his own children back home. Either way, she knew she would be safe tonight.

Joseph must have surely felt it too, because his sleep was deep.

*Please, Lord, no dreams tonight,* she prayed. *Let him sleep.*

Overhead, the stars blazed. Her thoughts turned to the mothers of Bethlehem. By instinct, she pulled Jesus in closer, rocking gently. The horrors of man's cruelty were too much to contemplate. How could those soldiers of Rome have obeyed such a wicked command?

Why did God not stop them?

If she had hid Jesus, if she had not let the shepherds visit, or the Magi, if she had not gone to the Temple for her ritual cleansing, would the babies still be alive? She alone escaped with her child. How the other families must hate her! Why hadn't Joseph gotten word to the other families?

But he was warned in a dream, by an angel. If he had gone door-to-door, telling every family of his dream, who would have believed him? He was a stranger from Nazareth who let his wife give birth in a stable, a husband who had invited shepherds to visit his newborn and had even allowed magi from the east to touch his child. She'd heard the rumors. Joseph was unclean. Unwise. Unprepared.

The night passed quietly, the stars slipping past her overhead as she dozed. A few tears escaped when she woke each time and checked on Jesus. The stress of the journey was seeping out around the edges of her life. She missed home and family. They didn't even know she was a mother now.

She tried to pray, but graceful words were hard. Could she just offer the truth?

"I never knew that I could hurt so badly and still be in the will of God."

She caught a glimpse of the moon before they rose and departed the next morning. She felt small and lost, like a child far from home. Her heart was in Israel, and she doubted she would ever see it again.

# CHAPTER FOURTEEN

Scrub bushes were at her feet, and palm trees were overhead as she entered the market. All around her, people wore animal skins for clothes instead of linens. Children roamed, looking hungry and dirty. Vendors in stalls shouted at her to buy their amulets for protection. Idols were for sale everywhere she looked. Seashells, baskets of them, sat on benches in the market, and women kept urging her to buy them so that she would have more babies.

Mary did not understand. Why would having a bag full of seashells increase her chances of having a baby? But everywhere there were superstitions and amulets and statues. Had someone dropped them into another world, a world of frantic, competing gods and vices?

Joseph wasted no time, navigating through the chaos of the market to locate temporary dwelling. After settling Mary and Jesus in a room at an inn (how she was relieved—she always had a fear of being turned away), he went to buy tools. He had to earn money.

When Joseph returned to the inn, he was frustrated. Good tools were expensive. He had not wanted to spend the magi's gold, but he had no choice.

"I think but I have no confirmation," he confessed, with a terse edge to his voice, "that the gold was meant for our needs, not just an offering for Jesus."

Jesus, sleeping on a straw mattress, stirred, smiling at the sound of Joseph's voice. It warmed Mary's heart.

She crossed the cramped, dark room and patted Joseph's shoulder. "We could never have foreseen all this. Imagine us…in Memphis!"

"I have all these tools at home," Joseph grumbled. "You have an oven there. You wouldn't have to buy bread every day. Are we wasting money?"

"You know the answer," Mary said softly. She let her hands rest on his shoulders.

All he said was true. But they had no home now. They had only this moment, and each other. That would have to be enough. Thank God, she thought to herself, for His provision.

Joseph pointed to a figure, a small carved bird, that rested on the floor underneath the dressing table next to the bed. He was, perhaps, too tired to even make conversation.

Mary sighed. "That is Horus, the god of the sky. He's an Egyptian god. I tried putting it outside our room, but the inn-keeper's wife was offended. This is her house. I threw it under the table where we won't see him." Horus was in the shape of a small winged falcon, to remind everyone he ruled the air.

Joseph's shoulders slumped.

Mary bent and kissed him on the top of his head. "Don't be discouraged. We knew Egypt would be a strange land. Remember that we are here by God's will."

"No one here expects the Messiah," Joseph grumbled. "They don't believe in Him."

Mary sat beside him, leaning her head against his shoulder. "And yet here He is."

Joseph chuckled softly, then tipped his head to rest against hers. "And here we are."

"'Trust in the Lord with all thine heart, and lean not unto thine own understanding,'" Mary recited quietly. "In all thy ways acknowledge Him, and He will direct thy paths."

She listened as his heartbeat drummed on in the quiet of the room, her thoughts on the days ahead.

***

Early the next morning, Joseph left to find work. Mary asked the innkeeper where to get water. After learning how to find the reservoir, she took one coin for bread, wrapped Jesus up, and walked to fill their waterskins. She was almost there when she was stopped.

"You are not Egyptian." A man, bald and shaved, with dark painted eyes, held up one hand. He wore an insignia around his neck that did not look like an amulet.

"No, I am an Israelite."

"Foreigners pay for water."

Mary looked around. Plenty of people filling their waterskins and buckets were not Egyptian. Why was she being singled out?

"No use looking around. No one will help you," he said. "Do you want water or not?"

What could she do but surrender the coin she had been saving for bread? She hated being a stranger in a strange land, with men like this ready to prey on her vulnerability.

She filled the waterskin and made her way back through the crowds to the inn. Hopefully, Joseph was having better luck. Memphis was the first major city upon entering Egypt. Maybe the people were tired of foreigners. She certainly was. She wanted to be home in Nazareth.

People here wore hardly any clothes. Every man had a bald head and no beard—it was scandalous. She knew it was because of the fear of lice, but she didn't like looking at men who had less hair than her baby. And they wore so much body oil that they glistened in the sun. Women wore brightly colored eyeshadow too.

Mary realized how plain she must look.

She returned to the inn to get another coin and go back to the market for bread. Her feet would hurt by evening.

The innkeeper's wife had no sympathy. Before she went up to her room, Mary explained about the man at the reservoir.

"You people come down here and bleed us dry," the woman groused, kneading bread in her kitchen. "He is only protecting our water."

"There are other Jews here?" Mary asked, incredulous. She hadn't seen any.

"I am not talking about race," the woman nearly spat. "I am talking about Rome. The Roman empire demands our grain and taxes and anything else they can load onto ships and carry away."

"I am not Roman," Mary said.

The woman shrugged. "Neither are you Egyptian."

Mary thanked the woman for her advice and left. Secretly, Mary was determined to win her as a friend, to change her mind about foreigners.

But there would be no time.

***

Joseph did not dream, not this time. Mary only wished it had been so.

"Are you sure?" she asked again.

"They traveled by ship," he said, quickly packing his new tools. "They were fast. We came by foot."

Roman soldiers in Memphis, looking for runaway Jews? Especially mothers with infant boys from the region of Bethlehem... The soldiers prowled the streets, looking for tidbits of information about any child their sword might have missed. Herod would pay a handsome bounty if they found a runaway mother and killed her child. Mary knew, as did Joseph, that there was no shortage of people who would sell them out to the soldiers. So many people here looked desperate for a good meal or a roof over their head.

Mary was so tired. She had only been in Memphis for two nights, but already it was too dangerous to stay. They had to flee.

***

Turning west, Mary followed Joseph on the dusty road that led toward the Nile River. From there, they would hire a boat of some kind and find a new city to settle in. Joseph had no idea yet where it would be safe. How far would they have to travel to escape Herod's wrath? He had no jurisdiction here, but that did not mean he did not have spies and mercenaries.

The road was busy, and for that she was thankful. Although they did not blend in with the Egyptians, there were so many people that it was harder to be seen. They stopped in villages where they could, staying long enough to let the caravan pass and a new one begin. They saw no Roman soldiers. As the weeks passed, their fears of being discovered faded.

A woman carrying a load of dyed animal skins on her back hobbled alongside Mary one afternoon, her weathered face squinting in the sun. Mary stole glances at her, and the walking stick worn at both ends by time and use. Arthritis gnarled the woman's hands. She moved with shuffling steps and hummed a tune under her breath.

"What is the song?" Mary asked finally. She hadn't spoken to another woman in a friendly way for a week or more. She missed having friends and wondered if she'd ever have another.

"The hymn to the Nile, of course," she replied, not breaking stride. "You do not know it?"

"No," Mary said, readjusting the wrap around Jesus. He was struggling to sit upright to see the woman's face more clearly. He had grown in strength since His birth nearly ten months ago. He loved to sit up and see the world as she carried Him. He loved, most of all, faces.

"Beautiful child," the woman remarked, her walking stick striking the earth again, propelling her body forward.

"Thank you. You have children?"

"Once. They are no more."

Mary's heart was pierced. "I am sorry." It seemed too insufficient to say when the wound must have been so great.

"Where are you traveling to?" the woman asked, her tone betraying no emotion. If she grieved, she kept her feelings tightly locked away. But Egypt was a brutal land, and perhaps she had adjusted to that.

Mary hesitated. Could she trust a stranger with even a fraction of the truth? Probably not most strangers, but this woman had known such heartbreak. Did that make her less likely to betray another woman? Or more likely? Mary had no way to be sure, but she was so lonely.

"Tell me of Egypt," Mary said finally. If she was lonely, she would just have to trust that to God. She couldn't risk Jesus's safety just because of her emotions. That hurt her heart, but it was the truth.

"Well, let me see," the woman said, her stick striking the ground over and over as they walked, lending rhythm to the dreary, hot journey. "Cleopatra has been dead thirty years now, but people are still wildly devoted to her. Egypt belongs to Rome in name only. Our hearts are our own. A Roman prefect named Aegyptus rules the Egyptians."

"There are so many gods," Mary remarked.

The woman chuckled. "Yes! And cats. Cats are everywhere and so respected. The sun is always bright and hot—we do not have many seasons here. The Nile is what rules our world, though, even more than our gods and the sun. The Nile has three stages—flood, growing, and harvest."

The woman stopped and removed a necklace she wore. She handed it to Mary with some difficulty because her fingers were stiff, and Mary saw it was an amulet.

"This is Tawaret. She protects mothers and their children."

Mary paused, unsure of what to do. She couldn't wear it, but she did not want to offend the woman. Looking up, preparing to hand it back, she saw tears forming in the woman's eyes.

"Perhaps if I had worn it long ago..." The woman's voice trailed off.

The amulet felt like an iron weight in Mary's hand, a useless burden. She knew she could not give it back to the woman. Instead, she slipped it into her bag, where it would be unseen, and determined to dispose of it later. Mary then placed her hands over the woman's.

She had no words. Tears trailed down the woman's face, clearing the dust away. Mary wished she knew what to say, but they did not share the same faith.

Jesus cooed. The old woman's eyes brightened then, and letting go of Mary's hands, she reached for Him. Touching His cheeks, she smiled.

"Beautiful," the woman repeated softly.

"Yes," Mary said. "He is."

The moment held, and the air seemed to shimmer between them. The woman's eyes cleared, and she looked at Mary directly for the first time.

"Thank you," she whispered to Mary. "Thank you."

The woman resumed her walk. Mary walked beside her, wondering what she had been thanked for. All she had done was let her touch Jesus. And that, somehow, had been enough to heal a broken heart.

***

"Travel the Nile at night?"

Joseph recounted to Mary the horror on the guide's face when Joseph asked for a quick departure. The guide would not leave before dawn, no matter how much Joseph tried to bribe him.

Mary stifled a giggle as Joseph threw one hand over his face, acting out the man's theatrics. She sat on the ground, under the refuge of a palm tree, nursing Jesus. She did not feel especially safe. The noises here along the Nile at night were unnerving and there was no inn. The Nile, she had quickly learned, was at flood stage, and this brought many animals to its banks. There was so much to learn about Egypt.

At first light, regardless of the dangers, she carried Jesus alongside Joseph and stood at the banks, ready with payment. The guide brought several men armed with spears whose only job was to look for dangers. Mary did not ask what other dangers might be, besides the obvious one of traveling against the current in this season.

Once the boat pushed back and the rowers began laboring, Mary settled herself and Jesus in the center of the boat. There she felt safer, flanked by the crew and Joseph. Along the banks, people danced and set out offerings.

"Our new year's celebration," the guide said over his shoulder as he scouted the water ahead.

Mary felt a splash of water as a fish flopped near the boat. Smiling, she wondered with awe at Moses's mother, who had the courage to set her son in this river. It was one thing to listen to that story—it was quite another to be in the river with her own son and contemplate the action. What a risk his mother had taken, and what a loss she had borne! Yet the Jewish people had survived because of her sacrifice.

Why did God ask such things of women? What sacrifices a tender heart made in His service! The praying, the seeking, the letting go...Mary knew she might never have to set Jesus in a river, but she knew what it was to entrust her child to God. She knew what it was to face an unknowable, frightening future, and act in faith.

The boat rocked side to side, buffeted by the currents. The guide looked at her as he gave instructions to his crew, and he ordered a crew member to offer her bread.

She had not eaten breakfast, but the currents made her queasy anyway. She did not like traveling by water. When the man offered a small round loaf of brown bread to Joseph, he broke off a chunk for her. Inspecting it, she saw light pops of grain on the surface. After biting it tentatively, she was relieved. Soft and light, it tasted like wheat and dissolved immediately, like pastry.

"Sorghum flour," the crew member said, tipping his head in respect. "It will settle your stomach. It makes for strong babies too."

Mary blushed. But of course, he must mean Jesus, whose tiny, chubby hands reached for the bread. Joseph tore off a bit for Him. He shoved it into His mouth and gummed it furiously.

"Sorghum is a cheap and plentiful staple," the guide said over his shoulder. "You can pop it over a fire or make a paste we call couscous."

The guide steered the boat through the center of the Nile until the sun set. Only once did he allow for a comfort stop, and insisted Joseph stay alert and by Mary's side when she relieved herself in the reeds. It was humbling to have no privacy, but she reasoned that being eaten alive would be worse. Not much worse, perhaps. She had wanted to have a romantic marriage to Joseph…and so far, every step in the Lord's plan had taken them far from that ideal.

Still, they lived together now as a true husband and wife. God's will had not been so severe that they could not have a full marriage. They just could not have a journey together they fully understood.

At dusk, the boat reached a camp that smelled strongly of rotting meat and wet fur. Still, it gave them shelter for the night. Sitting up to sleep, her back against a thick pillar of wood at the center of the run-down shelter, Mary held the toddler Jesus as He slept. He was nearly fifteen months, by her estimation. In the night, bats flittered past. She heard animal sounds that she had no words for and wanted to wake the guide to ask him what creatures were nearby. Joseph did not sleep. He heard the noises too. A scraping sound at the mouth of the camp caught her attention. She watched a thick snake slither past.

"A cobra?" she whispered. She'd seen one in the market in Memphis, curled in a basket, lured out by a charmer if one offered the charmer a coin. Joseph nodded, his hand slowly going to his belt, where he kept a knife.

What good would a knife be? They were woefully unprepared for this journey. She had to just trust God that the cobra would not slither close by. She had to trust God that none of the animals would attack. His creations were under His command, always and forever. Only humans had a choice when they heard His call.

"Two by two they went into the ark at the command of God," Mary whispered, remembering the scripture. It was more than a story—it was the holy Word of God.

Joseph cut a sharp glance at her. "I don't want to see two of those." Mary bit her lip to keep from laughing and waking Jesus.

She rested her head once more against the pillar. "The night is so alive here."

"I had no idea the countryside could be so loud," Joseph replied. He remained at the mouth of the shelter, watchful. "What do you think our families are doing in Nazareth right now?"

She bit her lip for a moment, pondering. "Your brother is snoring next to my sister, who is wide awake and scowling at him in the darkness."

"The men of my family do not snore," Joseph replied staunchly. She saw his shoulders stiffen and knew he was restraining a laugh.

"They don't? Hmm. I wonder what I hear when you sleep? There are so many strange animals here."

"It is a land of wonders," he answered lightly. "Such as I never thought I would see."

"Will we ever return?" Mary asked suddenly. "To Nazareth?"

Joseph shrugged, then looked back at her over his shoulder. "I do not know. If we did, what could we say? Who would believe us? We are not even the same people anymore."

"And we have Jesus." Mary nodded. She had seen so much—scorpions as big as her hand, dancing cobras, fat hippos, striped horses called zebras, and tall proud herons standing at the water's edge at dawn. All this wonder of creation had soaked into her soul, as surely as her skin had been browned by the sun. Egypt had marked her with its glory.

The next day, the river raced with churning waters that made the boat unsteady.

Pulling the boat into the reeds, the guide announced that they had to wait for the currents to slow. He suggested that they all stay in the boat, and he would pull a linen tarp across the top for shade.

Jesus stood at the front of the raft, His short, unsteady legs wobbling on the boat as it bobbed in the water. Mary watched Him eyeing the reeds that were taller than He was. He lifted a hand to touch one, and a great rush of noise exploded. The guide screamed as a huge gray beast thundered toward Jesus, trampling the thick reeds underfoot like straw.

Grabbing a stick, the guide yelled and smacked the sides of the raft, trying to scare the beast away.

"An elephant?" Joseph whispered, the awe in his voice evident.

"It can kill us all!" the guide yelled. "Stay back!"

Mary froze in fear and amazement. Jesus had not moved. He stood, hands outstretched like a child waiting for a toy, staring up at the elephant with curiosity, and perhaps even adoration.

The elephant blasted its trunk and a tiny elephant, a baby, pushed its way through the reeds to look at Jesus.

Shocked, the guide dropped his stick into the water. He clearly dared not stick his hand in the black current for fear of the crocodiles that swam along on the river bottom.

Jesus and the elephants stood still, examining each other, until Jesus clapped His hands in delight. As if that were a command, the bigger elephant retreated, using its long trunk to nudge the baby to follow.

Joseph's exhale of relief nearly rocked the boat from side to side. Mary collapsed back onto the bench that sat in the middle, weak.

"What is He?" the guide asked, pointing at Jesus as if the toddler were a terrifying apparition.

"He is the son...of Mary," Joseph said, stammering for a split second. Mary knew Joseph could never claim to be the father, no matter how much he loved the boy. And if he revealed Jesus's identity, it would put Him in danger.

"I will take you to Giza but no farther," the guide announced, then used his leg to push the boat away from the river's edge. "I want you out of my boat."

# CHAPTER FIFTEEN

Jesus wanted to stand, so Mary let Him stand next to her on the street. He bounced on His feet, swaying side to side.

"Do You think our people built these?" Mary asked, pointing up at a pyramid. The pyramids here at Giza were already 2,500 years old.

Joseph was walking in the main area of Giza, looking for work. Mary was trying to learn her way through the streets and find the market. The inn they were staying at was comfortable, but she had hoped to find a home to stay in. Giza was far enough away from Herod that she wanted to settle down for a few months, which meant paying for lodging at a home. An inn would simply be too expensive.

Jesus stared at the towering pyramid, but His expression was hard for her to read. His sweet face looked so serious, with a scowl that made a cute little wrinkle between His brows, but what could He know about the years of slavery in Egypt?

"Did You see it somehow? Has the Messiah always been with us?" she asked suddenly.

Jesus turned to her, His wide brown eyes luminous in the morning light. He babbled something she could not understand. He seemed glad to be here with her on a beautiful morning.

Mary sighed, staring at the pyramid. It was daunting, with an air of total silence around it, as if it had taken more from this world than it would ever give. Too many had sacrificed their lives for a worthless stack of brick, a monument to a man turned to dust.

Her people prayed for hundreds of years to leave this land of slavery. God must have seemed so silent to them. But God heard their prayers, and Moses led the great Exodus to the Promised Land. These very lands, this very dust under her feet, under Jesus's feet, had seen Moses leading the people out of dark captivity.

Where would Jesus lead them? If not to the Promised Land of Israel, what was waiting just beyond these years of silence?

A delighted shiver ran down her spine, and goose bumps appeared along her arms. Something very big, and very good, must come next. The next exodus, she knew, would be incredible. And her son would lead it. She looked down at Him, prepared to scoop Him up and kiss Him.

He was flat on his belly in the dust, admiring a beetle. He lay there, head on arms, watching the armored insect with happy intensity. He reached out a chubby finger to touch the back of the beetle delicately and giggled, looking up at Mary in wonder.

Mary sat beside Him. He would lead a great exodus, true, but today, He was just a child. And children were in love with creation. She would rest for the moment and let Him delight in the world God had made.

Egypt was a land of sun without shadow. The relentless heat made Mary faint in the afternoons. She struggled to find her appetite for bread. Or what the locals called bread.

Even mornings were hard lately, and she didn't understand why. Mary sat up from her sleeping mat, reluctant to begin the day. A busy two-year old, Jesus was already awake, playing with a rag doll puppy Joseph had bought at the market.

Joseph had been so happy last night, because he'd found work—work that paid well. Mary did not tell him, but that discouraged her. Had she harbored hopes to return to Nazareth? Perhaps. Her heart was a mystery even to herself. How could she ever hope to understand the heart of God, then?

The room spun, and she pressed a hand to her mouth to keep from being sick.

A basket of the unleavened sorghum bread was on the table near the mat. She grabbed a small cracker and nibbled at the edge, and it helped. Where would she find a doctor in Giza? One that did not practice witchcraft or the Egyptian magics? Surely she had contracted a fever on the Nile. Joseph would worry.

How could Gabriel have called her blessed and favored? Weak, Mary nibbled the bread as she recounted the losses—no home, no family nearby for support, no wealth of her own, no idea what the future held. Still, she wasn't bitter, just confused and homesick.

Being "blessed" was not a circumstance. If it was a circumstance, she wouldn't be here, sick to her stomach, alone in a blistering-hot room. God's blessing and favor was reality. She needed faith—so much faith—to believe it!

She returned her attention to Jesus as He played. He needed breakfast, even if she had no stomach for it.

Within the hour, they were both groomed, dressed, and in the market, hunting for the day's food. Most of the sights turned Mary's stomach. If she found a friendly face, she would ask for a doctor to prescribe a remedy.

One woman stood at her stall, baskets of dried fruits and roots all around. Her face was young and plump, her eyes bright. She looked really and truly alive, in the way so few people did. Mary liked her at once.

Approaching her, Mary fished in her bag for coins. Dried fruit would keep very well back at the inn for breakfasts.

The woman reached immediately for a gnarled brown root.

"Oh, I would like to buy raisins, and any other fruits you have," Mary said. She resisted naming them in case she embarrassed herself. Not everything here had the same name.

"By the looks of you, this is what you need." The girl laughed, cutting a chunk off. She handed a piece about the width of Mary's thumb to her. "Chew this. You will feel better."

Mary popped it in her mouth and chewed, her eyes watering. The root was spicy.

The girl smiled, watching.

Mary sighed, waiting for the stinging on her tongue to abate.

Jesus stood next to her and kicked off one sandal. Digging His foot into the sand on the street, His brown curls bounced as He wiggled and laughed at the sensation.

"You must enjoy being a mother to have another so soon," the girl said. "How much ginger would you like?" Her hand hovered over the bowl.

Mary's mouth opened in shock.

"You didn't know? But you looked at the other food stalls and nearly went green in the face!" The girl laughed. She grabbed a large chunk of root and pressed it toward Mary. "Here. A gift."

Mary's thoughts jumbled together all at once. An angel had announced her first pregnancy. She had not resumed her monthly cycles since she had been nursing Jesus, and she blamed the nausea on the heat and strange food. She wanted to run and tell Joseph, but he was working, and she didn't know where in Giza he was. And she liked this girl. Would Mary stay here long enough to have a friend?

The girl lowered her head suddenly, her eyes darting away. Mary turned.

A woman rode through the market in a litter carried by four shaved and oiled male servants. Veils tied to poles at each corner partially hid her from the crowd.

"What is this child?" the woman demanded, pulling back the veil that covered her face. Overhead, a thicker piece of linen shielded her head from the sun. She wore a wig that had thick braids brushing her shoulders, and thick kohl lines around her eyes.

Repulsion swept over Mary, like a brush against a rodent in the dark. But why?

She reached down and picked up Jesus, cradling Him to her chest.

Mary's new friend bowed. "We are honored to reply." She glared at Mary, as if urging her to say something too.

"His name is Immanuel, Jesus." Mary said. For no reason, her knees trembled.

"Do you worship the gods of the Ennead?" the woman demanded, fire lighting her eyes.

Mary shook her head.

The woman pointed a jeweled finger at Jesus. "When I saw this child, dark whisperings came to me. I dislike His face." The woman's gaze swept back to Mary. "I dislike you. Egypt may be a vassal of Rome, but we are not Romans." The woman paused, as if hearing another voice. "You are not Roman. What are you?"

"We come from Nazareth," Mary replied meekly. Still, she stood straight and met the charged gaze. "We are of the house of David."

*Oh*, Mary thought. *What have I done?*

"Nazareth? I have never heard of this place. But you are in Egypt now, not Nazareth. The house of David means nothing to us. Mind that you do not seek to supplant our gods. That would surely bring a bitter end to your child."

The woman motioned to her servants, who moved on.

Mary exhaled, her body folding in on itself after the encounter.

"She is a priestess," her market friend explained. "I don't know why your son provoked her. Perhaps He looks like an enemy she once had?"

Mary stared with sorrow as the litter disappeared into the crowded streets. She gathered up her thoughts and held them close to her heart.

Jesus caused such unexpected reactions from strangers. Hearts were laid bare in His presence.

---

The following week, Joseph returned from his work, a dark frown on his face.

"Men drinking at the inn spoke about a Jewish king that Herod was chasing."

Mary felt the blood run from her face. Her heart felt cold as stone.

"When must we leave?" she asked softly. She did not want to leave. Her new friend at the market was a delight. But Jesus was more than her son. He was the Messiah, and her duty was to Him. Besides, she had been the one to reveal her son's name. If Herod was astute, or his spies were, they would make the connection.

"In the morning," Joseph replied, sighing. "Let's eat a good dinner and then pack."

Joseph must have read her thoughts, because he spoke with great kindness next. "We still have gold, and we have not traded the frankincense or myrrh. We can afford to travel and seek refuge in another city. That is a blessing. And perhaps that is God's will, for you may find friends there."

She smiled softly. He knew she was lonely, especially during the day when he went to work. She hated to spend the gold, though. The wise men had given a gift to honor a king, and Mary felt conflicted to think that the wealth had been used to conceal His identity. Maybe that was what God had intended? But how could she know? Raising a Messiah was a terrain that came with no map, no guides, and no other experienced souls who could offer words of encouragement.

Traveling up the Nile, Mary was content to watch the dark waters swirl past. Crocodiles sunned on riverbanks, but none slid into the water as the boat passed. Their size astonished Mary. Were these the leviathans that Job described? She could not remember the exact passage. It had not been one she had even wanted to commit to memory. The feeling of dread had been enough, even listening in synagogue.

If only she could have known that someday she would see one!

She rested a hand on her belly. Joseph caught her eye and smiled. *His child*, she thought, *his first child grows within my womb.*

Tipping her chin, she let the morning light warm her face. She felt truly alive suddenly, seeing dangers and wonders she never would have believed long ago. With only Joseph and Jesus, she was surviving without her family. She had never imagined that either! Here in the land of the Exodus she had seen hints of a second exodus, one that would come through Jesus. Slowly, she believed God would piece everything together and that someday every step on the journey with Jesus would be rich with meaning and foreshadowing.

She felt favored and blessed at this moment, for no real reason she could describe. Even if they had to flee once again, they were together. They had each other and they had God.

Being blessed was very different from being happy. Smiling at the revelation, she remembered that once she had confused the two. Happiness was a fleeting emotion, based on circumstances or mood, or even the last thing she ate. But to be blessed was to be in close relationship. And here in the land of the Exodus, she had never felt closer to God, Jesus, or to Joseph.

"The Garden of Eden is rumored to be just farther south," the guide said. This guide was more familiar with the stories of the Hebrews.

Mary caught a sly smile on Jesus's face and wondered what He knew.

"What is the noise?" Joseph asked.

There was shouting in the distance, and what sounded like drums.

"Celebration," the guide said. "The Festival of Opet."

Joseph shrugged to Mary.

The guide noticed. "It's the major festival of the year. People carry statues of the god through the city and hand out free food. Free drinks too. There's music and dancing in the street. You picked a good time to travel to Thebes."

Mary's heart lightened. Perhaps Thebes would be more welcoming than Giza or Memphis.

Within the hour, the boat landed at the docks of Thebes. The guide was right. The city was in celebration. Bright yellow drapes hung from buildings, and as Mary set foot onto the street, someone handed her bread. Free bread! Joseph accepted a beer, although it smelled strange. She guessed it was made from an Egyptian grain. Still, it was safer to drink than the water.

Jesus looked at the city with delight, His wide eyes taking it all in. Several women stopped to tickle His chin, which made Him giggle and push their hands away with His chubby hands. He struggled against Mary, wanting to get down and run in the streets, but it was not safe.

"Wait until we have lodging," she said to Him. "Then you can run around."

Joseph took the lead. "I will find an inn."

Her heart caught in her chest. When, she wondered, would those words stop causing her such panic?

# CHAPTER SIXTEEN

Thebes was a city of brightest color and richest food and people who indulged in every way. Scholars roamed the streets, arguing the merits of recent scrolls acquired for the library in Alexandria. Musicians stood on street corners, playing songs in hopes of coins. The markets overflowed with goods. Mary noticed the city had very few beggars, and she wondered if the poor were better cared for here. It did seem to be a city of great wealth and energy. Perhaps the city elders had found a way to give them work and lodging. Outside the city, on the western border, was a huge mound. Jesus was in awe.

"What is that? What makes that?" Mary asked as Jesus pointed a chubby finger toward a tall mound of earth protruding from the ground.

"Termites," a man passing by replied. "If you travel south, they have giant ones."

"Giant termites?" Mary gasped.

The man slapped his thigh and roared with laughter. "No! Giant mounds. The termites there build mounds taller than you."

Mary laughed at her silliness, but when the man had left, she shook her head in amazement. Every day she learned something new, something that she could barely believe. Egypt was not so much a country as a condition of the imagination. It had to be believed, even when your eyes doubted what you saw and your mind struggled to think it could be real.

As the days passed, Thebes proved to be a magnificent city. Joseph had work, and Mary had company wherever she turned. Hesitant to make friends, she accepted companionship without pushing for intimacy. That seemed to be enough, and she found a new ease in dealing with other women. As her abdomen grew, the other women held Jesus for her when He fussed and carried her heavy market purchases back to the inn. And when the time came for her to be delivered, they did not mind that she did not want spells or amulets. They knew she was different.

Still, a midwife came that did not rely on Egyptian gods. Mary was so thankful for her help. And the pains came, terrible pains, pains unlike what she experienced with Jesus. She was out of her mind with pain. When she screamed, Jesus let out a brokenhearted wail that brought everyone in the inn running. He was inconsolable.

Finally, Joseph took Jesus to another inn for the night, shielding Him from His mother's agony.

Late the next afternoon, Mary delivered a boy.

Joseph's son.

She held him, studying his face with exhausted wonder. He looked like Joseph. He startled her, as if she had never given birth before, never even held a child. But perhaps she hadn't, not a child of her marriage, a child of earth. The baby looked nothing like Jesus.

Joseph entered the room, holding Jesus's hand. Jesus toddled forward, one hand reaching to touch the baby's face.

Mary hesitated. She was unclean. Jesus touched the baby, and the pair locked eyes. Brother stared at brother for the first time.

"James," Joseph whispered. "We will call him James."

"You have a brother," Mary said softly to Jesus.

His eyes flitted up to meet hers. He looked grieved, as if still worried for her. But He was just a toddler. How could He understand the pain of what a woman experienced in childbirth? How could He know that suffering was a natural part of life?

The thought was cold and hard, like a rock in her sandal. Suffering wasn't natural, was it? Jesus knew that, somehow. He was grieved, not just because she had been in pain but because pain was wrong. Eve and Adam brought that curse into the world. Would Jesus reverse it?

She drew Him to her side and kissed the top of His head.

"Mary," Joseph said, with just a light scold in his voice, for she was unclean.

"I know," she replied. "But nothing makes sense around Him...and then, everything does. Absolutely everything."

Thebes was the resting place she could not have imagined. Colorful, vibrant, and busy, the streets were always buzzing with energy. On nearly every corner stood an open-air temple with columns of dizzying heights and beautiful tiled floors. Thebes was a feast for the senses, and that made it easier for Mary to forget her heartache.

She missed the rural peace of home. And the plain, unadorned faces of her family and friends. How long had it been now since she had seen them? Months had flown by, then a full year, and another. Jesus would soon celebrate His third birthday. James had just had his first. And Mary had another child on the way.

Now was the time, she knew, to force herself to accept the inevitable. Thebes was home. Joseph had steady work. They'd rented a tiny house that shared a communal oven, and the other women had slowly begun to accept her.

She could accept them too, she decided, as her friends and family, the only ones she would have now.

The following week, Mary was awake before Joseph and the boys, a small miracle. She wanted to be the first woman at the oven today to bake the morning bread. As her pregnancy progressed, the heat of the day bothered her more.

As she sat up and stretched in the darkness, she noticed a change in the air. The tiny room was thick with an unusually fragrant spice, as if someone had been burning incense. Every breath, however, gave her body strength. She gasped quietly, suddenly realizing where she had remembered this smell. The Temple! This perfume was identical to the Temple incense that burned as a symbol of the people's prayers rising to God.

There was no Temple to Yahweh in Thebes. No one here burned that incense. Her skin prickling, she realized an angel had been near as she slept, one who stood in the presence of God. The scent of prayer was simply unmistakable.

Then her heart fell. When Joseph awoke from his sleep, she knew what he would say—he had dreamed. Again. An angel visited him in his sleep and revealed a message from God. Mary rested her hand on her stomach. What now?

Was Jesus in danger? Looking around the room, she decided what she could pack quickly. No. Surely, they were safe—they were so far south in Egypt.

Why couldn't the angels appear to her, just once more? She missed glimpsing another world, but perhaps being pregnant, she was too heavily tied to this world.

Joseph sat up, rubbing his eyes. Before he could speak, Mary asked.

"What did the angel say?" she whispered urgently.

The boys stirred on their mats. James had curled tightly next to Joseph, and he whimpered and reached a hand out for his father. Joseph patted him on the back, soothing him back to sleep.

Mary watched. Whatever the message from the angel, it was not bad news. No Roman soldiers would be beating down the door looking for Jesus. Was it just a few years ago that she lived in great fear for His life? Thank God, she thought, that those days were gone forever.

"How did you—" Joseph started. Then his mind seemed to clear, seeing the intensity of her expression. "The angel said to me, 'Arise, and take the child and his mother and go into the land of Israel; for those who sought the child's life are dead.'"

Mary sat back, exhaling forcefully. Herod was dead. It hardly seemed possible. And it was more than one man's death—the angel said all those who sought to end Jesus's life were dead. Something must have happened at the palace, more than just the passing of a ruler.

Jesus sat up. Mary scooped Him up in her arms and settled Him in her lap, adjusting His weight around her growing belly. James opened his eyes and stretched his legs.

"What do we do?" she asked. The news seemed over-whelming. They'd been on the run for three years, concealing their identity, hiding who Jesus was, pushing away any thought of home.

"I think we obey," Joseph said, sounding as stunned as she felt.

"Do you hear that, boys?" Mary asked. "We're going home. To Nazareth!"

The luxury of time made this trip so different. Mary and Joseph were not escaping to Bethlehem, trying to hide a divine preg-nancy. They were not fleeing to hide a baby from Roman soldiers. With no rush and no threat, they had thought through their plans and chosen their route based on convenience and comfort.

The Nile was too high to use for transport back to Memphis, and travel by foot would take at least four weeks. Joseph decided that waiting a month for the Nile to recede would be a better choice for the family. Mary agreed. After all, she could keep track of two boys on a small boat, but on the open road in Egypt, that would prove more challenging. Plus, the wildlife that hid in the reeds and shrubs would have easy access to the boys if her attention—or their feet—wandered even for a moment.

And secretly Mary was relieved that she didn't have to travel by foot or donkey for an extra three weeks. Making the journey to Nazareth was going to be long enough. At least she could skip that part.

Once the journey began, she took delight in watching the boys' expressions as they rode along the Nile. Jesus had been too young to remember His first trip. They clapped and giggled at the birds that flew overhead and gasped in wonder at the size of the crocodiles sliding past in the water. A hippo on the shore surveyed the boat with a cold disinterest, and that was the only time Mary saw the boat guide grow visibly scared. The hippo had babies with it, but miraculously, it was in no mood to charge and capsize the boat. Perhaps it sensed Jesus, but she would never know.

Jesus held James's hand when the currents pushed against the boat, rocking it roughly. James cried in fear, not liking the uncertainty of open water. Jesus, who was little more than a weaned child Himself, was a good big brother. Still, James dropped Jesus's hand and buried his face instead in Joseph's robes.

Jesus frowned, His lower lip quivering. Mary held out her arms, urging Jesus to come to her for a hug.

Mary wondered how this would work as the boys grew older and grew up together. With another child on the way, she had hoped that the children would be a tight-knit group. She had not expected Jesus to have a powerful effect on His own siblings, the same way He affected strangers. It hardly seemed fair.

And it hardly seemed like something she could overcome.

***

Once they arrived in Memphis, the port was not far. From there, they would return to Hykkos, then to Israel. Mary rested a hand on her belly as Joseph negotiated with a merchant for their dinner. He had already secured a room at an inn for the night. The boys stood at her feet, clinging to her robes.

Mary glanced back over her shoulder at the busy market, feeling like all of Egypt was behind her. *I never would have thought I could have survived all that I have seen and done since leaving home!* She recounted the whole strange journey. Giving birth without mother, sister, or the village midwife. Surviving the pain of leaving Nazareth behind forever—or so she'd thought. And the unexpected journey to the land of slavery, which would be their home.

The land of so much Jewish suffering now protected their Messiah. The tears that fell here, the bodies buried here, all were like seeds, and today she saw the fruit that those lives bore. A land that belonged entirely to God, always and forever, kept Jesus safe. If even one of those poor slaves had glimpsed this remarkable turn of events, how their suffering would have been eased! She bent to pick up a little broken rock and tucked it into the bag at her waist.

James and Jesus looked up at her, watching her do it.

"For our garden in Nazareth," she said. "A piece of Egypt to carry with us and remember."

"Remember what?" Joseph said, returning at that moment.

"Remember when we thought our exile would last forever," Mary said. "How word from an angel came to you when we did not expect it, revealing that God had prepared the way for us to return home."

Joseph nodded. "I like that. Pick up one for me."

Frowning, Mary rested a hand on her bulging belly. "Pick up one yourself. I have enough of a load."

He laughed loudly and grabbed both boys, hoisting them into the air, making them shout with glee.

"We better feed your mother, boys!"

Mary suppressed a grin and followed behind.

━━━━◆━━━━◆━━━━◆━━━━

At the campfire, Mary watched as the cook peeled an onion. They'd been traveling for a week now after landing in Hykkos. They were in Israel again but still had a long journey to reach Nazareth. Mary could hardly wait to see her family again and give birth to her third child there.

Egypt had such good onions. She didn't want to admit it, but she missed them! This onion was smaller than she was used to, and she hoped the flavor was not too sharp. As the cook peeled the brown skin away, the soft white layers were visible. He tossed each layer into the cooking pot, and the onion in his hand grew smaller. Mary and Jesus watched the cook work until the onion was gone. His hands were empty.

*Before Gabriel appeared to me, I was like an onion plant in the ground, full and thriving,* Mary thought. *But God pulled me away from my comfort. As I followed God, layer after layer peeled away,* she mused as she watched the flames under the pot.

*Yet, with every layer that was peeled away, I was not diminished. No, God grew larger, and that made my life so much bigger too. With God at the center, it does not matter how many layers life peeled away. If God is my center, I am constantly enlarged.*

*This is favor. This is the blessing,* she realized. *Life can be painful, but with every loss, there is more of God.*

And here, at the end of so much sacrifice and loss, she was ready to return home and have a peaceful life. She would raise her little family with Joseph and watch God unfold His plan for Jesus.

There was only one problem.

Joseph did not want to go to Nazareth.

***

"Jesus is the Messiah," Joseph argued for what felt like the hundredth time. "He belongs in a major city. Bethlehem or Jerusalem, one with a synagogue that has learned rabbis. The Pharisees in Jerusalem are the best teachers—you know that. We must make sure He has the best religious instruction."

"But I want to see my family," Mary countered. "He needs that too. Nothing is more important to our daily life than family. He can't learn about love from lectures."

"That's why He has us," Joseph replied flatly.

"You should pray about it," Mary said, looking away. She knew that was an argument that Joseph could not overcome. "Again."

Much to her surprise, God settled the argument with another dream.

Joseph waited two full days to tell her the details. It did not matter, as they were nowhere near Jerusalem or Bethlehem yet. Mary kept her silence and waited, but by his expression, the angel had not given him the news he wanted. Finally, as the boys went down for sleep on their traveling mats near the campfire, Joseph spoke.

"Herod's son, Archelaus, reigns in Judea in place of his father Herod. Apparently, he is a tyrant. Everyone hates him, even Rome. I heard that bit from the men in the caravan, not the angel in my dream."

"Hmm," Mary said, not willing to comment further. Joseph needed to have a scrap of pride left, after all.

"So we shouldn't settle anywhere in the region he rules, which is Judea."

Mary nodded, but in her heart, she thought of the cities that Judea contained, including Jerusalem and Bethlehem. Archelaus made them unsafe. She had won.

"Where should we go, then?" she asked, as if she didn't already know.

"Nazareth." Joseph sighed. "But it makes little sense, Mary. Why should Jesus be raised in a small town, one held in poor regard? He won't have access to the best teachers. And think— so much has happened, and we are such different people. Why would God call us back to the place it began?"

"Does it feel like failure?" she asked gently. No wonder he resisted returning to Nazareth. He thought God expected more from him, and now he could not provide it.

Joseph nodded. "One more thing. In two days, we will be back in Bethlehem. Have you thought of that? We'll see the graves for the sons who died because of Jesus, mothers who have no sons His age, and we are the reason."

"Herod is the reason," she reminded him. "You take responsibility for too much."

Had she ever understood how deeply he felt this burden of raising the Messiah? He must have considered challenges and possibilities and felt that it was up to him to navigate them both. She wished he had shared his concerns more openly, but perhaps he did not want to burden her now that she was pregnant again. And she had been so determined to have her own way, returning to Nazareth.

"I'm sorry," she said softly. "I wanted to return home, but I can see that you have so much more to consider than my happiness."

Joseph winced. "Oh, Mary. I wish I could think of only that! Sometimes I wish we were an ordinary married couple. I worry about how we should raise Jesus, and then I worry that I am cheating you out of happiness. How do I choose between being a Jew who loves the Messiah and being a man who loves his wife?"

This was the most he had said about their lives since they had first become engaged. She leaned toward him and kissed him.

She didn't know what to say, but a kiss seemed like a good answer. Maybe it was the only one.

# CHAPTER SEVENTEEN

Late spring made the hill country beautiful. Mary watched Jesus run through fields of wildflowers, chased by James on unsteady legs. She rode the donkey Joseph had purchased for the journey, not minding that the beast was so slow. She was too, these days. Her best estimate was that she would give birth in four months, but she might be wrong by a month in either direction.

Her heart lifted when she saw Nazareth in the distance, with its tiny houses cut into the hillside. Other houses made of stacked stones sat below rock walls farther down in the village. About fifty houses in total made up the little nest at the heart of the community. The houses cut into the hillside were the best, for they disguised the entrance in case of an invasion of angry Roman soldiers. Her parents lived in one of those.

She could hardly wait to see her parents!

"Remember our agreement," Joseph cautioned. They had agreed that they would keep the events around Jesus's birth a secret, if possible, until Jesus revealed Himself as the Messiah. He was the one who would lead the people, and they could not assume that authority. At least, in the absence of another command from God, this was the best decision they could come to.

Joseph's father saw them from a distance and met them on the path before they reached the stone wall. Joseph picked up his pace when he spied his father, so the two had a joyful reunion while Mary was still approaching. A joyful, loud reunion, Mary thought, for his father shouted in delight as Joseph pointed to his sons.

His father saw Mary in the distance but did not wave. Instead, he turned his back, and Joseph stood alongside him. That was unusual, and Mary frowned with concern. She was too far away to overhear or even read lips, but why would they not even want her to see their expressions?

A cold rock of fear dropped into her belly.

No.

Joseph turned and walked toward her.

No.

"My mother?" Mary choked out as he approached.

He was pale and hung his head with grief. "Both. I am so sorry, Mary."

She didn't remember what happened next, except that when she stopped her wailing, she was in the family room of Joseph's family home. His younger brother's wife was spooning broth into her mouth.

Mary sat up, the grief making the room spin again. Her parents could not be gone! They had never met either boy. They had never met the Messiah!

"Tell me," she said to Joseph.

"A tax revolt, led by a man named Judas. Roman soldiers killed him, then attacked and burned the nearby city where your father sold goods at market. Your mother was at the stall that day too, to be near your father. Your sister is alive, though, living in your family home. She is eager to see you."

It was days before Mary could bring herself to walk through the village. Many friends and family came to Joseph's parents' home to see her and Joseph, however. She did not come down from the loft bedroom to greet them but listened as Joseph introduced his sons, James and Jesus, to each villager. Only Miriam, her older sister, was allowed into the loft. The sisters held on to each other for a long time, without speaking.

Each had birthed children in the years apart. As they touched each other's faces gently, Mary knew her sister saw what she did—the new lines that had appeared around the eyes, the softness of a body filled out by age and motherhood, and the hands roughened by working every day to provide meals and refreshment for a growing family.

Mary grabbed her sister's hands and pressed them to her face, kissing them. How beautiful they were, with calloused palms that carried water jars every morning to and from the well.

Her sister blushed and tried to pull away. "Your friend Rebekah has servants."

Mary shook her head, and a tear fell away onto her lap. "Rebekah will never have hands as beautiful as these. Not to me."

"I have missed you terribly," Miriam said. "I want to know everything. Gossips have never stopped speculating about the reason you left on the night of your marriage. But Jesus is three. He's not so old that anyone would assume the worst."

Mary dropped her hands. What could she say? Pressing her lips together, she pondered.

"You know you can tell me anything, right?" her sister pressed.

"Of course!" Mary replied earnestly. "I just—I am tired from the journey, and the shock of the news of our parents. That's all."

But Miriam could read the deception in her eyes. Mary knew it and felt awful, but until she spoke to Joseph, she could not tell even her sister about Jesus's identity, Gabriel, or the night He was born.

And to think—her sister had been waiting all her life for the Messiah, and He was here, under this roof. How could Mary conceal that from her own flesh and blood?

Yes, she and Joseph had planned to keep this secret, until such a time Jesus chose to reveal it. But Mary had not realized how much she would need to unburden herself once she returned home.

When Miriam left, Mary stood at the window and watched her walk back to her married home. They were not children anymore, huddling under the covers together, sharing the secrets of little girls.

How she missed those days.

---

The weather in late spring was beautiful. Mary delivered a baby girl in the fall, and was enjoying her first outings with the boys, keeping the baby tightly wrapped at her chest. Nazareth was chilly at night, but the days were gloriously warm. Mary walked with the boys every morning, showing them the wildflowers peeking up from the grass. Chickpea fields were in bloom and olive groves were green, with grape vines flourishing along fences. At night they ate fish brought from the Sea of Galilee.

The midday wind came in from the Mediterranean Sea. That sea was not an idea to her any longer. She had walked along its shores. So many things that were once only ideas were now very real.

Like the Messiah. He sat at her table, His small tender face in concentration as He tried to remove the bones from a dried fish. He was four now. Next year He would begin His formal education at the synagogue.

"So many," He muttered. "I just want to eat."

She suppressed a grin of rebuke. God had put all the bones there after all.

James chomped his fish and crunched the bones. Joseph lightly smacked him on top of his head. "That is not safe!"

James shrugged.

Mary glanced between her boys and saw that their differences were plain. So was the animosity, at least from James.

But on the long, pleasant walks during the spring days, Mary looked at the familiar faces peeking from doorways and wondered who would believe her about Jesus. It was still not her place to reveal His identity. Besides, her own identity had caused something of a scandal when she first returned home.

Mary's old childhood friends, including Rebekah, had needed time to grow accustomed to her appearance, for it was different. When she returned from Egypt, she was darker, her skin tanned by long days in the Egyptian sun. Her jewelry and robes from the Egyptian years were unusual by Nazareth standards, but she did not have the money to replace her wardrobe just to blend in with the local women once she was back at home. She refused to trade the remainder of the wise men's gifts just to buy familiar-looking clothes. She wasn't even the same girl in her heart.

Her sister had accepted that Mary carried secrets. Mary wished for the days of total trust and togetherness, but raising the Messiah carried a high price, one that had to be paid daily and in a thousand different ways.

Rebekah invited Mary to visit, but their friendship faltered. Common interests were hard to find. Still, Rebekah refused to bring up the subject of Mary's sudden departure from her own wedding, or the suspected pregnancy. Mary blessed her silently for that kindness.

Besides, Rebekah was far more interested in advancing her husband's standing among the elite of Rome. The fortunes of Rebekah's in-laws had taken a sharp downturn, and wealth threatened to dissolve under her very feet if she did not hurry.

Mary once envied her for the ease of wealth, but now she was grateful that she did not have to work to keep it. Plus, Mary got to look upon Jesus's face morning and night. He spoke to her, and she listened, and when she sang the psalms, He glowed with happiness. And wasn't this one more way she was favored by God?

She saw the face of God every morning at her table. Even on the days when she was weary, when money seemed scarce and her worries seemed plenty, He was there.

Smiling.

Mary missed Jesus in the mornings when He was at the synagogue. He was such a helper around the house, always entertaining His younger sister, or ready when needed in the workshop, handing Joseph the correct tool every time.

James glowered in anger that Jesus got to go to synagogue first, and it did no good to explain the age difference. James was determined to prove himself better than Jesus.

Mary admitted to herself that both boys spent their mornings well. Jesus excelled at synagogue, amazing the teachers with His grasp of scriptures and His hunger for learning. When other boys fidgeted and fussed, Jesus always wanted to hear more. And James? James had a talent for building that exceeded even Joseph's. What delight Joseph took in showing James every tool and technique! Before James turned five, he knew the basic steps of constructing a solid joint and a hinge.

The first year of synagogue went well, except for one comment by Joseph's parents. It was like a seed dropped over a garden wall. Mary could not retrieve it but only watch helplessly as it grew. Mary was expecting again, and one night at the evening meal, Joseph's mother made an observation as Mary served the dinner.

"Jesus does not look like His brother or sister."

The old woman pushed her lentils to one side of her bowl using her flatbread, looking for a scrap of lamb. Mary used little lamb, as prices were high. Joseph worked hard, but providing for a large family and his parents proved difficult. They had stashed away what was left of the magi's gold, in fear of anyone discovering it. It was not Roman gold. It bore the marks of the Persian empire, and the Persians were enemies of Rome. It would raise so many questions and suspicions that it was far, far safer to keep it hidden. Although no one looked for Jesus to kill Him—thank God that danger was over now—the Roman government would never be kind to families who hid gold from other enemy empires.

Joseph looked sharply at his mother, then at Mary. Mary froze, her hands around the serving bowl held in midair. Who would dare question Jesus's paternity in front of Joseph? In front of her?

"Do you not think He favors your side of the family?" Joseph asked, a bright, false smile on his face. He leaned back, one hand stroking his chin.

Mary knew he was pretending to study Jesus's face.

"You know," Joseph continued, "the rabbis say Jesus is the most gifted student they have ever taught. There is a younger boy in Jerusalem named Saul, taught by Gamaliel, who might be almost as smart, but Jesus far surpasses even him, and that boy is a Pharisee descended from Pharisees. But if you don't see the resemblance..."

"Oh," she said quickly, "I do. Obviously, He favors my side of the family. The other two favor Mary's. That's all I meant to say."

James hung his head as Mary clutched her hands under the table in aggravation. When Jesus finally revealed His identity as the Messiah, would it be too much to ask that He tell her mother-in-law first?

Jesus grew taller and stronger, and He loved wrestling with His friends. Some boys in the village ostracized Him and bullied Him because He refused to make fun of the weaker boys or harm animals for entertainment. He was careful with everyone and all life.

"And you always let the smaller boys win?" Mary asked.

Jesus smiled sheepishly. "Yes."

Jesus had to keep His identity hidden until it was time. Mary wrestled with God's timing, but how much more Jesus must struggle!

And as the years passed, Mary gave birth to three more sons, Joseph, Jude, and Simon, plus two daughters, Adinah and Rachel. Her home overflowed with bustle and laughter. James continued to prove his talent for building, but what brought the villagers to the workshop was Jesus. It amazed Mary that Jesus found more ways to serve the village. He made toys out of scrap wood for the children, which won Him enormous favor with the mothers. Joseph was more than pleased, for when the mothers adored Jesus, they insisted their husbands use Joseph's workshop for their building needs.

Mary loved the tender years between the start of synagogue and His arrival on the brink of maturity. Jesus was a wonderful older brother to His sisters and brothers, although James begrudged Him the adoration that came so easily to others.

One evening that was especially dear came as Mary prepared the evening meal. Jesus recounted the story of Noah and the ark to His siblings gathered round, using animals made from scraps of wood to illustrate the march to the ark. The children listened, wide-eyed with wonder, then collapsed into giggles as Jesus described the antics of the animals and all that Noah and his sons had to do to keep them fed and quiet when it was time for sleep. His capacity for detail seemed endless. It was as if He had been there, among them.

Even James laughed at his brother and the stories. Mary treasured the moment, knowing that the following year it would be time to go to Jerusalem and present Jesus at the Temple for Passover.

*Where did these years go?* she wondered.

The days had seemed so long, sometimes, especially the afternoons. But the weeks, the months, even the seasons flew by. Jesus had grown taller and wiser. He loved going to synagogue. James did not love it the same way, which caused yet more conflict between the boys. James preferred working with his hands in the workshop or the garden. Jesus did the same work, but Mary knew His heart was with the scriptures and the people.

Jesus could listen for hours as people talked, anyone at all. He listened to the beggars at the market telling of fighting in long-ago battles. He listened to lepers who cried out from a great distance and then wept to Him about living on the edge of the world as an outcast. He listened to tired young mothers and talkative old men.

Jesus loved the children in the village too, even the younger ones who wanted to tag along with the older boys. Jesus did not mind being seen with the ones who still soiled themselves or were not fully weaned. That made Him a target for the older boys, who thought Him weak or odd.

He could skip rocks though. Maybe that was the reason the older boys never hurt Him, the reason they did not pummel Him daily. They wanted to learn His secret. When the boys went to the river after synagogue lessons, they grabbed stones for a rock-skipping contest. Jesus won, every time, His rocks practically dancing across the water.

James glowered at Him over dinner every night.

"He won't tell any one of us His secret," James always complained. "I want to skip rocks like that. But He must keep all the glory for Himself."

"It's not a secret." Jesus shrugged. "I just do it."

"How?" James demanded.

"I just close my eyes and tell the rock what to do."

The answer infuriated James.

Did Jesus fully understand who He was? Was it her place to explain? He knew all about the night He was born—what child didn't ask for those stories?

Maybe that's why James disliked Him so much. James had been born in a lovely inn, with a proper midwife. It had been perfect. It was a boring story. No shepherds visited, no signs appeared, and no priests arrived bearing gifts. James did not understand what made him different from his brother. He did not know yet that Jesus was the Messiah. He only knew that Jesus's birth—like everything about His life—had been more interesting than his own.

Mary and Joseph wanted Jesus to reveal His identity to His siblings and His friends in His own time and in His own way. The weight of the truth was far too great for anyone but Jesus to carry. She could not ask James, or anyone else, to carry that burden. Not yet.

But Mary had told Jesus everything she knew, from experience and scripture. She had taken Him to synagogue and let the rabbis instruct Him in everything they knew too, although they did not know He was the Messiah they spoke of. If Jesus needed more knowledge, that day was quickly approaching. He would turn twelve, and they would go to the Temple in Jerusalem for Passover. Jesus would be acknowledged as a man, no longer a child.

Jesus had yet to tell anyone who He was…but the time was coming. She was sure of that. For now, she would let Him skip rocks and enjoy the simple pleasures of being young. Because soon, very soon, that would all change.

Jerusalem waited to receive her King.

# CHAPTER EIGHTEEN

As they traveled to Jerusalem, Mary quizzed Jesus on the Temple, just as her father once did with her.

"This Temple is missing something. Do you know what it is?"

Frowning, He chewed His lower lip as He walked alongside her. His strides matched hers easily. He would be close to her height when fully grown. Joseph was quite tall, and by all judgment, James would be too. Jesus would probably be of average height. Truthfully, she wished He would be taller. It seemed fitting for the Messiah to be tall, strong, even undeniably handsome. Jesus was average in all superficial aspects. Only His heart and mind made Him unforgettable. It was regrettable that many people didn't pause long enough to encounter the heart or mind when dealing with others.

She hoped He was ready for this, this unveiling of His destiny at the Temple.

"The sacred objects," He replied finally.

Mary smiled to herself, for she was becoming just like her father, peppering her child with endless questions, treating each moment as if she were a teacher and her child a student.

"True! The holy ritual things, the incense tongs, and goblets for the drink offerings, all are missing. Soldiers looted those and carried them away, probably to an evil king's court.

But what do we grieve the loss of most of all? What is the one loss that seemed unbearable?"

He stopped midstride. "The ark of the covenant." He turned away from the bright sunshine, as if He needed a moment to grieve.

Adjusting the shawl that hung from her head, she pondered the fate of the ark. No one knew who took it or where it was. Rumors abounded, of course. The ark meant so much to her people. They prayed for its return. She had seen the drawings of it. It must have been a thing of great beauty.

God Himself had given the pattern to Moses with incredibly detailed instructions. Every measurement, every line, was planned before the work began. The beauty was not just from the gold that overlaid the acacia wood frame. The sculptures that rested on it must have been breathtaking too. The ark had a lid with two angels, their wings outstretched to overshadow the lid, which was called the mercy seat. God's overshadowing presence, glory, would be visible between the angel's wings.

Inside the ark was a copy of the stone tablets of the Law given to Moses on Mount Sinai, a jar of manna, and Aaron's rod that bloomed and bore almonds. God gave the Law, daily provision, and an unexpected sign of His power.

The ark was so much more than an object. It was their connection to God's overshadowing shekinah in creation.

Overshadowed…how the word resonated in her heart! She rested a hand on Jesus's shoulder, gently turning Him to face her.

Looking down at the soft lines of Jesus's face, she remembered how God's presence overshadowed her once. The thought that His shekinah glory had overshadowed her, a common woman who had not even offered a sacrifice for purification before the overshadowing, seemed almost scandalous. God's presence was not confined to a Temple any longer. Maybe it never had been. Looking at Jesus, she knew it never would be again.

Jesus nodded, as if He knew what she was thinking, as if He was thinking it too. The shekinah glory had led the people out of slavery—but it was deadly to anyone who looked upon it when unworthy. The glory of God was a dangerous beauty not of this earth.

Her thoughts came in a jumble. She had seen the shekinah glory and lived! Who would believe her? She still could barely believe it herself. Holy men approached the ark with trembling fear and awe, and only once a year, after much preparation.

When the high priest went in on the day of atonement, he burned incense, then sprinkled the blood of a bull for his sins, then the blood of a goat for the people's sins. Only then was it safe for him to approach the glory-cloud in the Holy of Holies. Only a priest who was properly cleansed had ever seen the glory cloud resting over the ark and lived.

And to think—that same shekinah cloud had overshadowed Mary. She had not paid for any sacrifices to be made at the Temple on that day, or even that month. How could she have been considered clean? How could God have visited His glory upon her and allow her to live?

"Do you think we will ever see the ark again? On earth, I mean?" she asked Jesus.

"I don't know," He said, His eyes peering at the horizon, the holy city in the far distance. She looked at His ruddy cheeks, and the soft dark curls falling around His ears. He might have answers to her questions but not today. Today He was still her son.

She rested a hand on His shoulder. "You remember what I told you about the road outside the city?"

His face darkened. "I will not look."

"And do not let the younger ones look at the crucified men either." She nodded. "Now go and join your cousins."

His cousins were anxious for Him to walk with them the rest of the way. She watched as He was swallowed up by the group of children, all clamoring for a chance to walk alongside Him.

She was glad to be alone with her thoughts. What she really wanted to ask but dared not was a scandalous question. Why had God never returned the ark to His people? Because now Jesus was here? Was He a new and living manifestation of shekinah glory?

But to talk of the glory of God was to invite the wrath of those who were charged with keeping His law. Until they had their Messiah, they would treat her questions as blasphemy. She had to be patient and allow Jesus to show them the truth of who He was.

She was caught in an uncharted land between what had been long ago and what God was doing now.

It was a land of few explanations and many dangers.

The crowded streets of Jerusalem were always a shock to Mary, with their noise, the smells, and all the different languages spoken. She heard Hebrew, even Latin, plus Aramaic, Greek, and a few words of that strange Egyptian tongue, Demotic. The language of the Egyptians continued to change with the influx of immigrants and the rule of the Roman empire. What would be left of the Egyptian empire? she wondered, with a pang of sweet memory for that land.

Jews were scattered throughout the Roman empire, and the Roman soldiers patrolled the streets of Jerusalem to be sure no one talked of revolt.

She parted with Joseph and the boys at the gate to the Temple. After kissing Jesus on the forehead, she paused only long enough to exchange a look with Joseph. This was the day they had long awaited. Jesus would be a man, and the Messiah would enter the inner courts of the Temple.

What a day for the people of God.

She watched as Joseph led Jesus and the boys into the men's court. She turned and made her way to the women's gate and courts. They would not be together until tonight, when they met back at the inn for dinner. She could hardly believe this was happening. She could hardly wait for the hours to pass, to hear the news from Joseph! What a stir this would cause, what celebration, what utter and total disruption. Her heart would be in her throat until she knew it was done.

Just a few hours, she thought, and she would lay her burden down. The world would know Jesus was the Messiah. Praise God.

The walk home was quiet. Mary could barely stand to look at Joseph, so great was her disappointment.

"Are you sure you made the right offering?" she asked again. "And did they recognize He was now a son of the commandments, ready to take on a full life at our synagogue?"

"Yes," Joseph said, an edge in his voice now. He was probably tired of answering the same questions. But nothing had happened! They had recognized Jesus as a full participant in Jewish law, and ready to proceed with all the education that remained. There was nothing left to do in Jewish law except grow in knowledge. All the rituals, the offerings, the sacrifices that were required to be a part of the community, all were complete.

And still Jesus had not proclaimed Himself to be the Messiah.

What *was* the Messiah? Mary asked herself for the first time. Had she misinterpreted the scriptures? Had she misheard Gabriel? If Jesus was going to deliver people from their sins, would they ever even know His name? A great despondency fell over her, and she walked for hours without talking. Joseph must have felt the same, for he walked alongside her in a similar mood. The only relief from their confusion and sadness was that they were not expected to care for their children. The cousins preferred to walk together, with Jesus in the middle of the pack. James took the lead, naturally, which made his father Joseph proud, and the cousins were always flanked before and after by the adults. Traveling to Jerusalem for

Passover was an adventure on the open road for the children, an escape from chores, and a chance to stay up late into the night telling tales by firelight.

Mary was glad they were enjoying this trip and entertaining themselves. She did not have the heart to be merry. She barely had the heart to say her prayers. As she tried, a nagging feeling prodded at her, but she dismissed it. She'd done everything she could to get Jesus recognized. Nothing else could be done. She had to dismiss these nagging feelings and doubts.

The third day, the nagging was no longer so polite as to stay at the edges of her prayers. It roared in her ears as she walked along singing a psalm.

She clutched Joseph's robe. "Jesus!"

He stopped, confusion in his eyes.

"Jesus is not with the cousins!"

Joseph ran to check, and when he returned, she could tell by his expression that her foreboding was right. They told the family to take the younger siblings and travel on without them while they returned to Jerusalem. James was bright with embarrassment to think he had led the cousins for three days, not noticing his own brother was missing.

They ran more than they walked, not even bothering to hire a donkey. None could be had anyway. Everyone was traveling out, away from the city, leaving after the holiday. They needed the donkeys to return home.

"We have to get to the gates before they close at dusk," Joseph said on the second day. They had made good time, since they had no one to care for and no one to wait for.

"I don't want to leave Jesus alone in that city for another night, but neither can we risk being alone in these hills with the wild animals and thieves."

Mary thought she would pass out from a lack of water and food. What she would have given for even one gold coin from the magi! Joseph was so sparing when using those coins. Thankfully Joseph had a little left over from the journey, or they would have perished on the way back into the city.

They moved so fast that this was the only time she paid no attention to the dying men on their crosses, calling for mercy.

They arrived at Jerusalem just as the sky turned deep blue and the walls glowed gold.

Spying a soldier, Mary ran to him. "We have lost our son. Three days ago."

Dark circles hung under his eyes and the stink of stale wine was on his breath, the same vinegar-soaked smell clinging to his clothes.

"You are Jewish," the soldier replied.

"Yes," Joseph replied, raising his voice to be heard over the crowd. "We last saw Him at the Temple."

"How old is He?" the soldier asked, disinterested. Mary felt she might as well have told him she had lost a goat.

"He's twelve. Please, help us," she begged.

He looked at her, blinking several times.

"Come with me," the soldier snapped. He roughly pushed people out of the way. Those who saw him coming moved quickly out of his path, his sword making everyone afraid. Rome had that effect.

Coming to a stop at the entrance of the Temple, he grabbed Mary's hands, and tears formed in his eyes.

Joseph lurched as if to protect Mary, but the soldier rested a hand on a dagger at his hip. Joseph stopped. Mary's heart beat faster as the soldier leaned close, his fetid breath washing over her cheeks.

"Years ago, I killed Jewish infants in a town not far from here. All boys. Their faces never leave me. They would be twelve this year if I had not obeyed my commander. That is why I brought you."

Mary saw in his face the grief of following the wrong command. What devastation the wrong leader had wrought in this man's life, and in the lives of so many families.

But revulsion for this man and what he had done came over her and she jerked her hands away. "If only you had had the courage to say no."

He looked at her, one hand still resting on his dagger.

"My name is Timmaus, and since that awful day, I have begged the gods for a way to repay my debt."

He walked away, and Mary felt the sting of shame. He had no way out, no way to atone for his sins, and the wrath of God weighed heavily on him. The Messiah would deliver the Jewish people from their sins, but what about the Gentiles, and the criminals, the murderers?

What would God do for them? Weren't they lost too?

The soldier led Joseph away toward the men's court. Mary paced nervously, wondering if they would find Jesus. Should she stay and wait, or look elsewhere? The sky darkened as the sun set. Oh, and they had no place to stay for the night. Would they be able to secure a room at an inn? She prayed they would, for most of the travelers had left since the holiday was over.

Where was Joseph? Had he found Jesus? The wait, alone, was excruciating, as she watched families reunited after their time at the Temple hurrying back to their lodgings for the night. She wanted to run into the women's court to pray, but she had to stay here. Every time she caught sight of a boy with the same height of Jesus, her breath stopped, her heart caught in her chest…and her body collapsed in on itself when she saw his face. It was not Him. It was never Him. Where was He? Was He even here? Sickening memories replayed in her mind…the slave traders, the bereaved mothers who they said would pay for a child His age.

"Mary!"

"Mother!"

The voices were familiar and wonderful, releasing her from torment so quickly that she felt light on her feet, so light she thought she might float away. Then she glared at Jesus, her anger swift and hot.

"Where have You been?"

Jesus looked up at Joseph, astonished. Joseph held out a hand to soothe her.

"He was sitting with the teachers. They were having quite the conversation." Joseph looked at Him fondly, ruffling His hair with one hand. "All the rabbis praised Him to me, said no finer student had they found in all of Jerusalem. They said His understanding goes far beyond His years."

Joseph was mollified by sweet words from men, but Mary was furious. She stomped a foot and spoke to her son. "How could you do that to us? To me? We were worried senseless looking for You."

"Why were you searching for me?" Jesus asked, peeking at her from behind Joseph as if He didn't recognize this side of her. Maybe He didn't. He had never made her this angry before.

"Didn't you know I had to be in my Father's house?" He said softly, His sandal tracing the stone at His feet.

Mary sucked in her breath. Jesus's words had the power to cut Joseph to the core, for Joseph was not His father.

Joseph gently rested a hand on Jesus's shoulder. "Let us find lodging for the night. Your mother hasn't eaten for hours, and You know how she gets when she's hungry. We had a long journey to find You." He spoke tenderly to Jesus, who smiled broadly looking up at him.

Mary's heart softened.

Nothing had gone according to plan. Not hers, at least. If God had a plan for this stage of Jesus's life, He had not chosen to share it with her. Was her usefulness in the life of the Messiah over? Tears threatened to spill as she thought about letting Him go, letting Him become a man with a larger destiny than she could ever understand. She had done her best for Him, but He wouldn't need her forever.

As they trudged along the stone streets to find an inn, Jesus held her hand. His palm was warm, and she felt the calluses from hours in the workshop. He wanted to hold her hand as they walked along a dark street, and she suspected that it was now for her sake. The comfort that she took from this simple kindness was too great for words. It was all that she needed to know.

Her time in His story was not done. He loved her. He would always love her. That was what their story was about, what it had always been about.

For tonight, that was enough.

# CHAPTER NINETEEN

Rebekah was the one who brought it up. Mary was enjoying a midday meal in Rebekah's garden as the friends caught up on news and family.

"Who will you betroth Jesus to?" Rebekah asked casually.

It was the following year after losing Jesus at Passover. Jesus was nearly fourteen.

"He's young," Mary said lightly, more lightly than she felt. She'd always assumed He would declare Himself to be the Messiah far before now. No one had thought He'd be this old and still just a carpenter's son.

How could she evade the problem of marriage? Why should she even have to? If ever there was a time for Jesus to announce Himself—

"Are you even listening?" Rebekah asked.

"I'm sorry," Mary replied. "I was lost in my own thoughts."

Rebekah set the bowl of olives down and reached across the table, taking hold of Mary's hand. "I know you are worried about money. We all worry about money these days. That is why you must betroth Jesus now. Do not wait. You can choose from all the maidens in the village and pick one who can bring the most money into the marriage."

Mary leaned across the table. "What will I tell Jesus? Good news—your bride has the teeth of a donkey and the voice of a hyena, but she's rich."

Rebekah scoffed, sitting back. "I've never heard a hyena, so I can't judge. But money can make anyone attractive."

"No, it can't." Mary laughed.

"Well," Rebekah argued, starting to laugh too, "if there's enough money for motivation, anyone can learn to lie."

Mary picked up an olive and threw it at her friend. "I have to be getting back. Joseph is returning home from Sepphoris this afternoon. He installed a custom door on the government building. Meanwhile, he left the boys alone in the workshop to finish a few projects."

Rebekah stood and kissed her on the cheek. "Until next week, then."

"Until next week, or until you get another brilliant idea." Mary laughed.

"If there's money involved, I'll get an idea, don't worry."

<hr>

"Don't be so downhearted. You know the role you've played," Mary said to Joseph the following week. He had returned from Sepphoris, frustrated by the number of questions he'd received about Jesus's future. Joseph needed to announce a plan for his oldest boy, but he had none. Jesus had to make the plan, but Mary and Joseph could tell no one that.

The gossips were already speculating as to why Jesus was not betrothed. Was Joseph too poor? Was Mary too controlling? Was Jesus too…uninspired by the girls in His own village? Perhaps He thought too highly of Himself. After all, Mary seemed to value Him quite a bit, pushing Him in His studies, expecting exemplary behavior, not even blinking when He displayed talents or aptitudes that other boys did not possess. She assumed He was born for greatness.

Mary was stung but not surprised. She continued stirring the lentil soup. It filled the kitchen with fragrant notes of rosemary and sage. She threw in a clove of garlic, a spice they'd fallen in love with in Egypt, and so easy to grow here.

Joseph shook his head. "It is more than wounded pride for our good name that plagues me." Standing, he grabbed a spoon, walked to the soup pot, and stole a taste. Nodding in appreciation, he continued. "Jesus has flourished under our care, protected from the Romans. He is still a child under their law. But what happens when He becomes an adult under their law? We won't be able to keep Him safe."

That made little sense. "The Romans haven't been interested in Jesus since the time of Herod."

"And in those days, we could pick Him up and run," Joseph replied, pacing in the little kitchen. "What happens when He is a man? We won't be able to pack Him up and carry Him out of the country in the middle of the night."

"Why are you so plagued by these thoughts?" Mary asked softly. It wasn't like her husband to worry like this, of things so far in the future.

Joseph stopped, then looked at her with a stricken expression. "I do not feel well."

⸺◆⸺◆⸺◆⸺

The dawn rose gray, the clouds thick as wool.

Mary went downstairs to fetch a cup of water. Every step was hard, weighed down with sorrow and grief. Returning to Joseph's bedside, she listened to his rattling breath. His heart had given out yesterday, suddenly. He hung on by sheer will, or a pure miracle. She could not tell which. The older two boys had been away installing a door for a customer and had only just returned. As the morning turned toward noon, Joseph opened his eyes and grasped her hand.

Mary ran and called for James and Jesus to come to the bedchamber. James entered the room first, and Mary stood back, wanting to be available for his questions. She knew how hard this was going to be. Jesus stood at Joseph's bedside, but at a distance, letting James come the closest.

"My son," Joseph began, looking at James only.

James knelt by the bed, taking Joseph's hands in his. "You are so cold, Father."

"You are my firstborn son, James."

Jesus hung His head, not in shame, Mary knew, but in agony. The words hurt, because they were true, and Jesus loved Joseph so much. They loved each other so much.

James flinched. "No. You have Jesus, remember?"

Joseph laughed, and the chuckle launched a spasm of coughing. James looked back at Mary, his eyes wild with pain.

She knew he was terrified that Joseph was losing his mind as he faced death.

"I must tell you the truth," Joseph said. "I must tell you why Jesus does not look like me but you do. I must tell you who He really is."

James looked at Jesus, then Mary, then back at Joseph, fear and pain in his eyes.

"We tried to shield you from this for so long," Mary said, continuing the story so that Joseph could catch his breath. "We wanted Jesus to tell you first. But now that Joseph is…growing weak, we cannot wait. You will take over the leadership of the family. And you will become part of a story that is unimaginable. It can be a heavy burden."

Joseph's eyes misted over. Mary watched as his breathing slowed. But it was not death that approached now, it was memory.

"There have been angels," Joseph began, his voice trailing off. "Gabriel appeared to your mother when we were betrothed. Then the angel of the Lord appeared to me too."

He coughed and fell silent. His face softened and became radiant, and Mary knew he was remembering those days, the days of their young love, when angels walked in and out of his dreams.

His breathing settled into a steady pattern. He was sleeping.

James knelt at his side for a very long time. Jesus said nothing, but watched Joseph with an expression of helplessness that broke Mary's heart. Finally, Mary decided the task of telling the story had fallen to her. She had to do it and do it now. Joseph had started the story, and he was caught in the telling. He had to let go but could not. She would finish, and he would be at peace.

With legs that did not even feel like hers, she walked down the stairs and into the kitchen, motioning for the boys to follow. She had sent the other children to her sister's, so the house was quiet. The boys sat the kitchen table, but the tension between them might as well have been a fortified stone wall.

Mary unfolded the story neatly, as if it were a stored linen, and the creases were intersections of lives and prophecies. She reminded James of the prophecies about the Messiah and told him of the angelic visitations. It was difficult to meet Jesus's eyes as she spoke, and her voice did not even sound like her own. She was aware of her heart breaking, of her heart floating away in pieces, like chaff on a river, as she spoke.

She told James of strange visitors when Jesus was born, and Herod's wrath against the family, resulting in many cruel murders. Finally, she told James of Egypt, that land of wonder, and how she had finally and fully given herself to the truth of the Messiah and His mission there.

"Outrageous," James said quietly when she had finished. Mary studied his face for a clue to his emotions. The lines on his forehead deepened.

"It is an outrageous lie!" he blurted.

Mary's mouth fell open. He accused her of lying. He accused his own father?

"What rabbi told you Jesus was the Messiah?" James snapped. "How did he convince Abba to go along with it?"

Had he even been listening?

"Your argument is not with me," she said, reaching for his hand. He pulled away immediately. "Your argument is with God. Ask Him for wisdom. He will give it to you generously, I promise."

"My father is dying." James hung his head. "And you saddle me with this outrageous story. Why?"

"Because you are the eldest son of Joseph. You will take his place. And you cannot take his place unless you know the whole truth. We could not tell you when you were a child, for the wrath of Rome is merciless, and children say things they ought not. We weren't hiding anything from you—we were protecting you. All of you."

"Really?" James said, looking at his brother with disdain. "If Jesus is the Savior of our people, tell me this—why doesn't He do something? Our father is dying, and the Messiah doesn't care?"

Mary opened her mouth to speak, but she could think of nothing else that needed to be said. Oh, there was much she wanted to say, but that was another matter. What needed to be said had been said. Her part was done. She could not explain herself further, and she could not explain the will of God. She had never understood that herself.

But there was one thing she needed to know too. Would James forever associate this time of searing grief with the shocking revelation of his brother's identity?

Would he believe in Jesus, or blame Him?

She went back upstairs, leaving her boys to their pain.

Joseph was gone, she already knew. Their love story was finished.

———————

Mary washed Joseph's body carefully, preparing him for the burial that would take place later in the morning. Her hands touched the body that had sheltered her own, and Jesus, for so long, and every touch was an act of prayer. She touched the hands that had held hers since they were children. The arms that had held the infant Jesus. She rested one hand on his chest, over his heart that beat so strong, so true, in life. Joseph had been so much more than a husband. He had been a shield and a confidante in this mystery she held.

He was gone and she was alone. The children were downstairs with the mourners. James sat with the elders of the village, receiving words of comfort and counsel. He had accepted his role as the eldest son. Mary sighed, wearily, the threads of that story finally slipping from her hands. The Lord had finished His weaving, using her and Joseph. Now it would be up to Jesus and His heavenly Father, His true Father, to complete this tale.

She wondered, her mind so dull with grief that each thought was as heavy as a stone sunk in mud, whether Jesus could endure the gossip that would come next. He was the oldest son in the eyes of the village, not James.

But Jesus was not even here. After Joseph died, Jesus went into the hills to pray, leaving Mary alone with her questions, doubts, and fears. Alone with the mystery of God's will.

How would she face the future without Joseph? Who would she tell of the ponderings of her heart?

God had revealed His plan to her, once, long ago. It had been a day that changed her life, and Joseph's, forever. That day had changed the story for the Jewish people. And now Joseph's story had ended.

She bent and kissed Joseph's forehead, the skin cool to the touch.

"My love," she whispered, "I would have lived a thousand stories with you."

# CHAPTER TWENTY

James worked in the cool of the morning, rising before Mary. She rarely saw him before the evening meal, and he was not talkative after a long day of hard labor.

As the years began to click by, he continued the carpentry and building trade, and Jesus worked alongside him dutifully. James asked no questions about the story that Mary told him the night Joseph died. Mary wondered if he believed it. Jesus Himself said nothing of it.

She worried as Jesus passed into His late teen years. He seemed to be a lonely boy, despite the throngs of children who adored Him. His friends in the village ridiculed Him as they married and moved on with their lives and asked Him privately if it was Mary who refused to let Him go. She knew because He confided in her late at night, when the sisters were in bed and James worked late in the workshop on a project. James often liked to work alone. Jesus accepted the subtle rejection with grace. Alienation did not harden His heart toward others, Mary noticed, although it crushed her very soul.

Maybe that was what made her boy special—He could bear so much pain without bitterness.

When James asked to be betrothed to a girl named Annah, she knew Joseph would have been thrilled. Annah was a delightful, quiet girl who brought out the tender side of James. Mary herself had not seen that side of her boy since his youngest days.

Brighter days were ahead. James would be married. Mary might soon have grandchildren. And Jesus?

The Messiah and His timing were a mystery to her, even now.

Even more so now.

---

"You are sad today," Jesus remarked.

Mary shuffled around the table, making a few last-minute adjustments. James's wife was busy stirring the lamb stew. Jesus's younger sisters had finally married off this past spring. How different the house seemed now.

"John has begun his ministry," Mary told Jesus, ignoring His comment.

Annah ladled lamb stew into a bowl for supper. Jesus thanked her, then nodded to Mary. Elizabeth had died a few years past, and John had been raised by the Essenes. Both Mary and Jesus had speculated that John would become a teacher.

Mary was surprised, however, that John was reported to be a wandering teacher, rather than one that taught at a school or synagogue. His father had been a temple priest, after all.

She watched Jesus eat. Finally, He set His spoon down.

"What is it, Mother?"

She swallowed. What could she say? That she was getting old and Gabriel had appeared to her when she was young? She thought her life would have been so very different than this! Gabriel never warned her she would become an old woman, waiting for her son to reveal His identity to the world. God had made His intentions for Jesus clear. Now she knew that intentions were not the same thing as a plan. She'd grown old waiting for the plan.

Jesus was nearly twenty-nine. His best years were gone, at least by the standards of Rome, who worshipped pink-cheeked youth. What was He waiting for? Had something gone wrong? If He were any other man, a normal man, He would have been married with children by now. His best and strongest years were past, as were hers.

What was God doing?

How is this blessed, she wanted to cry out, to watch your child wither on the vine, His promise unfulfilled? How is it blessed to wait, past all hope?

Mary wanted to remind herself that the blessing was the relationship, not the circumstance. But the pain of the moment was just too much. She took a moment and breathed, closing her eyes, wishing for Joseph's steadying hand.

Opening her eyes, she looked at Jesus and saw her own pain and confusion reflected. He must have been feeling many of the same things. She'd never considered how hard it must be for Him, waiting on God's signal that it was time to begin.

Somehow, walking with God through this painful mystery had been her chosen path, just as surely as it had been Jesus's.

Mary knew then that her greatest contribution to His life might have been her presence. She had been there on all the thousands of quiet days that passed without notice, without signs from above, falling one after the other with numbing certainty. She had been favored, and she let that same favor flow to her son. The presence was the blessing.

*Lord,* she prayed, *let me stay strong in that belief. Let me remain constant.*

If it was these long, lonely days that led Jesus deeper into the will of His Father, then it would be these days that she must help Him endure.

---

"This will be my last Passover leading the family to Jerusalem," Jesus said to her one morning as they packed for the journey.

Mary paused, her hand in midair. She was folding a linen for her new grandchild, James's first son. How the little boy reminded her of Jesus! Only yesterday she held him as the light of a thousand angels was reflected in his eyes.

She nodded, unable to say anything. The time had come for Jesus to begin. She had waited for years, yet at this moment, the pain was so unexpected, so sharp, that it left her breathless. No matter how long a mother has to prepare for her child to begin a new life, it is always too short.

On the way to Jerusalem, the family heard the bleating of sheep being led to the slaughter.

Mary shivered, as she always did, listening to the poor creatures. Jesus looked troubled.

"Will it hurt very much?" Jesus asked her under His breath.

Mary rested her arm on His back, patting Him for comfort. "I doubt they feel much. The priests do it swiftly."

Jesus did not seem comforted.

"I'll buy it," James scowled and brushed past Jesus, his shoulder bumping Jesus rudely.

Jesus picked the lamb up and held it tightly, whispering words she could not hear.

James scowled but continued, leading the family toward Jerusalem. Mary pondered all of this in her heart.

⚜

Jesus was probably dead. Everyone told her that.

He had disappeared, and no one had heard from Him or seen Him for weeks. Mary refused to entertain those dark thoughts, though. She kept them to herself, penning them in her heart like wolves, refusing to loose them to do any further damage. But night and day they gnawed at her, and she ached.

It was spring of the following year after the last Passover together, and James's wife, Annah, was expecting again. Mary and Annah sat in the courtyard early one morning, talking with the other wives of the village. Everyone seemed reluctant to return to their chores. The spring sun invited them to sit and enjoy themselves a while longer.

Why hadn't she heard anything from Jesus? He had gone to see John, His cousin, who was baptizing people in the Jordan River. It was going to be a sweet reunion.

Jesus never returned.

Suddenly, James tore past the women and stormed into the house, where his young son was sleeping. Or had been, Mary thought. Annah jumped up and followed. Mary followed, her stomach in knots.

She overheard his words, spit like gravel found in bread, at his sweet wife.

"First, He leaves with no warning. Now He comes back and announces He's leaving for good. He says it is time to begin His ministry. Can you imagine? My own brother, proclaiming Himself as the Messiah of our people? Wandering around, begging for food, attracting the wrath of Rome? If Herod once murdered infants who could be the Messiah, can you imagine what his successor will do when Jesus says He is that man?"

Mary held back at the threshold, wanting to hear more.

"And now the entire business falls to me. I will do double the work for the same money!"

Annah soothed him with soft words. Mary crossed the threshold and slipped into the room.

James looked up at her, his eyes holding the pained expression of a young boy who feels betrayed. She knew he did not understand that he was reliving the night of Joseph's death, trying to make sense of what was happening.

"We must let Him go," Mary said.

"He's been collecting disciples," James said, nearly spitting the word out. "And are they scholars? Serious students? No. They are fishermen."

Mary shrugged lightly. "I do not understand that. But James, I have understood nothing for nearly thirty years." She laughed and took a seat at the table. Suddenly, she felt very weary. She missed Joseph and wished he were here to see this moment. It was all unfolding so strangely. But then, this was Jesus. Nothing about Him had ever been expected.

"How can you laugh?" James winced. "He is claiming to be the Messiah."

"He is the Messiah." Mary slapped her palm on the table, startling them both.

James became quiet.

"So it begins," Mary said softly.

---

Jesus arrived at the wedding in Cana with His new friends. He was much thinner than He was when He left home, but He looked well. He introduced Mary to His new friends, including Philip, Nathaniel, Andrew, and Peter. To her great shock, women accompanied Him. The entire wedding crowd was scandalized. Men did not travel with women.

Mary saw that something else was different about Jesus, something with a familiar feel—she remembered the power of a divine encounter. Jesus seemed to be flooded with that same power. It was as if the shekinah glory of God rested on Him now.

Jesus approached James with arms opened for an embrace.

James turned away, engaging a wool merchant in conversation.

Mary saw the grief pass over Jesus's face. His own brother wanted nothing to do with Him, not since He left. Mary hurt for both her sons and noticed the gossips in the crowd turning to one another and speaking in hushed tones. She did not want her family drama to ruin a wedding. Worse, this day was a wedding for Rebekah's family, a sister's daughter. Mary owed Rebekah so much for not gossiping about her when she was pregnant at her own wedding. She did not want to see this wedding ruined by her sons. Especially since the gossips were already inspecting the food tables and canopy. Mary overheard the comments about previous weddings from this family.

"Why is the feast so small?"

"Why does the canopy not have fresh flowers? Why is it not dyed and beaded linen?"

Mary flinched at the thought of Rebekah's pain. Whether it was right or wrong to love wealth, it was wrong to gossip so cruelly.

Mary liked Jesus's friends very much, but Peter was her favorite, because he seemed the most out of place. He was a big man, and not good at conversation. His face was sun-weathered, but he had an easy smile and twinkling eyes. She could tell he had a kind heart.

And yet a small pain lodged in her heart like a thorn—her son's world was no longer hers. He had new friends and a new life, one she did not share. Hadn't she prayed for this, though? But her heart as a mother could not reconcile with God's will so quickly. She'd need time, and the thought made her smile wryly. Once, time had been her enemy.

After the ceremony, people were drinking heavily, which made them hungry. When the food ran low, the people drank even more. She overheard the servants' panicked whispers—the wine had run out.

"They have no more wine," Mary said to Jesus. She did not bother telling Rebckah's family. What could they do at this hour?

"Woman, why do you involve me?" Jesus replied. "My hour has not yet come."

Mary grinned. She saw the sparkle in His eyes as he spoke. Of course, He would address her as if she were Eve—the Messiah was here to reverse the Fall. She was not pushing Adam to eat the forbidden fruit—this Eve was pushing the Messiah to unlock the gates of Eden.

Not even bothering to reply, she motioned for the servants to come near. "Do whatever He tells you." She clapped her hands together in anticipation. Thirty years! Thirty years she had waited for this moment!

Jesus said to the servants, "Fill the jars with water."

He pointed to six stone water jars, used for ceremonial hand washing. They stood nearly to her waist, holding enough water to flood the Nile, she thought happily. The water made hands clean, at least symbolically. The servants struggled to fill the jars.

Then He told them, "Now draw some out and take it to the master of the banquet."

As they did, Mary saw that the water was now a dark red color, bloodred. Her heart stopped and she looked at her son. He nodded, His eyes soft. Yes, He seemed to say.

The wine looked like blood to her. The water never made men clean, she saw that now. In a flash of understanding, she saw that what would unlock the gates of Eden would be...

She shuddered and turned away.

The master of the banquet tasted the water that had been turned into wine. He exclaimed in delight, and everyone had another cup of wine.

Mary sat under a fig tree and pondered this in her heart, the sight of wine running down the side of a wooden cup, of red running down wood, and how that struck fear in her heart.

And she had urged Him toward it!

The women of Nazareth seemed offended. A few refused to say good morning to her when she walked to the well. Rebekah was the one who dug for details and explained the situation. The offense was nothing Mary did. Rather, it was who she was, or claimed to be.

Mary trudged along the path, her empty water jug in hand, hoping she didn't run into anyone. It was all so awkward.

If Jesus was the King of the Jews, then Mary was the Queen Mother, who would hold vast power and influence. In Jewish tradition, the Queen Mother was second only to the king. Any woman related to a man of great power held power herself, but especially the mother. She could open or close doors, influence and assign places. Mary shook her head. That was not her role nor her place. The glory of God had rested upon her briefly, an act of stupefying grace. How could she claim the right to parcel out the gift of God? She needed God's continual presence and blessing as much as they did, maybe more.

Not less.

Her world felt smaller, and not just because Jesus was off ministering and teaching. Reports about Jesus's activity had offended many of the faithful attendees at the synagogue. Jesus had attacked merchants at the Temple in Jerusalem, and wild reports spread about healings and miracles that surrounded Him. Miracles—and yet He had never done anything to heal His friends or family in Nazareth, the people groused.

She filled her jar and turned for home. Rebekah stood with a jar at her hip, startling Mary.

"Your son is provoking Rome," Rebekah said, her tone flat. "I've done everything I can to protect you, but really, Mary. This has gone too far."

Mary nodded and picked up her jar, now full. Of anyone in Nazareth, Rebekah's husband and family had the most to lose if Rome retaliated against a Jew claiming to be the King of the Jews. Her family did the most trade in neighboring towns.

"I don't know what to say," Mary replied.

She did not understand why her son had broken with both tradition and law. Jesus was a Jew. He loved the Jewish people and His faith! Mary did not want Jesus to come between her and her oldest friend.

Excusing herself, Mary hurried to the carpentry shop, where she found James, just as she hoped. James could escort her to see Jesus and ask Him about the swirling rumors and accusations.

"Jesus is not far," Mary told James. Her son scoffed but made no other noise. He continued sanding a tabletop.

"We might go and see Him," Mary suggested. "There is a rumor that He healed a nobleman's son. Other rumors are far more…outrageous, as you would say."

"What's outrageous is you, Mother!" James sounded exasperated more than angry. "How long will you listen to these lies? How long will you persist in this delusion that my brother is the Messiah?"

Tears formed in her eyes.

"You remind me of your father in so many ways," she countered softly. "When I first told him I was with child, he was furious with me. We were not yet married, and I was with child. It was indeed outrageous."

James hung his head. "Please do not repeat that story, not to me, not to anyone!"

"Why are you so afraid of scandal?" Mary asked.

"Why are you not?" James countered. "Our lineage is of the line of David—how could I even think to bring dishonor to that name? Whatever happened before your marriage, keep the secret and take it to your grave, if you care at all for me or the grandchildren."

"You don't understand. It is not a secret to be hidden. It was a gift. And a gift that was meant to be shared. If I take it to my grave, my life will have had no meaning. I am not afraid of the shame that comes from the revelation of God. I am afraid of going to my grave without having told everyone I know who Jesus is."

James did not want to travel to see Jesus, and so Mary could not. She was not young anymore, and travel was unsafe for an unaccompanied woman.

She missed Joseph.

# CHAPTER TWENTY-ONE

Mary busied herself cooking for Jesus and His ragtag band of friends. He had not attracted the best of companions, she noticed, but she was so happy to have Him home for a visit that she said nothing. They all looked poor and rather dirty. Mary instructed her daughters-in-law to run to the well and bring fresh water, lots of it, so the men could wash before dinner.

"And the women," the youngest and newest daughter-in-law, Dinah, said brightly. Dinah was a good match for her son, Jude.

Mary bit her lip. "Yes, the women. Why don't we set jugs of water on the far side of the courtyard? The women can wash and eat outside. It will be lovely weather."

"Jesus is putting us in an impossible situation!"

Mary recognized James's voice at once. She sighed, knowing James was right.

"Who are these people?" he continued. "And who are those women? They are certainly not honorable women. A man would never let his wife roam about the countryside with a nobody like Jesus."

She flinched at the venom in his voice then turned and rested one hand on James's cheek.

"You are zealous for our good name as a family," she said kindly. "And I know that if you search your heart, you are not angry with your brother. You are worried for Him."

James's face softened. "Did you know this was going to happen? When He was young, I mean?"

Mary chuckled. "You mean, when I had vast amounts of time to think, in between fleeing for our lives, evading angry elephants, snatching Him from the jaws of Nile crocodiles, and traveling with spice merchants and slave traders so unworthy they sought to steal Him if I slept a wink?"

James looked at the ground.

"No, I did not know how His ministry would unfold. I knew I had to keep Him alive. I knew I had to raise Him with the best knowledge of scripture that I could. But having done my best, having lived the will of God, I am at a loss for what to do now."

Jesus was still in danger, but He no longer needed her.

"How do I stop being a mother?" Mary whispered to herself.

James draped an arm around her and pulled her to his side, comforting her.

She rested her head on his shoulder. "I have done what God asked. But God never told me that the hardest part wouldn't be raising Jesus. The hardest part would be letting Him go."

On the Sabbath, they went to synagogue. Mary felt so delighted to have her whole family there, and even James was on his best behavior. Jesus had been so loved here as a student, the place brought back wonderful memories for everyone.

Jesus stood up to read, and the scroll of the prophet Isaiah was handed to Him. When He had unrolled it, He began in a clear, rich voice.

"'The Spirit of the Lord is on me, because He has anointed me to proclaim good news to the poor. He has sent me to proclaim freedom for the prisoners and recovery of sight for the blind, to set the oppressed free, to proclaim the year of the Lord's favor.'"

As He spoke, the tenor of the room shifted, from sweet sentimentality to uncomfortable speculation. Mary could feel the air change all around her.

Finished, Jesus rolled up the scroll, gave it back to the attendant, and sat down. The eyes of everyone in the synagogue were fastened on Him. "Today this scripture is fulfilled in your hearing," Jesus announced evenly.

James glanced up at Mary. She shifted in her seat in the gallery, nervous. The crowd was whispering, pointing out to each other that Jesus was one of their own. A Nazareth boy, Joseph's son, the carpenter.

"Surely you will quote this proverb to me: 'Physician, heal yourself!'" Jesus continued.

Mary's hand flew to her mouth. What was He doing? It was as if He was reading their minds and having a conversation without them speaking out loud.

"And you will tell me, 'Do here in your hometown what we have heard that you did in Capernaum.'"

The crowd's whispers turned ugly now, low and urgent.

"Truly I tell you," He continued, "no prophet is accepted in his hometown. I assure you that there were many widows in Israel in Elijah's time, when the sky was shut for three and a half years and there was a severe famine throughout the land. Yet Elijah was not sent to any of them, but to a widow in Zarephath in the region of Sidon. And there were many in Israel with leprosy in the time of Elisha the prophet, yet not one of them was cleansed—only Naaman the Syrian."

Jesus walked out, and only a few followed Him. Mary stumbled over the other women trying to get to Him. Some needed healing, and those who asked, received. James was immediately engulfed in angry men who demanded that he censor his brother. Mary left him in the synagogue to deal with them.

Jesus laid hands on people, and they were healed—Mary saw it. Speechless with awe, she watched as glory flowed from her son's hands to these people.

They were healed! The shekinah glory of God flowed onto the people!

The doors to the synagogue burst open, knocking down people begging for healing. The angry crowd drove Jesus to the edge of a cliff. Mary stumbled, crying out, unable to stop them or help her son.

She saw him slip through the middle of the crowd, unseen. He nodded to her and left.

When the crowd realized He had escaped, they turned on her.

"Did you know Joanna, the wife of Herod Antipas's steward, is traveling with your son? She claims He healed her when

Herod's physicians could not. Think of what that means! Someone close to Herod is saying Jesus has supernatural power. At any moment, boot steps of Roman soldiers will be heard in the streets of Nazareth!"

James rushed out and pulled Mary free.

"How many of our children will die then?" the crowd continued to shout. "How many of our children will die for your son?"

"None," Mary replied softly. "But He will die for yours."

Had the villager's fears proved true? Herod, never one to be challenged, arrested John.

Mary worked cleaning the home, preparing for a visit from the rabbi. James would be here any minute to attend the visit. Mary wanted the home to look presentable. The family's reputation was in tatters, but at least the home would be cared for. The work was good for her.

Why Herod had not come for Jesus, Mary did not know. But grief pierced her heart, thinking of Elizabeth's boy in prison. The prisons were horrid places, and so few were released. Prison was only a place to wait for execution. There was no justice.

Jesus should have left the area, should have been more discreet. Instead, He had picked eight more disciples. It was well into the second year of His ministry.

Mary wondered where this would all lead. Jesus was not claiming any right to Herod's throne, even though He was the King of the Jews. His teaching was powerful, His miracles were astonishing. He healed those who asked. Even a Roman centurion received healing for a servant.

"You know that I have always loved your family," the rabbi began.

James had offered him a cup of wine and Mary's best bread. He had declined both.

Mary nodded, keeping a pleasant smile on her face, as if she didn't know why the rabbi was visiting on this fine afternoon.

"I taught your sons," the rabbi continued.

Mary nodded again. He was dosing her with honey, which could only mean something bitter would follow. She did not reply. Why help him in his plan?

"We love the synagogue," James asked. "We are people of faith, and you have taught us well."

The rabbi cleared his throat and reached for the wine. Mary knew his problem was not a dry throat.

"I heard from another rabbi some news about Jesus," the rabbi began then waited, looking at Mary expectantly.

Mary held her hands in her lap, where he could not see, and wrung them tightly. It was such torture to not react defensively when her son was gossiped about.

Surprisingly, James did not speak either.

"Jesus has been collecting quite a group of misfits who follow Him around," the rabbi began, smiling.

The sight of his teeth reminded Mary of the wild dogs in Egypt.

"But I have always thought that Jesus had a love for people who do not amount to much, and compassion for those who cannot attend the synagogue. But the news…" He sighed. "The news is that Jesus has called a tax collector named Matthew to become a follower."

James grimaced. Mary understood. No one liked a man who collected taxes for the occupying government. The men often lined their own pockets and showed no mercy. Why would Jesus call such a man? Was He hoping to weaken the local government and evade taxes?

The door flew open. Her youngest daughter, Adinah, tore across the room and threw herself in Mary's arms.

"What is it, child?" Mary gasped. "What has happened?"

"He's dead!" Adinah wailed. "They killed him!"

Mary saw the rabbi's face as those words crossed Adinah's lips. In his eyes, she saw a glimmer of satisfaction. Her stomach turned into a cold pit as dread slowed her thoughts. She felt the room spinning.

"Who is dead?" James demanded, reaching for Adinah's arm and shaking her.

"Cousin John!" Adinah wailed. "He was taken from the prison only last night and beheaded!"

Mary slowly pushed the girl off her lap and turned away to vomit.

The rabbi lurched up from the table. Maybe he didn't want to be unclean. Maybe he was excited to share this news with his fellow leaders at the synagogue.

James stood, pointing to the door. He wanted the rabbi gone.

Mary's mind flashed back to the moment Elizabeth had laid her hand on Mary's swollen belly, and how both babies had leapt in the womb, delighting both mothers. John and Jesus were connected in that invisible realm of creation.

And the connection was severed.

"I have to go to Him," Mary said.

"I will escort you," James replied softly. "It is no longer safe for Jesus to be challenging authority in public. We have to bring Him home."

Mary knew Jesus too well. He would not quit. Instead, she had a terrifying awareness that death was near. Just as God had once hovered over the dark waters to bring creation to life, death hovered over Jesus. It was all around Him.

The enemy had drawn first blood. John was dead.

Would Jesus be next?

New rumors filtered to Mary every day. Throughout the region of Galilee, Jesus taught with the authority of the greatest teacher and performed astonishing miracles. Some said He had multiplied one boy's lunch to feed thousands. The crowds had grown to never-before-seen numbers.

Herod must be furious—or nervous, Mary thought.

James had become less angry and more reticent when discussing his brother. People came to Jesus from Judea, Jerusalem,

Idumea, and the regions across the Jordan and around Tyre and Sidon. James simply didn't know what to think about this growing phenomenon that was Jesus.

But there was a crisis boiling, and everyone in the family knew it. The Romans talked about Jesus. The Pharisees talked about Jesus. The Jews and the Gentiles talked about Jesus. It was all Mary could have ever hoped for, and it felt as dangerous as a knife at her throat.

James approached her one evening as she tidied the kitchen after supper. James was wrong about Jesus. He thought Jesus was unwell. But, Mary conceded, he was right that they needed to talk to Him about His methods. James had lost a significant amount of work since the incident at the synagogue. No one wanted to be associated with the "madman from Nazareth." He explained his plan, and she agreed to accompany him.

They had no trouble finding Jesus. So many people were on the road! And these people were clearly not traveling for business. They were broken, in body or spirit. They were walking to Jesus and led Mary right to Him.

The other people on the road, the merchants and traders, had befuddled expressions as the broken travelers passed by. Those people had always hidden in the shadows, on the out-skirts of the villages. Mary understood how strange it was to see them come into the light at last.

She always gave them alms, but they didn't want her money now. They wanted her son.

Could He really heal them, all of them, with merely a word?

James warned her not to reveal her identity. Too much attention was already focused on Jesus, and the mood among the religious leaders was souring. He was no longer their brilliant pupil.

To them, He was a madman and a threat.

Jesus was inside a house, and Mary had no hope of pushing through the great crowd of people desperately trying to get inside.

"I will tell Jesus we are here," James said. He pressed his way through the crowd, making his way to the front door, stepping over mats spread out for the sick, and restless children hoping for a look at this man called Jesus.

She heard a commotion from inside the house. James had clearly reached Jesus and gotten His attention. Two women exited, fanning themselves in the heat. Mary studied them. One was obviously a woman of great wealth. Her robes could be sold for a year of James's wages. Perhaps this was the wife of Herod's steward, rumored to be traveling with Jesus now. And the woman next to her, although markedly poorer in fashion, seemed familiar somehow.

Mary craned her head to get a better look at the woman's face. Then she recoiled, shocked. That was the demoniac woman who had once wandered the streets.

A cloud rolled over the sun, casting a shadow over the crowd.

What was Jesus doing with women like that?

The shadow sweeping over the crowd was a cold and dead thing that made Mary shiver. She worried that death might be where Jesus was leading them all. It was as if an enemy were whispering in her ear.

"Though I walk in the valley of death," she reminded herself, "I will fear no evil. For Thou art with me."

The woman looked straight at her then and smiled kindly. There was a light in her eyes, a steadfastness, that shocked Mary again. This was that same woman, but she wasn't. She was entirely new.

Mary smiled back, understanding suddenly. Jesus would rescue His people, but He had already saved her.

Suddenly, the crowd began to snicker and whisper. Both women turned their heads as James marched out of the house, his face dark with fury.

"I told His 'disciples,'" James said, nearly spitting the words, "that we were out here to speak with Him."

"Why are the people talking?" Mary glanced around as the whispers continued from person to person.

James smirked. "He didn't reply to me, or even acknowledge me. Do you know what He said? He said, 'Who is my mother, and who are my brothers?'"

"Then," James continued, as angry as he was disbelieving, "He pointed to those standing around Him. He said, 'Here are my mother and my brothers. Any one of you who does the will of my Father in heaven is my brother and sister and mother.'"

Mary's heart sank.

"It's outrageous," James snarled.

"No," Mary said slowly. "It is truth. But it might also be one thing more. Let us return to our home, and I will explain on the way."

"I'm not leaving without Him," James snapped.

"Unless you want to fight this crowd, that's exactly what you're going to do," Mary snapped back. It was time to be firm with James. He was the head of the family, but he was also very wrong. He was wrong about Jesus, he always had been, and he couldn't see it.

She would do her best to explain this to him as they walked home. *One more time,* she thought, *I will tell the stories that James does not believe.* The stories of angels and prophecies, of a Messiah that was in every way unexpected—but very real.

Mary silently weighed Jesus's words as she picked up the hem of her robe to make her way back to the road. She knew Jesus would never insult her. He was teaching, even then. Even then, He was loving and protecting.

But why did His lessons have to be so bold? He captured their imagination, that was true, but it was easy for people like James and the rabbis to be offended. "But it is true." Mary sighed. "We all belong to Him now. All of us." Looking around, she repeated the words. "We all belong to Him."

His kingdom was growing, but she didn't recognize any of the faces. The Messiah had been sent to people she did not know. People she would have passed over. He was her son, but He belonged to them.

And what she would explain to James, when they were out of earshot of the crowds, was that with Roman soldiers and angry rabbis nearby, perhaps Jesus did not want to publicly call her forward and make her identity so obvious. It would be just like Him to protect her, even as others misunderstood.

The rabbis were angry and the people agitated, thinking of the fate of Sepphoris. They did not want to attract the attention of the Roman soldiers. Why couldn't Jesus say what the rabbis wanted to hear? they whispered. Why did He provoke them? Why did He insist on calling God "My Father"? The rabbis had one word for that—blasphemy.

The people called it trouble.

# CHAPTER TWENTY-TWO

Mary had only been home a few weeks when a messenger arrived, a young boy who shifted his weight from foot to foot and would not meet her eye.

"What is it?" she asked. He wore an amulet around his neck, a lion-like monster she guessed was a foreign god. The boy was not from her people or any nearby town, which only heightened her confusion.

He thrust out a tattered piece of parchment.

After opening it, she studied a figure written on the parchment. It appeared to be a sum of money.

"My masters say you must pay this," he said, his voice catching, perhaps from nerves. It was a great sum of money.

She chuckled and held the parchment out, expecting him to take it, but he did not.

"You must have the wrong family," she said. "We owe no one. And this sum of money is not a debt we could ever pay, regardless."

He chewed his lower lip.

"Come in," she said. "Rest. You must be tired."

Moments later, he was seated at her kitchen table drinking fresh milk and shoveling bread into his mouth as fast as she could break it off in wedges.

He told her a story that made her stomach do flips. After refusing to acknowledge her and his brothers in the nearby Galilean village, Jesus had traveled to the Decapolis region. Just the name struck fear in Mary's heart. No one traveled there willingly. No wonder this poor boy wore an amulet for protection!

As Jesus arrived in the Decapolis region, two demoniacs confronted him. They had long terrorized the people. And Jesus's response? He healed the men. Completely. They washed, put on clothes, and tried to speak to the villagers. Of course, the villagers were reluctant to get anywhere near the men.

"I still don't understand why I owe this debt," Mary said. "Who are your masters?"

"Pig keepers," the boy replied. "Your son destroyed the herd."

"That does not sound like my son," Mary countered. Jesus loved animals and was kind even to the unclean ones.

"Jesus commanded the evil spirits to enter the pigs, and the pigs went wild with fear, and ran off a cliff. All of them. My masters seek payment for the loss of their herd."

Mary thought for a minute. "Tell your masters that they have profited by my son. Now traders will travel safely through their region. It's time they prepared for a robust new business."

After the boy had left, Mary debated whether to tell James. She needn't have worried. That night, James came into dinner with a wild story all his own. Apparently, Jesus's disciples claimed Jesus had calmed a mighty storm with just a word.

He had control of creation, including the weather.

As if Rome needed one more reason to seek His imprisonment or death. James was sick with worry, and this time, Mary could tell that James worried for his brother, not just the family. James loved Jesus, even if he didn't believe Him. If only James would open up to her, she would tell him that she understood. Some claims were hard to accept. Even his father, Joseph, had struggled.

Mary slept fitfully that night. Nights like these, alone with her thoughts, could be maddening. Why had Gabriel only given her instructions, and not explanations?

In the third year of Jesus's ministry, Mary's youngest son, Simon, married a beautiful girl from Sepphoris. Mary was relieved that a family entrusted their daughter to them after the gossip surrounding Jesus. Reports of the miracles had an unpredictable effect. Some were sour with doubt and others excited with wonder. Perhaps those who were sour simply lacked the courage to go and ask for what they most needed. Everyone needed some kind of miracle, but few people had the courage to ask. Or did few people have the courage to believe?

When she saw Jesus the next time, she would ask His thoughts. She was most curious too about a disciple named John who followed Jesus. Was this John anything like Elizabeth's boy? She yearned to spend time with Jesus and His friends. She'd labored her entire life for this season of His!

But getting away from home to see Jesus was increasingly difficult. With a large family, her home was overflowing. Her four married sons and their wives lived with her, plus the grandchildren from the older two boys, James and Joseph. Jude and his wife were expecting their first child this fall. Mary didn't know she knew this yet, but the signs were unmistakable even if it was so early.

She loved having a full house, and she loved that her daughters lived in Nazareth as well. She could see them at the well or at the market or have them stop by for cake. But she missed Jesus. She missed the future He could have had, one of marriage and children. She knew it was silly to miss what was never meant to be. God's will wasn't easy to accept, even if it was perfect.

With Jude's wife due this fall, travel for the Feast of Tabernacles would be impossible, at least for Mary. She hated missing the feasts. But she would never miss the birth of a grandchild.

***

"We should go early," Mary said to James at supper. She made herself busy with serving, trying to look innocent. She'd heard the reports, as surely as the rest of the family had. Jesus had raised yet someone else from the dead. This time, it was His dear friend Lazarus. A dead man came back to life at her son's command. Her scalp tingled when she considered that.

The daughters-in-law looked at Mary with wide eyes. They knew her too well. Mary suppressed a grin.

James frowned. "Go early to Jerusalem for Passover? Why incur the extra expense?"

No doubt James was doing sums in his head, adding up costs for the inn for the whole family, the costs for the stable, the meals, plus the sacrifices.

"I had to miss the Feast of the Tabernacles," Mary replied. Abigail had been close to delivery and could not travel or be left alone. "I deserve a few extra days in the city, don't you think?" Mary didn't want to reveal the reason. It would only upset James.

She'd heard that Jesus was arriving in the city early too. And she'd been so busy with the new baby that she hadn't seen much of Him the past few months but only caught scraps of gossip and news at the market and well. That was hard on a mother.

James stared at her, one eyebrow cocked. He knew.

She giggled.

"Yes!" she blurted. "I want to see Jesus. He will be there early too."

Everyone looked at James. The name Jesus was usually enough to make his face turn red with silent anger. Not today. James pushed back from the table.

"I want to see Him too," James confessed. "The story about Lazarus was so outrageous that I traveled to Bethany to talk to Lazarus myself. Lazarus and his sisters were... Something happened to them. They aren't lying when they say Lazarus died and was raised. But to believe that Jesus is the Messiah? The Son of God? Are we ready to make that leap?"

He looked around the table at each member of the family.

When his eyes met Mary's, she knew that he saw her answer. But she couldn't find fault with him for being so cautious. After all, she had been visited by Gabriel, who had explained who Jesus would be. Angelic visitation had given her a head start.

James had not arrived wholeheartedly yet, but he was on the right road. Mary wondered, briefly, what Jesus's life would have been like if His brothers had believed and supported Him. The sting of sorrow shot through her heart like an arrow from the hand of her enemy. Regret over a past she couldn't retrieve or influence—that was always a tool for the enemy to fashion into a weapon.

But the future? Ah, the future was the province of the Lord. And what was impossible for the Lord? Absolutely nothing!

*Lord,* Mary prayed, *may Jesus's brothers believe and become men of great faith!*

Excitement buzzed in the streets, more than the usual energy that surrounded the Passover holiday. Mary was uneasy. It was a feeling she had not been able to shake.

Mary was on the road into Jerusalem with her family. She searched the faces of the pilgrims, looking for someone to stop and ask. What was the excitement about?

She convinced James to stop a merchant passing them, one who had a gleam in his eye. Happy crowds spent good money.

When James asked what the excitement was about, the merchant answered with one word—Jesus. Other travelers, not so eager to race ahead into the city, filled the family in on the details, not knowing their identity. The King of the Jews was approaching Jerusalem! The noise overwhelmed the screams and calls of the dying along the road, the men crucified by Rome.

Mary's heart squeezed in pain. *Those pour souls.*

The Roman Empire was merciless, and this city would crown her son as King.

The Messiah crowned as King, at Passover, in Jerusalem. This was exactly as it should be. Right? But she knew that Rome would draw its sword.

Approaching the gates, she remembered entering when she was pregnant with Jesus, how she felt apprehension over the unknown future, how little she knew. She laughed, ruefully. *How little she still knew!*

The people shouted "Hosanna!" Children climbed palm trees and tore the branches, tossing them down. The crowds laid the branches in the street. Other people took off their cloaks—their cloaks!—and laid them in the road.

Mary saw Jesus enter Jerusalem, riding on a donkey, trotting over the palm branches and garments, but a shadow crossed her heart. These people were impulsive, and impulsive people could turn in a flash.

Was this why Jesus had predicted His death?

*No,* she thought. *The crowd adored Him! They could not possibly turn on Him now that they had proclaimed Him as their king.* Mary hoped that this vast number of people who honored Jesus would keep Him safe. Surely the religious leaders would not strike Him now and risk alienating the entire city just before Passover.

But the shadows weighed on her mind. Rome weighed on her mind. She stayed invisible in the crowds. If she revealed herself as Jesus's mother, she would be celebrated. She could ride a donkey alongside Him as the Queen Mother.

But Jesus would never have a queen at His side. She had to recede even as He moved into His full power and authority.

So she threw a palm branch into the street as Jesus passed by on a donkey. He knew she was there—His gaze searched her out immediately in the crowd. She nodded in acknowledgment and followed His progression through the city. Her youngest daughter grasped her hand, overwhelmed by the crowds. Mary smiled at her.

The smile hid her lurking unease. It did not feel like Jesus was walking toward a throne, even though the crowd proclaimed Him as their king. Although it made no sense as she surveyed the celebration, she sensed a shadow moving over the city, a darkness invading, creeping out of the stones beneath her feet, seeping out of the walls, a decayed and poisonous root, rising.

Did her son, this Messiah who would lead His people on a new exodus, understand what was happening? Did He ride confidently toward His doom?

Mary from Magdala appeared on the opposite side of the street. She and Joanna had been following Jesus at a distance.

Mary from Magdala pushed her way through the crowd, pulling Joanna with her, to get to Mary's side.

"Do you feel it too?" Mary from Magdala asked. "Something is coming together in the city. I can't explain it any better than that."

Mary inhaled sharply. "Yes." She had hoped it was only her imagination. But Mary from Magdala was acquainted with evil in a way that few others were. If she sensed it too, then it was real.

Jesus was about to face a great enemy.

Her daughter's chin trembled, and Mary put her arm around her.

The women all grasped hands and prayed.

* * *

The innkeeper had a lovely room set up, and all the guests partook of the bitter herbs and unleavened bread and passed the cups of wine—then passed more and more wine.

One chair was set aside for Elijah, as was the custom every year in the hope that the great prophet would show up. Mary's heart ached looking at the empty chair, thinking of Cousin Elizabeth and her son, John. Both were dead. The chair would always remain empty, and these people did not even recognize that Elijah had already come!

The noise in the room grew unbearably loud. Her family enjoyed the feast, it seemed, but she could not.

Mary excused herself and went outside to get some air.

She nearly toppled over as a man rushing past bumped into her. The street torches had not been lit yet, so her eyes hadn't adjusted to the darkness.

"Judas?" she asked, alarmed. "Is everyone all right? Why are you not at the feast?" She glanced up at the inn's window, thinking she could call James. If Judas needed a doctor, James could help him navigate these streets quickly.

Judas looked stricken to see her. "Everything is fine," he said, but his face was a sickly shade of gray. He had the pallor of death. "Enjoy the feast."

With that, he hurried along. The jingle of coins echoed in the empty streets as he shuffled quickly away. In a crowded city, he should worry about thieves.

As she returned to the Passover supper upstairs, an uneasy feeling had settled into her stomach, and she could eat nothing more. Taking her daughters-in-law, she escorted them to the room, and the women prepared for bed.

Tomorrow there would be shopping, a visit to the Temple, and a chance to see Jesus.

More than anything, she wanted to see Jesus.

* * *

The next morning, the crowd in the streets below was so loud that she woke far too early. Stumbling in the half light, trying to find her robe, she went to the door and cracked it open. The innkeeper's wife was in the hallway, holding an oil lamp, whispering with another guest. Mary craned her head, trying to hear.

An arrest had been made. A notorious criminal. A crowd was forming at Pilate's residence to demand justice.

Mary closed the door softly to avoid waking the girls. What concern was that to her? She had no dealings with criminals, and she avoided Rome at all costs. Those people were foolish to form a crowd and demand anything from Pilate. He was not a man known for consistency. He might lock them up if he was in an ill humor.

Besides, it was Passover. She had more important things to do. This was the most wonderful holiday of the year and a beautiful event to contemplate. God had delivered her people from slavery.

Why would she bother persecuting a man she did not know?

It was Peter who told her.

Later that morning, in the breakfast room at the inn, the adults in the family gathered to hear what Peter had to say.

Peter, with the weathered face, burnished from sea winds and sunburns, his arms as thick as Ephesian stones. Peter, who never faltered, on this morning could not look her in the eye as he spoke. She had to ask him to repeat himself twice.

"Jesus," he said again. "They arrested Jesus."

Mary laughed even as her blood ran cold. "That's impossible. What crime could He have committed? He heals. Teaches. Feeds. Is there a law against feeding the hungry?"

Peter scowled and looked up. "Our religious leaders cannot do those things."

Jesus had damaged the Jewish leaders' pride. He had threatened their security. He had destroyed their idea of the Messiah. For those invisible crimes, He was arrested.

Desperation made her voice sound high and hollow. "Pilate cannot rule on a Jewish matter. Pilate is Rome. Rome cannot rule on Jewish law. Pilate let Him go. Of course Pilate let Him go. Right?"

Peter hung his head, and a tear stained his robe as it fell.

Jude's wife shot from behind Mary and grabbed hold of Peter. Mary did not even realize she had been in the room listening.

"What did Pilate do to Him?" she screamed.

Peter's eyes cleared. "Pilate sentenced Him to death." Looking at Mary, he whispered, "Crucifixion."

That was the last thing Mary remembered before the room went dark and she fell.

---

Crucifixions were done all along a stretch of the main road going into Jerusalem. The grisly sights reminded pilgrims traveling into the holy city for Passover of the penalty for defying Rome. No one could focus on the beauty of the Temple when the agonized groans of the dying were on either side of the road. Even on the rare empty stretches, holes in the ground held a main wood beam, waiting for the condemned to carry the cross beam to the site.

Everyone kept to the center of the road, and mothers drew their robes around their children. No one wanted their children to see the dead—or worse, the dying.

Mary had forced the girls to stay behind.

She and the other women pushed through the pilgrims entering the city, earning confused glances from the faithful. It was, after all, Passover weekend, and for a Jew, there was only one place a faithful Jewish woman would want to be.

But Mary was Jesus's mother, and she would be here. Her daughters had fought to accompany her. Someday they would forgive her for insisting they remain behind with their older brothers. Mary had seen victims of crucifixions after the revolts in Sepphoris.

She knew the horror that awaited.

After arriving at the stretch of road that rose high and gave a vantage point to all, called the Place of the Skull, scarcely breathing from dread and the stench of death that permeated the area, Mary clutched her chest in terror.

Joanna took her in her arms, shielding her as the guards shoved Jesus through the crowd.

Joanna looked as if she would vomit from the sights and smells. Mary had already emptied her stomach, although she had only bile. She hadn't eaten since hearing the news.

Her mind couldn't make sense of anything. This was the long-awaited Messiah! He was going to rule the people and usher in a new era of peace. He was going to lead a new exodus into a glorious future. Where was that Messiah? This one was bruised and broken, bleeding with every step.

The cross fell to the ground, stirring a cloud of dust that clung to the soldier's feet. A dark-skinned man stood weeping over the cross, his robe torn and his shoulders raw.

Roughly shoving him aside, a soldier scorned him. "You did what we asked. Now get out of here before we turn our attention to you."

Mary watched as the man fled, the one man who had assisted Jesus, carried His burden, when all others had fallen away. She said a silent prayer for his blessing, knowing that the wrath of the enemy would be upon him.

She felt the sharp pains of the enemy's scourging in her heart, as if a thousand blades hit her every second. The pain was unbearable. She couldn't breathe.

John came and wrapped his arms around her and Joanna, sheltering their faces as Jesus screamed. Mary heard metal strike metal, and a dull wet response from flesh. They were nailing Him.

She buried her face into John's robes, begging God to save His son.

"He will not save Him," John said, perhaps knowing how she prayed, perhaps praying the same thing. "He is saving us."

Jesus screamed, and Mary's mouth opened in an agonizing wail. She did not want Jesus to save anyone, especially not these vile men. She did not want a God who loved murderers and torturers and those who were cruel. She wanted God to show

His power—a power of wrath, not of love. Love had no place among these men.

Moving her face to catch a breath, she caught sight of her son being lifted on the cross.

Oh, Love did have a place. And today, that place was a cross.

Jesus's head hung in exhaustion and suffering, blood dripping from His scalp, blood running down His legs, blood pooling on the dry ground.

Her heart shattered again, stopping her breath.

Jesus's screams were like shards slicing through her mind. She could not even pray now.

Mary fell to the ground, slipping through John's embrace. Unable to bear the weight of Jesus's suffering, she crouched on all fours, rocking back and forth, moaning in prayer. This grief was so great, so powerful, it was like being taken over by a force beyond herself. She had never known grief like this—the horror of sin, the cruelty of man, and a body torn apart for sport.

The other women gathered near, hands resting on her back. It was, she remembered, the same pose that she experienced when giving birth to Jesus.

His birth had been foretold, had been marked by strange signs and wonders. But this? His death? This was marked by blood and agony—and the deathly silence of heaven. Where was God?

In response, the sun refused to shine, its light suddenly snuffed out. Mary looked up, stunned by her sorrow, looking into the faces of her companions. Their pupils were dilated wide in the darkness. They saw everything, with no way to go back to the light they had only hours ago. That light was gone.

God had created the sun on the first day of creation—and now, on the last day of the earthly Christ, He extinguished it. He reversed creation, taking the light, dimming the moon. Darkness swept over everyone, causing murmurs and cries.

God had once hovered over the darkness and created new life.

Was He still here?

# CHAPTER TWENTY-THREE

As Jesus suffered, soldiers cast lots and divided His clothes. Mary's mind went back to His birth, how she wrapped Him in throwaway rags. Now soldiers valued His clothes, not Him. They didn't want to save Him, they wanted to save His clothes.

Above Him on the cross was a sign that read THE KING OF THE JEWS, written in Latin, Aramaic, and Greek.

Jesus said, "Father, forgive them, for they know not what they do."

Mary heard the words of Isaiah resounding in her soul: *"Yet he bore the sin of many and made intercession for the transgressors."*

Shaking her head, she refused. This could not be the plan of God! *If Gabriel were here,* she thought wildly, *I would refuse! It cannot be this way!*

Scribes and elders from the faith were there, mocking. She heard their taunts.

"He saved others, but He can't save himself?" "He is the king of Israel, so let Him come down now from the cross, and we will believe in Him. He trusts in God, let God deliver His Son, if God desires Him. He said 'I am the Son of God.'"

The men hanging from crosses on either side joined in—but one stopped, talking to Jesus. Mary strained to hear what was said but could not. She saw a look of shock pass over his face, and he was utterly transformed into a man at peace with death.

---

Three more hours passed. Mary survived only by a primal call to stay alive for Him.

Jesus slowly slipped away as the third hour passed, crying out to God.

"My God, my God, why have You forsaken me?"

She no longer recognized the voice of a man—this was the sound of a child lost in the dark. But Jesus had never been lost in this world. He had created it. What was happening?

These were the very words of David! He cried out to the Lord in his great anguish. *Oh God*, Mary wept, *why must Your King suffer? Why was Jesus born to rule a people who did not love? Why must He endure their sin without punishing them for it?*

She stood and rushed to Him. He could not leave her! She fell at the foot of the cross, begging God to save Him. To save her because she could not bear this loss. The announcement of His birth had changed her entire life, and His death was destroying what she had built. She had built a life of trust and obedience. But this crucifixion—unjust, undeserved—undid all of that.

Jesus looked at her, His eyes swollen and red. John stood alongside and then knelt at her side, lifting her up.

"This is your mother," Jesus gasped, every word forced out of a hollow, bloody chest. "Mother, behold your son."

Then Jesus closed His eyes. "It is finished. Father, into Your hands I commit my spirit."

Mary let out a wail that seemed like a call for the heavens to tear the earth apart. When Jesus breathed His last breath, there could be nothing more of this world, she was certain.

This wasn't just Jesus dying. It was so much more. The old order was gone.

As if in confirmation, the ground shook so violently, the foundations of the earth trembled before a dead Messiah. Many people ran. Mary didn't. She willed the earth to shake even more violently, to split beyond repair.

She never wanted to live in this world again. It had fallen long ago.

A soldier lifted his spear and stabbed Jesus in the side. Blood and water spilled out. All that once made Him human spilled out on the dry, stained ground. And the rocks split and the ground shook, the humanity of God the Creator shattering the natural order.

"My God, my God," Mary whispered, repeating her son's words to herself, thinking of her son's birth.

When He was born, her own blood and water had been spilled. He had completed the cycle of birth and death. And yet on that day in the stable so long ago, hadn't new life begun? The blood and water had marked a beginning, not an end. On that day long ago, He had been hidden no more and had begun a new life among men.

Could that happen again? Mary dared not let her mind think that, else she might go mad.

***

Two days later, Mary awoke in darkness, unsure of what had roused her from the deep and dreadful sleep of a bereaved mother. As her mind slowly regained awareness, the crushing agony of losing her son fell again like a weight against her heart. She gasped for breath, the pain like a hot knife searing through her body.

Blinking, she peered into the darkness at the women sleeping near and around her. They had all fallen asleep in the same room, all had surrounded Mary like a hedge of protection. What blessings they were, and how utterly useless to stem the flow of her heart's blood. She thought she would bleed forever.

Jesus had said He would rise again. What did that mean?

Downstairs the door softly closed, and Mary sat up, studying the mats around her more carefully. Mary from Magdala was gone. Salome was standing in the corner, pulling on her robe. The women were getting up, but it was not even dawn.

Mary sat and reached for her robe. She knew they had meant to let her sleep, had meant to do one last service for her son. But she couldn't sleep when He was gone. She would go.

In the darkness, the women made their way toward the tomb. The stench of the crucifixions hung in the air, and Mary pulled her robe over her nose. Not even the strong scents of aloe and myrrh could dampen the horror of death. Mary from

Magdala was so far ahead on the path, she was not even visible.

In the east, the sun burned white as it rose, the light blinding. Around her, the landscape looked pale, rimmed so brightly in light that all color blurred and disappeared into a white burst, like a flower opening on the horizon.

Mary held a hand over her eyes, unable to stare directly into the light of the morning sun.

Then Mary Magdalene screamed.

Mary Magdalene raced ahead to the tomb. In a blink she came running back to report that it was empty. Mary ran to see as well, but she found only John and Peter. Peter had lost the foot-race to the tomb, John said, and Mary even then wondered how men could be boys. But they were laughing, dazed with the knowledge that Jesus was alive.

Alive!

The sun was bright yellow, radiating a warm glow. Sitting on a garden bench, too drained to walk back home, Mary let the sun fall on her face and neck. The air smelled fresh and sweet, like the air on a spring morning after a night of storms. Looking around, she noticed the broken rocks on the ground. These rocks had been split only three days ago, torn by the ravages of God's own grief. She picked one up and felt sharp edges against her palm. She turned it over and saw a dazzle of purple crystals. Looking around, she picked up another, finding more breathtaking beauty. When she had heard the rocks splitting as Jesus died, she had wept! But the breaking revealed a beauty hidden long ago.

Mary Magdalene came up the path as Mary set down another geode, still marveling.

"He is alive!" Mary Magdalene gasped, her hand pressed to one side, her face bright with tears of joy. "He is risen. I must go tell the others!"

"I know!" Mary said, but the other Mary did not hear. She was already running again, the other women trailing behind. The chaos of the resurrection was joy, splintering in all directions like a sunray.

Mary sat under a flowering tree staring at the empty tomb from a distance. The guards discussed in hushed tones the story they would tell the authorities. Peter stood inside the tomb, and then he brought out folded linens. John shook his head in amazement. Grave robbers would not unwrap a body. Even if they did, who would take the time to fold the cloth?

Mary stared at the dark cave, remembering how the glory of God had descended on her and filled her womb with a miraculous new life. This tomb had witnessed the same shekinah glory. She envied the darkness, for it had seen a great light.

Jesus had said He would rise again. This tomb was proof. He was alive. Turning, she felt the tears washing down her chafed cheeks. Her eyes were hot and scratchy from the constant flow of tears.

She made her way to the disciples, clutching her arms to her chest, as if she could keep herself from disintegrating. She believed, but she had no son to hold. The memory of what those men did, the sight of her son in agony beyond words, and the silence of God…how could she ever be made whole? The woman she once was, was gone forever. That woman had died when her son breathed for the last time.

What was the promise for that woman, the woman who watched evil win? Would Jesus resurrect her?

Peter and John bowed their heads in respect as Mary walked inside the tomb and sat, then pressed her hands to the cold walls. She stretched out on the rocky shelf that His body had rested upon. There was no stench of death.

*There is no death here,* the voice of God seemed to whisper to her heart. And she realized that for the first time this voice sounded very much like her son's.

Long ago, she had been thrown into the glory and mystery of a life God planned, not the life she wanted. And here, once again, she was on the threshold of that same choice.

Would she still choose to trust?

Jesus appeared in the room. Mary, surrounded by the disciples and women, saw Him first.

He was wounded. The heinous scars, the proof of man's blind cruelty, still marked His body. But here He was, resurrected.

She went limp with joy and relief, her body unable to sustain both emotions that swept over her with the force of a howling storm. She extended her hands.

"Shalom," Jesus said. Peace. He was a wounded Messiah, yet fully healed and all powerful as He stood before them.

Jesus crossed the room, taking her hands in His and lifting her up.

*Why,* Mary thought, her eyes searching His, *must He still bear the scars?* Why did God's resurrection miracle not wipe them away?

She touched the wound on His side—was this where the rib was taken from Adam to create a woman? Was Jesus pierced at the very spot woman was created? Had the enemy scorned her, and all women, with that final indignity?

And yet Jesus stood, having conquered that enemy, and now transcendent, glorious, with no pain.

She nodded, tears streaming down her face. Jesus was showing her the way to go on. Jesus was revealing His power to walk in this world while she awaited the resurrection.

Yes, total peace and joy. Jesus was flush with the beauty and vitality of new life!

If He could be at peace with scars, so could she. This was how she would live the rest of her days with the memories, the sights, and smells of that awful, sunless day. She would bear the scars but walk in peace.

Mary rested her hand on His chest to feel His breathing. The rise and fall was a balm to her soul. He kissed the top of her head as she pressed her face to His chest. How precious His first breath had been, and how painful His last. But this breath, this supernatural breath, would last forever.

Jesus had the breath of life, of the first and the final dawn. He was not done creating, Mary knew. She would be made new too. When she breathed her last breath here, a new breath, His breath, would fill her lungs, and she would know at last what it meant to be alive.

"Joseph?" she asked, looking up and into Jesus's eyes.

He smiled, that mischievous delighted grin that she remembered from His boyhood years, when the other children would ask about the animals on the ark, or how the stars were named.

Jesus knew the mystery. He knew how it ended.

As if He read her thoughts—and perhaps He did, because His power had no limits—He shook His head no.

"Not an ending, not at all." He grinned. "A beginning."

All of life was ready to begin.

She held Him a moment longer, then released Him to minister to the others. And she knew—whatever this was that she had now, this thing called life, it was a pale imitation to what He created with His death. A whole new world had been born.

She stood next to Him and knew she stood on the threshold of heaven itself.

<hr>

Mary was old now, older than she had ever expected to be. Looking in a polished brass mirror, she tucked her silver strands behind her ear, remembering the young woman she once was. She remembered how she fought with her curls as she prepared for Rebekah's wedding so many years ago, knowing she would see Joseph. How she had hoped to catch his eye, and how she had been blessed later to have his heart! What adventures they had shared. Even as children, they had loved nothing more than wandering in verdant fields, marveling at creation. And to think—God's greatest work yet had been entrusted to her, and to them.

She had never solved the mystery of why God had chosen her. But she had long ago made peace with it. Being favored was painful. The evil of men was great. But when God moved, He drew the most unlikely women into the story. She closed her eyes briefly, praying for the women yet to be born, those who would someday join the story. She wished she could tell them so much.

Her soul had been pierced by a sword, just as theirs would be. But that space, that deep wound, had become a window in a dark world. Since that awful day on Golgotha, light had flooded the world. She would tell those women not to fear the darkness nor their deepest wounds. She would tell them to trust, for a woman's trust in God is a potent weapon.

She continued her grooming, although her eyes were dim, and her hands shook. Joseph was waiting. He seemed so close, as if he were in a field of Nazareth wildflowers, calling to her.

"I am coming, my love," she whispered. "Wait a moment longer."

She and Joseph would again explore the wonder of a city made verdant by God's presence. And she would see her son, seated at the right hand of God.

Yes, she had walked with Jesus in her earthly years. But soon, with her beloved at her side, she would bow before Jesus in heaven.

And what greater favor could ever be given a woman?

Letter from

# THE AUTHOR

Dearest Reader,

I loved Mary's story so very much, and I walked away with a profound respect for her as a woman of great strength and courage.

Every Christmas, we see Mary portrayed as a sweet young girl, with twinkling light cascading all around as she smiles at her holy infant with a tender expression.

But make no mistake—Mary was a mighty spiritual warrior.

Like many of us, she knew God's intentions but not His exact plan. Yet unlike us, she encountered the shekinah glory of God and as a result, experienced hostilities and adversities that must have felt unbearable at times. She loved her son deeply but had to surrender Him fully to God. Most mothers can relate to that, but for Mary it was soul-shattering. Evil did its worst to her son. His sacrifice on the cross was His gift to us all—and His resurrection was astonishing, but she probably never forgot the sights and sounds of that terrifying day. She survived, but I doubt those wounds ever fully healed. Only heaven could do that, I suspect.

Mary taught me how to live and love with all my heart, and with all my faith, even as I let go. As I wrote this, my oldest graduated college and started his new life, and my youngest graduated high school and prepared to move to college. Mary was a wonderful and wise companion for my journey. Whatever journey you are on right now, I pray she encourages you mightily.

He is faithful.
You are favored.

Ginger Garrett

Book Group
# QUESTIONS

1. What does it mean to you to be blessed or favored? Did Mary's story change your perspective?

2. How did Mary change in her spiritual life from her betrothal to Joseph to the woman who saw Jesus at the resurrection?

3. If Mary kept a prayer journal, what do you think she would have most often prayed for and about? Were any prayers unanswered?

4. James, the brother of Jesus, later became a significant leader of the Christian church. Do you think he struggled to forgive himself? If Jesus forgives us, why is self-forgiveness so hard?

5. What advice do you think Mary would give young mothers today?

# A SCHOLAR'S VIEW
# OF NAZARETH

Mary would have a hard time finding her way around Nazareth today. The city is in the same geographic location it was more than two thousand years ago in Mary's time, when it was only a tiny village. But now the ancient town has become a virtual metropolis. Streets twist and turn through the neighborhoods with no seeming pattern. Everything from religious stoles to Moslem barnuces hang from stalls like prizes in a carnival. The brilliant reds and yellows or plain white colors of jibabs, nigabs, and hijabs blend with the smell of roasting chestnuts or fresh pita bread.

When people ask if Nazareth is the actual town where Mary and Joseph raised Jesus, the answer is yes. However, today Mary would find her bearings by looking toward the Church of the Ascension that towers over the city. The spire of this church was designed like the upside-down bloom of a local morning glory. Then Mary could look to the sky and find her way home by walking toward the Church of the Annunciation. Mary's world has been preserved inside that Church.

In the Holy Land, ancient sites are studied to see if they are only a fable, a legend, or a historic reality. The Church of the Holy Sepulcher in Jerusalem is one such genuine site: that of the burial of Jesus after the crucifixion. The Church of the Annunciation is of the same order—the place where the angel Gabriel told Mary that the Holy Spirit would overshadow her and a Messiah would be born.

To find her residence, Mary would have to enter the church and descend the stairs to the grotto which encompasses the area where Jesus grew up. People are often surprised to discover that Mary and Joseph's home was in a cave, not a wooden house. In the first century, most people lived in such makeshift circumstances, particularly if they were poor. One doesn't have to walk around Israel but a few steps to discover a land of rock and stone. Many dwelling quarters had the family's animals inside sleeping at night with them. Mary's abode where the angel visited looks today about the same as it did two thousand years ago except that it is now covered by a magnificent Cathedral with marble floors and striking frescoes. Magnificent paintings line the church walls.

The city always had a controversial reputation. Even in Mary's time people gossiped, "Can anything good come out of Nazareth?" (John 1:46) After Jesus began His ministry, He found Nazareth was not conducive to his miracle ministry (Mark 6:5-6). Consequently He did no "mighty works" there. In fact, when He returned to His hometown and stood up to proclaim his calling, the elders of the synagogue tried to kill Him. Those memories linger even to this day.

Today one needs a good guide when walking the streets. Ambitious entrepreneurs claim to own everything from the exact spot where the angel visited Mary to Joseph's carpentry shop. Never mind that much of the current city was rebuilt through the centuries and you may be standing five to ten feet above where Mary first walked. However, one street relic stands out as unquestionably authentic. Called Mary's Well, it is the only such water well in town. You can be sure that a stone-lined hole in the ground never moved. Undoubtedly, Mary, Joseph, and Jesus drank from this well.

The town of Nazareth looms large in Christian history. The earliest Christians were identified as coming from there. Some of the earliest writings in Rabbinic literature refer to the believers as *notzrim,* indicating that they came from this town. The phrase "Jesus of Nazareth" appears many times in the New Testament. The Koine Greek New Testament referred to Jesus as the *Nazoraios.* That name is used repeatedly in the Greek version, which means it might have been the earliest form of the name. At one time, Paul was accused of being a leader in a sect called Nazarenes (Acts 24:5). Even in today's world, the city's name is used to identify a Christian denomination. The Church of the Nazarene is a large denomination that uses the title.

History tells us that Nazareth was occupied by the Romans through the Roman Period into the Byzantine time. Jesus must have grown up seeing soldiers on the streets and might have known some of them. He certainly would have known them as a hostile presence. Of course, the attempted overthrow of the Romans in AD 70 would have had repercussions in the town. The Bar Kokhba revolt in AD 132 destroyed the country. Not until Constantine's mother, Helena, came in 323 AD did the nation and Jerusalem become reestablished. Unfortunately, we know little of Nazareth during this period, but the town carried on.

However, recent excavations in Capernaum reveal how important these towns were even immediately after the resurrection of Jesus. The house now identified as belonging to Peter's mother-in-law recently had a church built over the site. The residence was so identified because of the unusual decorations on the walls that indicated that even in the first century the house had been set apart as a place of worship. Nazareth would have had equal prominence with many first-century Christians.

During the crucifixion, Jesus released Mary to John for him to care for her. (John 19:26-27). We have no record of her returning to Nazareth, but according to Christian tradition, Mary traveled with John and was finally buried in Ephesus. Undoubtedly, her memories of Nazareth lingered with her during those final days.

Today's believers can walk those same streets with Mary and allow their imaginations to reconstruct what that ancient world must have looked and felt like. Humble people with a strong devotion to their God constructed daily life around their beliefs in the Torah and the history of Israel. Mary must have spent hours instructing the boy Jesus about heaven, angels, and His heavenly Father.

As the New Testament tells us, Mary was especially favored by God.

The Reverend Robert L. Wise, Ph.D.

Fiction Author
# GINGER GARRETT

Ginger Garrett is the author of multiple inspirational novels with Guideposts, including *An Unlikely Witness: Joanna's Story and Missionary of Hope: Priscilla's Story*, as well as many other books.

A popular speaker and media guest, she's been featured by national media, including Fox News, USA Today, Library Journal, The Fish, and more.

Nonfiction Author
# ROBERT L. WISE, Ph.D.

The Rev. Robert L. Wise, Ph.D., is the author of thirty-five books and numerous articles published in English, Spanish, Dutch, Chinese, Japanese, and German. On the internet he weekly publishes *Miracles Never Cease* and monthly presents live interviews on YouTube with people who have experienced divine interventions.

*Read on for a sneak peek of another exciting story in the
Extraordinary Women of the Bible series!*

# SINS AS SCARLET: RAHAB'S STORY

## BETH ADAMS

Hazi was afraid. Even in the dim lamplight, Rahab could see it in his eyes as he stepped inside. The heavy wooden door slammed behind him, but he didn't seem to notice. The traders gathered around the table looked up from their stew and turned toward the sound.

"Welcome back." Rahab walked around the wooden table and toward the door to greet her guest. Hazi, a trader of furs and leather goods, traveled throughout the land and was one of her more frequent guests. He stayed at her inn whenever his business brought him to Jericho, and she often enjoyed hearing the stories of his travels and the people he met. But she could see that something was different tonight. It was in the set of his shoulders, the way he pressed his mouth into a thin line. "Let me take your cloak."

Hazi handed his traveling cloak to her without a word. This was very unlike him. Hazi was friendly and loved to talk, sometimes beyond Rahab's desire to listen, and he was never rude. Rahab hung his cloak on the hook by the door and guided him toward the long table.

"Your things are in the courtyard?" she asked.

He nodded. Hazi knew to tie up his donkey in the courtyard below the main floor of the inn before coming up the steps to the door. He would have left his cart there too. Rahab would lock the door as soon as the city gate was closed for the night.

"Please sit." She gestured toward the dining table, where her three other guests also sat. "Meet Alam, Hashur, and Adrahasis."

Hazi nodded to them but did not greet them. Something was definitely wrong.

"You are in luck," she said, keeping her voice light. She walked back to the serving table, poured cool water into a thick earthenware cup, and carried it to him. The night was warm, and the cooking fire made it warmer. "There is lamb stew tonight."

Lamb stew was Hazi's favorite dish. He always asked for it when he stayed at her inn, though he knew she did not make it often. She only had meat when Haran gave her a good deal, but if he knew that he did not let on.

Hazi did not respond. He was looking down at his hands, jostling his leg up and down beneath the table. The air inside the room had gone still, thick, choked with smoke and sweat and something else she couldn't identify. The pure, animal scent of fear, maybe. She went back to the serving area and scooped a portion of the stew into a bowl and carried it to him.

"What is wrong?" She slid the stew in front of him. He looked up and nodded, thanking her. "What has you so frightened?"

Hazi didn't answer for a moment, but then he gestured to the bench across from him, indicating that she should sit down.

Alam, the spice trader, scooted over so she could sit. It was not a large table, and the traders were all watching Hazi with interest.

"I have just come from the valley of Moab." Hazi's eyes were wide. Rahab nodded. She knew that his trading route often took him through all the cities throughout the region. There were several large cities in that area—Dibon, Heshbon, Jahaz—all of them with markets where Hazi had good luck trading. Hazi was a very wealthy man, to hear him tell it. "They are gone, all of them."

"Who is gone?" Rahab did not understand. Heshbon was a large, powerful city on the far side of the sea, several days' journey from here. It stood in the shadow of a mountain, and on the edge of a desert, and was said to be one of the richest and most powerful kingdoms in the land. Rahab had not been there. She had not been anywhere, but she heard about so many places from the travelers who came through the inn. Jericho was in the valley, on one of the main trading roads, and she hosted people from all over the world.

"The Amorites," Hazi stammered. "The people of Heshbon and all of the surrounding towns. The cities have been conquered. The people destroyed completely. All of them are dead."

"That's impossible," Alam said immediately.

Alam was right. King Sihon was one of the most powerful kings in the land, and Heshbon was an important city. It could not have been taken. It could never happen. And if it had, they would have heard.

"And yet it is true. I have seen it with my own eyes."

"What do you mean they have been conquered?" The metal trader, Hashur, turned to Hazi. He was thick and squat with wide-set eyes and an easy laugh. Rahab had just met him that night, as he had not done business in Jericho before, but he'd declared the shared rooms perfectly suitable. He shook his head. "I am afraid you are mistaken. That is not possible. I was just there not two moons past."

"No one could conquer Heshbon," Alam added. Alam came from the east, carrying spices of colors and scents that dazzled the eye and the nose. They held flavors Rahab could only imagine. "The Amorite king cannot be beaten. King Sihon is far too powerful. His cities have strong, thick walls, and his army numbers in the thousands. The city cannot be taken."

"Heshbon has been taken before," the third trader, Adrahasis said. Adrahasis came from Jerusalem and had fine features and dark eyes that missed nothing. Rahab was not sure what his business was, only that he always paid up-front for his stays and that he did not like to talk about what he did while he was in Jericho. "King Sihon himself took the city from the Moabite king."

"But King Sihon has armed his cities well," Hashur said. "The walls are guarded heavily. They say his army is invincible."

"They are wrong," Hazi said. Tiny wisps of steam rose up off the surface of the stew, but he didn't even seem to notice the food in front of him. "Heshbon is destroyed. I have seen it with my own eyes. King Sihon is dead, his army gone, the people all vanquished. The invading army settled in the area and then marched on. They have also taken Jazer and driven out all the people who are there—all the settlements as well."

"What would they want with Jazer?" Alam asked. "It is not a big city. Hardly worth taking."

"It is on the river," Adrahasis said, shrugging. "Good access to water." The oil lamp on the table cast flickering shadows over his face, making his expression appear dark.

Alam nodded, considering this. But Hazi was not done yet. He spoke again.

"After that they marched toward Bashan."

"Bashan?" Hashur questioned. "They went to Bashan?"

Rahab felt a stab of fear. The region of Bashan was much closer to Jericho, just two days' journey to the east. King Og, who ruled the area, was said to be a good king, kind to his people, not demanding too much in taxes nor treating his people badly. King Og had two royal cities, as well as sixty strongly fortified towns, under his control.

"Surely King Og defeated them," Alam said, though his voice betrayed the fear his words did not. "His army is strong, his cities secure."

"They say King Og met the invaders with his full army at Edrei." Hazi took a long drink from his cup, and when he set it down, his hands were shaking. Edrei was one of King Og's royal cities, perched on a hill, surrounded by thick walls. "King Og was defeated, him and his sons and his whole army."

"No." Hashur could not seem to muster any more than this. Rahab understood why. It was unthinkable. Unbelievable. This invading army could not have struck down two of the most powerful kings in the land.

Rahab did not want to believe it. She could see the men at her table were struggling to believe it as well. She had never known Hazi to stretch the truth. But this seemed impossible. What people could have truly destroyed the kingdoms of the Amorites?

"But who are they?" Alam had already finished a second bowl of stew and was eyeing the pot as if hoping for more. "There is no army capable of such a thing."

"They are called the Israelites," Hazi said. "They also call themselves the Hebrews."

"The Israelites?" Alam said, shaking his head. "I have never heard of them. Surely we would have heard of them if they were powerful enough to do what you say."

"Their leader calls himself Joshua," Hazi said. "They claim their god has given them this land as their own."

Hashur laughed aloud at that. "Is their god more powerful than the other gods?"

"It's not possible," Alam said again, shaking his head.

"The Israelites?" Adrahasis had narrowed his eyes. "I have heard of the Israelites."

"*I* have never heard of them." Hashur crossed his thick arms over his chest. He narrowed his eyes and lifted his chin up.

Adrahasis continued. "I heard of them when I was at Kadesh. They are migrants. A pathetic, ragged bunch of wanderers. They have no homeland. They have been walking around for many years, with no direction, no plans. They set up camp in places no one else wants to stay. They certainly have no army capable of destroying the kingdoms of powerful kings like Sihon and Og."

"And yet, apparently, they do," Hazi said. "For they have taken the land for themselves and destroyed all who live within."

"It cannot be true," Alam said, shaking his head. He did not want to believe it. Rahab did not want to believe it either, but Rahab's life had taught her that denying unpleasant facts did not make them any less true.

"It is said their leader is considering where to go next," Hazi said. "He is sending out men to scout the whole land of Canaan, looking for his next conquest."

"He must be insane. Demented." Hashur's eyes were wide.

"It is greed," Alam added. "Pure greed."

"It would be a very stupid thing to do, to drive that ragtag army into a place like this," Adrahasis said. "He would be risking everything they've already gained."

"Canaan is not like those other places," Alam said. "The cities here are big. The kings are powerful. The armies here are well trained."

Rahab felt unease grow within her. If what Hazi said was true... If these Israelites and their god were powerful enough to do what Hazi said they had done... If this Joshua was planning to advance into Canaan...

"Do you think he will come to Jericho?" Rahab couldn't stop herself from asking.

No one answered for a moment, and in the stillness, Rahab heard the low groan of the city gate being raised, closing off the town for the night. No one seemed to know what to say. These men were traders. They wandered from place to place, calling no city home. Rahab had lived in Jericho her whole life. This was where her family was. If the Israelites came to Jericho—

"You do not need to worry," Hazi said quickly. "Even if they do come this way, the walls of Jericho are strong and thick." He leaned back and tapped the back wall of the room with his hand. The inn was built into the city wall itself, and the back wall was made of rough plaster, which covered solid stone.

"Other armies have tried to take Jericho in the past," Adrahasis said. "None of them have succeeded."

Rahab knew he was right. Twice in her life, foreign kings had marched on the city, hoping to claim its fertile soil and green hills for themselves, but they had not succeeded either time. Still, scores had been lost in the fighting, and many had starved to death in the siege, when the gates had been sealed up tight.

"He is right," Alam said, gesturing toward Hazi. "You will be safe from the Israelites. Jericho is secure. Nothing could get through these walls."

Rahab took some comfort from his words, but she felt unsettled. She hoped he was right.

*Find inspiration, find faith, find Guideposts.*

# Shop our best sellers and favorites at
# **guideposts.org/shop**

## Or scan the QR code to go directly to our Shop

Printed in the United States
by Baker & Taylor Publisher Services